Praise for Marie-Nicole Ryan's *Too Good to be True*

"Too Good to be True is a very enjoyable story with a lot of twists and turns along the way. The heat between Rilla and Mac is sizzling... I would not hesitate to pick up another one of Marie-Nicole Ryan's books when I am looking for a good read."

~ *Tanya, Joyfully Reviewed*

"Too Good To Be True by Marie-Nicole Ryan is a gripping, edge-of-your-seat tale filled with smart, fast-talking characters... There is plenty of scorching hot sex, so this book really steams up the pages. This is one story that certainly won't ever be thought of as boring!"

~ *Kay James, Romance Reader at Heart*

"This story was interesting and enjoyable... On the whole, the story was intriguing and an entertaining read. "

~ *Rista Tompkins, Romance Readers Connection*

Too Good to be True

Marie-Nicole Ryan

A Samhain Publishing, Ltd. publication.

Samhain Publishing, Ltd.
512 Forest Lake Drive
Warner Robins, GA 31093
www.samhainpublishing.com

To Good to be True

Print ISBN: 1-59998-648-5
Digital ISBN: 1-59998-460-1

Editing by Linda Ingmanson
Cover by Scott Carpenter

First Samhain Publishing, Ltd. electronic publication: March 2007
First Samhain Publishing, Ltd. print publication: September 2007

Dedication

To my editor Linda Ingmanson, who is one tough cookie when it comes to editing, thank Heavens! Linda has provided valuable input and suggestions to strengthen my story and my writing.

Prologue

The sniper lay concealed in the brush with his high-powered Bushmaster .223 rifle propped and steadied on a tripod. He stroked the weapon and waited for the mark.

He never missed.

Liam glanced at his watch. If his intel was correct, the mark would come down Highway 22 and turn into his driveway to take his mother to her weekly bridge luncheon.

The familiar thrill coursed through him. He sucked in a deep breath and let it out. Steady nerves meant steady hands. Another tool of his trade.

A black and tan vehicle with Clinton County Sheriff emblazoned on the door panel turned into the drive.

The sniper squinted and peered through the sights. A tall, lanky man stepped from the vehicle. Dressed in a tan uniform, the sheriff wore his white hair in a buzz-cut. Another minute and it would be over. As soon as the contractor verified the hit, Liam would be on to his next job.

The mark obliged by walking to the mailbox and stopping long enough to peruse the mail.

Perfect.

He squeezed the trigger. A mist of blood sprayed into the air as the mark crumpled and fell.

Job done, he stood and walked through the wooded hillside to a black SUV. He opened the rear gate of the hired vehicle and broke down his weapon, stowing each well-oiled part in the carrying case.

Once his task was completed, he slid a cell phone from his pocket and punched one on the speed dial.

The contractor answered on the first ring. “Yeah?”

“’Tis done.”

“As soon as I verify, I’ll wire the rest of your fee as arranged.”

“Fine.”

“Don’t hang around. Town like this…folks notice strangers.”

“I know what I’m about. No one has seen me. I’ve been in the area fifteen minutes, and I’ll be gone in one.”

Liam broke the connection. He’d wasted enough time.

True to his word, less than sixty seconds later, he eased from his hiding place and drove away from Cherokee Springs, a boil on the arse of America.

Chapter One

Today was make or break. Would the DEA give him another chance or not? Mackenzie Callahan watched Chief Inspector Havers' scowl deepen the longer he read the physicians' reports.

"The doctors say you're physically ready for another field assignment..." Havers hesitated and Mac forced his noncommittal expression into stone and returned the C.I.'s glare.

Never let 'em see you sweat. Wasn't that the key? Would it be the old heave-ho or a new assignment? He wished it didn't matter so much and he had some kind of life outside the Agency. But it did. The Agency was his life.

"I'm not sure." Havers shook his head. "You've had six months to consider your future. What do you think?"

"I'm ready."

"You may want to rethink after you hear the assignment."

"Doesn't matter what the assignment is. I'm ready."

Havers' gaze narrowed. "Better be. It's your last chance."

Mac swallowed the growing boulder in his throat. He had to go back in the field. He had to. "So what's the deal?"

"The deal?" Havers' ironic tone tainted the innocent choirboy expression on his face. The Chief Inspector had risen through the ranks, and his proficiency was legendary. When it came to screw ups—and that's exactly what Mac had done—Havers was ruthless.

"The deal is this. We've had our eye on a low level operation in Tennessee for quite a while. The sheriff wasn't pulling in the dealers and marijuana growers like he had for years. When the numbers drop, something's going on. We were ready to send in someone else—you were still in rehab—when the sheriff was shot in his own driveway. Since then, there's been a change. Meth lab busts are up, but we've received information which indicates party drugs are rampant. We're looking for a new source."

"Was the sheriff's death a hit?"

"Had all the signs of one."

"Someone new in town got rid of the competition and upped the ante." Mac shifted his stance; the tension in his shoulders relaxed. Didn't sound like such a bad assignment. It would make a good reentry into field work—something he could handle with an arm and a leg tied behind him. "Any contacts on the inside?"

The boss's mouth drew into a thin line. "I'll leave that to you."

"Who's the object of my investigation?"

"Sheriff's replacement. His daughter. She keeps two bank accounts. Nothing suspicious on the one she's had for years, but there's a second account opened the same month the former sheriff was killed. Big deposits—more than she normally makes in a year—hit, then transferred quickly to the Cayman Islands."

"His daughter?"

Fuck. The last thing I need is another undercover op with a female at the center. Not after last time.

"And this one's cagey. Former detective with Metro Nashville."

"You think she ordered a hit on her own father?"

Havers shrugged. "He's dead, and she's serving out his term. Combined with hinky money transactions—what do you think?"

"One cold bitch. So, who am I?"

Havers did something he rarely did when briefing. He laughed. "You're a suspense writer with lots of money to throw around."

"Lots of money sounds good, but a writer?"

"Your website has already launched. You've written four books. Get used to being famous...for a while."

"Cool." Not. A female suspect and a profession he knew nothing about.

"Get busy. The particulars are in your PDA. And don't get shot this time."

"Thanks for the vote of confidence."

Havers leaned back in his chair. "Look, kid. I've been where you are. I know you can stay undercover so long you start to lose who you really are. But this is a test. Don't ever think it's not. You screw up this one, and you can find a new line of work."

"I get it."

Mac nodded, turned and left Havers' office. Nothing else to say. At least the C.I. hadn't reminded him to keep his pants zipped.

As soon as Callahan exited Havers' office, Havers picked up the phone and punched in Agent Quinlan's number. "Roxy, Callahan took the assignment, but you'll be his controller. Keep a low profile until it's apparent whether or not he's on track. No need for him to know you're there unless it's necessary.

"Got it. Just how am I supposed to keep a low profile in a dinky-assed Tennessee town where everybody knows everybody?"

"You'll be working as a waitress at a truck stop about three miles from town."

"A waitress, huh?" Her tone purred in his ear, but the undertone of steel was unmistakable.

"Won't be the first time."

"No, but I swore the Oklahoma gig would be the last. Damned near whole place was flattened by a tornado. I said then, 'No more waitress jobs and no more Oklahoma.'"

Havers chuckled. "Indeed you did, my dear. You're already in character. I hear it in your voice."

"I couldn't resist." Her tone and accent changed back to her normal huskiness. "Are we still on for *La Bohéme*? Or do I have to leave tonight?"

"Not tonight. I'll pick you up as usual."

"All right, sweet thang." She disconnected before Havers could object...or laugh. Damn, but she was the most intriguing woman he'd ever known.

A chameleon...one of the best.

An hour later, Mac had packed. Car and house keys would be waiting at the Agency office in Nashville. Bank accounts already opened. Credit cards—everything which would document his cover.

He'd hop the red-eye to Raleigh-Durham then connect to Nashville.

He looked around his spartan studio apartment. It was nothing more than a place to change his clothes between operations, but this was the life he'd chosen. No family, no pets and damned few he would call friend.

His cell phone tweeted. Damn. He hated the sound.

"Yeah?"

"Heard you were back on the job. Got time for a tall one?"

"'Bout that." It was one of the few...one he couldn't turn down. Seven years ago, Colton Drake had taken a bullet meant for Mac on their first undercover op. Earlier, they'd both been in Special Forces and served together in the Balkans.

"O'Malley's in ten?" Colton suggested.

"I'll be there."

O'Malley's Pub was so Irish Mac expected to see some guy prance out in tights and start step-dancing on the bar. A Chieftains CD was playing, and the smell of Irish hops penetrated his consciousness. Through the crowd, he spotted Cole in the far corner.

A tall mug of dark Irish beer already waited for him. "How you drink this stuff, I'll never know."

"'Tis mother's milk, don't you know." Cole winked and shoved the mug to Mac's side of the table.

He sat down and stretched out his legs. He hesitated then took a long swig of the warm brew. "Hmm. Better than I remembered. Must be developing a taste for it."

Cole laughed and leaned forward. "I don't guess you had much of a tipple in rehab?"

"None."

"Son, don't you think it's time you got out of the business? Go freelance like me. I make a good living. Not as many rules to follow—that's the best part."

Mac shook his head. "Undercover's all I know."

"Dude. You've been pretending to be someone else all your life. Don't you think it's about time you did something for yourself?"

Mac shrugged. "Peeking in motel windows isn't my idea of a job. No offense."

"None taken, but there's more to it than that."

"Sorry." Mac took another long pull on the draft beer. "Say, how'd you know I was back on the job?"

"Just because I'm no longer officially with the Agency doesn't mean I don't have contacts." Cole's expression grew serious. "Are you sure you want to take another chance this soon?"

"Doctors say I'm fine. I've a twinge or two, but I'm ship-shape."

"My advice to you is, keep it zipped this time. No woman's worth losing your life."

Mac clenched his jaw. "You sound like you know what went down on my last op."

"That I do." Cole slapped Mac's shoulder. "It's no lie what they say about the female being more deadly than the male."

"No shit." Stalling for time, Mac shelled a couple of peanuts and ate them. "It's not like I have a choice. This life is all I know."

"You're not in your cups yet, and you're already repeating yourself. I'm telling you. You have choices—a lot of 'em. Come to work with me. We'd be a good team—like we were before."

"Nah. I'm not ready for something so routine. I don't know how you do it. Aren't you bored out of your mind? I know a lot of it is behind a desk—computer research."

"The technology plays a big part, but I'm ready for the security of a desk job." Cole leaned forward, his expression intent. "But in some ways, it's not very different from what you're doing now, but at the end of the day you can go to a real home...to a woman, even."

"That's not my style. Don't see myself mowing the yard and painting a picket fence."

Cole threw back his head and laughed. "You're hopeless. Call me when you're tired of risking your ass for little money and no respect. We could be partners. I know you're bound to have some money socked away. We could go big time."

"P.I. Inc.? Don't think so." Mac glanced at his watch, downed the rest of his beer and stood. "Gotta go. Thanks for the brew."

"Yeah, whatever."

Cole had given him a lot to think about. Maybe he did have options, but home and hearth were the farthest things from his mind. And a steady woman? Get real. He'd never let another one get that close.

A blinding summer sun reflected off the hood of the Silver Porsche. Mac topped the hill outside Cherokee Springs, Tennessee. It wasn't much more than a village of green trees, little traffic and well-maintained houses. Their main street was a step back in time with rows of shops clustered around a town square.

So this sleepy little town was a hotbed of drug activity?

He dug in his pocket for the scrap of paper with his new address. Two-eighty-five North Main.

Hell, he was almost home.

The farther he drove up North Main, the larger the houses were. He pulled into the driveway of an old Victorian and parked.

He strode leisurely up the flagstone walk and noted the fresh paint and new landscaping. The porch wrapped around to one side and looked like something off a book cover. How fitting, since he was an author now. Sliding the key in the lock, he turned it and stepped inside a warm and welcoming foyer.

Damn. Home might not be so bad after all.

The house certainly possessed all the basic necessities—and then some. Hardwood floors, a library on the right. He walked through the dining area to the kitchen which was outfitted like some kind of restaurant. French doors led out to a three-level deck, and the backyard swept downhill in a lush green carpet. He headed upstairs and found his bedroom at the back of the house. The bedroom was furnished with solid, well-built furniture. Nothing frilly. Thank goodness. But the room took up half the entire second story, if you included a walk-in closet meant for someone with more clothes than he'd ever needed in his entire life and a bathroom on steroids.

Well, at least the bed looked more comfortable than the one in rehab. Satisfied with his sleeping arrangements, he turned and checked out the rest of the second floor. Hall closet with stacks of linen. Another bathroom. An empty bedroom. Another set up as an office. The DEA wanted him to be comfortable for this operation. Nice of them.

Must be some serious drug money going down for them to sink this much money into this op.

Chapter Two

Sheriff Rilla Devane's day was shot to hell the second Buster Villines unbuckled his belt, unzipped his pants and dropped trou. "Hold on! Don't do that in here!"

"But you need evidence, don't ya? Ed Tatum's dog 'bout gelded me."

She rolled her eyes and prayed for reason. "Dillon!" she yelled at the nearest deputy. "Think you could quit holding up the wall and take a picture of the *evidence*?" She lowered her tone. "Somewhere else?"

She pushed back from the desk, stood and patted her gun. "Meanwhile, I'll be checking out a suspicious character at the supermarket. Miss Tweedy thinks she's I.D.'d a serial killer in the vegetable aisle. She's afraid he's going to follow her home."

Miss Tweedy was a retired, old maid school teacher and notorious among the Clinton County deputies for the number of suspicious characters she'd reported to the authorities. Not content to watch soap operas and tend garden in her golden years, she "helped out" in the grocery store twice a week.

The deputy's hoot of laughter followed her out the door.

Miss Tweedy leaned forward and whispered in Rilla's ear. "Now, Sheriff, he was right over there sniffing and manhandling the vegetables, and after I called you, he headed over to the fruit aisle. Ain't natural—a man doing his own shopping."

Rilla held back the giggle which threatened to erupt any second. “Maybe he’s a vegetarian, Miss Tweedy.”

Maybe he’s just single. Not that she was interested, and certainly not after her last breakup.

“We don’t have any of those around here. Not legal, are they?”

Rilla bit back a groan, but then the former school teacher gave a droll wink.

Give me strength. If she’s not seeing intruders in her garden or terrorists in the vegetable aisle, she’s trying to match-make.

“Don’t you worry. I’ll check him out. I’m sure he’s perfectly harmless.”

“But, Rilla, you don’t understand. He’s not from around here. He’s got an accent.”

Rilla left the elderly woman to her muttering, rounded the potato chip display and headed to the rear of the store.

Quarry spied, she took her time cornering him as the view was exceptional. As reported, said suspicious character was loading his shopping basket with a large pineapple which joined a bunch of carrots.

He was tall and tanned with broad shoulders which stretched the fabric of his black T-shirt. A strong back tapered down into a muscled butt. His jeans were faded and fit like a second skin. If he had a face to go with the rest of the body, she might just have to follow him home—in the name of public safety, of course.

“Ahem.”

He turned around, and the breath caught in her throat. He had the bluest eyes she’d seen this side of a movie screen, although his raven hair needed a trim. A strand fell across his tanned forehead, meeting his thick, dark eyebrows.

"Sheriff." A lazy, lopsided grin took up residence on his lean face above a jaw so square she could've used it to build and level a deck. "Am I breaking some kind of arcane local law?"

His deep voice jolted her heart over the speed limit. As for his accent, Miss Tweedy was right. He definitely wasn't from anywhere below the Mason-Dixon Line. That fact in itself was enough to set her poor old teacher all atwitter.

"No, the cashier thought you were—uh, suspicious." She grinned to soften the statement. The man before her sure as hell didn't look suspicious. No way. He looked for all the world like a mischievous boy up to no good. But then most men were no good, whether they meant to be or not.

"I see." He added two red bell peppers to his basket. "And...?"

"Based on my years of experience with hardened criminals and other minor miscreants, I think Miss Tweedy was mistaken."

He flashed a smile this time which showed his soap opera star white teeth.

"You're new in town." It wasn't a question—she knew everybody in town.

"Yes, and for the record, I'm Mackenzie Callahan. My friends call me Mac."

She extended her hand. "Sheriff Rilla Devane."

He took her hand in his. His grip was strong...and warm. "I recently bought the old Victorian on North Main."

She knew the exact house and smiled. "She's had a lot of work recently. I wondered who bought her." Then she remembered to breathe and slid her hand from his. Dammit. The last thing she needed was another charmer like the up-to-no-good, scheming rat she'd left behind in Nashville.

"She had good bones." Mac agreed with a nod. "Would you like a tour sometime?"

She sucked in a breath, then let it out slow and easy. She'd love to see the inside of the old house, but... "Sure. Just let me know when you're all settled."

"Oh, I'm settled." His dark brow arched and it matched the half grin angle for angle.

"You're already unpacked?" She'd lived at her place for two months and still had a room of boxes whose contents had yet to see the light of day. What was his hurry?

He shrugged. "It's a character flaw, but I can't work when there's a lot of clutter."

"So you're stocking up the fridge?" Could she be anymore inane? Doubtful. Seemed her polite conversational skills had deteriorated since moving back to the Springs.

"Yeah. I've O.D.'d on Papa Tommy's Pizza and Colonel J's Fried Delight."

She nodded. "Lot of that going around."

Mac reached to the back of the vegetable bin and added a healthy bunch of romaine to his basket. He turned around and treated her to his boyish grin again. "Would you like to have dinner when you come for your tour?"

"You cook?" A man with a great house and he cooked? Must be gay. Yeah, that was it. At least she wouldn't have to worry about his hitting on her.

His lazy grin kicked up another notch. "I can manage a salad, and there's a grill on the rear deck. You won't starve."

Considering how long it'd been since she'd taken time for a real meal—and the cook was a hunk, gay or not—she didn't hesitate. "Sounds great."

"Tonight?"

"Tonight?" Damn. He sure didn't waste any time. What was he up to? Maybe she ought to rethink dinner. He couldn't be *that* bowled over by her charms—could he?

"If you're off duty?"

"Uh, yes. Sure."

"Eight?" He gave her a satisfied smile, as if he'd known all along she'd accept his invitation.

"Yeah. Eight's fine. Want me to bring anything?"

"Just yourself." His gaze slid up and down the length of her body. "Drinks at seven-thirty?"

His long heated glance set her back. Maybe he wasn't gay after all. "Yes. I guess. Seven-thirty." She checked her watch. Five hours to find something to wear...and run a background check.

Emotions off-kilter, she nodded good-bye and trudged back to the front of the store to confront Miss Tweedy.

"Well, did you read 'im his rights?" the good woman asked.

"No, but I haven't completed my investigation yet. I'll keep an eye on him." Yes, indeed, she would be keeping an eye on him. One way or another.

For all she knew he was a drug dealer or a serial killer. Killer blue eyes or serial killer? Or maybe he was just a hunk of a guy who was interested in her. And she wasn't sure which scared her more.

Slow it down, girl. Your imagination's working overtime.

Mac Callahan sucked in a deep breath to steady his breathing. Hot Damn. *That* was the sheriff.

Damn. He watched her walk away with an I-mean-business stride that brooked no nonsense. But even the masculine khaki uniform didn't hide the curve of her slim hips. About five-seven, he guessed. Her high cheekbones and the glistening, black hair she wore pulled back in a single braid hinted at Native American ancestry.

Did she ever let it down? The thought of running his hands through the silken strands revved up his heart another ten or fifty beats.

What was he thinking? His agenda had nothing to do with getting the sheriff in bed for some mattress mambo, but one glance from her warm brown eyes and bedding her was *all* he could think about.

No way he'd forget what happened last time. No more getting too close to his suspect.

How could he forget? He still had the scars.

Back in her office, Rilla scanned the data as it filled the computer screen. Mackenzie Callahan had no outstanding warrants in Tennessee. She checked the FBI web site. And he wasn't one of the ten most wanted. Not that she actually thought he was.

How about a Google search?

"Bingo." There were dozens of references. Her Mackenzie Callahan? Seems one Mackenzie Callahan was a writer with his own web site. Same one? She clicked on the link...

Sure enough. He'd posed for the camera in a fisherman's knit sweater. He was even wearing a pair of horn rimmed glasses.

Okay, anyone could set up a web site. She surfed to *Amazon*. Did he have anything listed there?

Hm. Four books.

That settled it. She'd just have to check him out—up close and personal. What she wanted was one of his books in her hand with his photograph on the dust cover. Then she'd believe he was legit.

Detective Katherine "Kit" Bellows tapped on the open door of Rilla's office. "What's up, Sheriff? Surfing the 'net?"

Rilla frowned at her new hire. None of the old-boy crap would do for the new sheriff. Yes, she'd known most of her father's men since she was a kid. And she trusted them...to a point. Kit had moved from Chicago a month earlier, presenting impeccable credentials, and Rilla had hired her on the spot as soon as her references cleared. "Just doing a little research on someone who bugs me."

"On the Internet?"

"Yeah, new guy in town. I'm picking him for sort of suspicious. I want to see if he's who he says he is."

"But why the Internet? You've better resources."

"I know. I've already checked for outstanding warrants. Just being careful. I met this guy at the grocery today—"

"And...?"

"...and he invited me to dinner at *his* place."

A wicked grin flashed over Kit's pretty face. "Dinner at his place, is it? I like a man who works fast."

"I don't know if he's up to something or if he's just bowled over by my charms."

"That has to be it." Kit's shoulders shook with barely repressed laughter.

"Let's keep this between us, Kit. It's *just* dinner."

"Seriously, it's time you had a date. I don't think you've had once since I've been here. And no one will think less of you if you had your tires rotated once in a while..."

Rilla rolled her eyes. As much as she enjoyed the light banter with the only other female in her department, the real reason she was sheriff of Clinton County intruded with a sick rush.

Her father's murder.

"I don't know, Kit. Sometimes, I think I'm losing focus. I'm here for one reason. I have to find who was behind my father's death."

"Listen to me. You're not letting anyone down if you have dinner with this guy. I didn't know your father, but I'm sure he'd be the first one to say you should go out and have a good time."

"I know."

"Then get out of here and slip into some of those girly clothes you must have packed away somewhere. Show that dude what small town girls have to offer. R.J. and I are both on duty tonight. Trust me, we can handle it."

"Of course you can, but..." Why was she hesitating? Was she that much of a control freak? R.J. and Bellows were more than competent. Still, something nagged at the fringes of her mind.

"Then let us." Kit smiled and raised a questioning eyebrow. "Well...?"

Rilla nodded. "Fine." Intellectually she knew Kit was right. Going on what would likely be a boring dinner date shouldn't make her feel disloyal to her father's memory or the job. Still it stayed in the back of her mind. She'd agreed to serve out his term so she could root out the bastard who'd ordered the hit. She couldn't afford to lose focus.

Not now.

But if her uncharacteristic reaction to meeting Mackenzie Callahan was any indicator, she just might.

Listening for the police scanner with one ear, Rilla stood in front of her closet and dismissed her present wardrobe with a trenchant "Crap."

What the hell did she have in her closet—something appropriate for touring a fabulous old Victorian house? Too dressy and he'd think she was trying to impress him or worse...desperate. Too casual and he'd think she didn't know how to dress.

And she couldn't shop for something new. As the highest ranked law enforcement officer in a small town, her every move was under scrutiny.

Look again. Maybe there was something she hadn't worn since she moved back home.

Finally, she found a short red skirt and a white off-the-shoulder blouse. She added a pair of red, strappy stilettos and dangly gold earrings and a set of bangle bracelets.

Then she tried them on and stood in front of the mirror.

Geez, she looked like a working girl ready to stroll down Dickerson Road.

No way. Trying too hard.

Why on earth was she being such a *girl*? She tossed the red skirt back into the closet and pulled out a pair of white slacks. She kept the blouse, but tugged it over her shoulders. No sense in showing all that skin.

And forget the stilettos. She wasn't boogying in Music City. This was only a steak dinner on North Main in the Springs. And her leather sandals would do just fine.

She glanced at her watch. Damn, she'd spent too much time rummaging through her wardrobe, there was barely time to shower and do something with her hair. Damn, damn, damn.

Mac stepped outside onto the tri-level deck and breathed in the sweet scent of the honeysuckle growing along the back of *his* property. He'd never seen anything like Cherokee Springs. He'd grown up in D.C., and his early life was nothing like this. No bicycling or playing hopscotch along shady sidewalks. After his step-father killed his mother, hopscotch was a game he played in a series of foster homes.

Hopscotch, indeed. He'd learned to fit in early, not like some kids who'd fought, cried, kicked and screamed. He'd learned to dodge the kicks and turn how many—he'd lost count—foster mothers' angry expressions into smiles with his quips and humorous antics.

The first time it happened, it was a fluke. Thelma Biggs had swatted at his behind at the age of six for spilling a cup of milk, but he'd turned a somersault in order to get away from her quick hand.

She loomed over him...and giggled.

He turned another one.

"You monkey, you." She gave a laugh and proceeded to clean up his mess. The fact he ran for the paper towels and bowed liked a fancy-pants guy in the movies when he handed them to her hadn't hurt a bit.

Later, he'd learned he could charm his way out of trouble, especially with women. All he had to do was grin and shrug, and presto-change-o, his sins were forgiven...until the next time.

Frequent moves between homes and schools had kept him aloof with few real friends. Sports had had been his only passion...until he'd discovered the softness of a girl's skin and the wet heat between her legs.

Leanne.

The basketball coach's daughter been a year older—seventeen to his sixteen—when behind the stage, she unbuttoned her blouse, let him feel her breasts and begged him to shove his dick deep inside her. She was slick and tight. Her muscles gripped his dick so hard he came in two quick strokes. The second go-round was better.

That was then. Now, if he screwed up this op, he wouldn't be able to clean up the mess with a whole roll of paper towels or a charming smile...and his dick would be in a wringer for certain.

"What the hell am I doing?" Inviting the sheriff to dinner and a tour? True, he needed to get close to the sheriff, but was this the way to go?

But who could blame him? Sheriff Devane was as sexy as they came. According to her dossier, she was in her early thirties, but she looked younger. Tall and slender, her body was buff, and it was obvious she was no stranger to working out. And eyes so dark they reminded him of ripe olives. But there was a sharp intelligence in those eyes. Not many women possessed her air of authority.

He couldn't help remembering the throaty quality of her voice. It sent a rush of heat straight to his groin. No doubt about it. His *cojones* were getting the better of him.

He set the wine in the cooler. Everything was ready for his second meet.

Yeah, that's better. This is an operation, not a date.

If only she weren't so damned hot. Why couldn't she have a big mole on her chin or be cross-eyed?

One thing for certain, he'd already spent more time in this town than he wanted. Small towns were seductive with all the peace and quiet and neighborly residents, but underneath it wasn't any different from a D.C. ghetto. Everyone was out to make a buck and screw anyone who got in the way. But small town folks did it with a smile.

With the Porsche sitting in his drive and the high profile rehabbing of an old house, he was much more visible than he was used to. Instead of blending into the woodwork or flying under the radar, here he was—preparing dinner for the local head of law enforcement.

Come into my parlor, said the spider to the fly.

Damn shame, too. More than anything he wanted to loosen the sheriff's braid and let her silky black hair spill across his pillow.

Dammit. He had to stop obsessing about her hair.

Still, she was his kind of woman.

At precisely seven-thirty-one, Rilla lifted the lion's head knocker and banged it once against the polished mahogany door. The beveled-glass sidelights revealed a well-lit foyer.

The door opened and Mac Callahan stood in the doorway with a lazy smile on his handsome face and a devilish twinkle in his eyes. "Come in, Sheriff Devane. Steaks are on the grill."

She laughed to cover exactly how nervous she was. "You'd better call me Rilla. Sheriff's a little on the formal side, don't you think?"

"Rilla? Unique name."

"Yeah, well. I don't tell many people, but it's short for Marilla." She shook her head, wondering, why she chose to tell *him* of all people. "Blame it on my mother. It was her bright idea." Apparently the only one the woman ever had before she ran off with a Ricky Skaggs roadie.

"I like it. Come on in."

She followed him through the wide entry hall, passing a well-decorated living room on one side and leather-rich library on the other. The furnishings all said comfort and money...and out of her class.

He took her by the hand. "Kitchen's back here. Would you like a glass of wine?"

Tempted, Rilla thought for a minute, then shook her head. "Sorry, I'm on duty—at least I feel like I am. Small town, you know."

"Bottled water or tea?"

Always the gracious host, was he? But she managed a polite, "Tea."

He nodded and busied himself with pouring the tea into a tall, frosty glass of ice. "I've discovered sweet tea is something of a southern staple. Why don't you sit down while I work on the salad?"

"Why don't you let me do the salad?" She flexed her fingers in front of her. "I can just about manage something that simple."

"Sure thing." Mac turned to the refrigerator and opened the door. He gathered the salad-makings and set them on the granite counter. "I'll check the steaks."

She looked at the salad greens. Geez Louise, here she was acting like some kind of a Martha Stewart clone. What in hell was she doing in this strange man's house? Okay, granted, he was a hunk, but still a stranger. What did she know about him? Web site notwithstanding, he could still be up to no good. Or was the paranoia of the job getting to her?

"Careful," Mac warned with a chuckle from behind her. "You look deadly with that knife. I'm sure the romaine will surrender without a struggle."

"Oh." She looked up into his eyes, her gaze held by his vivid intensity, and took a deep breath. He still had a mischievous-boy thing happening. No man had any right to be so damn good looking. Not that his features were perfect. His nose had an arrogant arch, and she could make out a tiny scar below his left eyebrow. Yet, those tiny imperfections made him a little more human and approachable.

"Actually..." He eased the knife from her hand. "...lettuce should be torn, not cut."

Once he completed the salad, taking more care than she ever would've, he motioned for her to follow him outside.

He flipped two large sirloins over to brown on the other side. Apparently satisfied with their progress, he sat down beside her on the top step of the deck.

Close enough, but not *too* close.

On and off glimmers of lightning bugs flitted about in the early evening dusk. Rilla breathed in the scent of honeysuckle. God, it took her back. "I used to catch those and put 'em in jars with holes in the lid, but Daddy always made me let them out. He always said no creature or human being should ever be locked up who didn't deserve it."

"Sounds like a wise man, your dad."

"He was the best."

The crackle and pop of meat juices hitting the charcoal along with the smoky aroma of charbroiled steak made Rilla's mouth water. And the deep blue eyes of her host sent her heart into the high-speed car chase range.

Dammit. What was she doing here? Hadn't she had enough heartbreak with Don the Jerk? Enough to last a life time.

He took a long drink of tea, then set the glass down beside him. "Tell me about yourself. How...?"

In spite of herself, she laughed. Men were so predictable. "How did a nice girl like me end up as sheriff?"

"Yes, something like that."

"My father was sheriff before me."

"So you took over when he retired?"

She looked down and hugged her knees. "He didn't retire. He was murdered."

"Sorry, I didn't know."

She stared into the approaching night sky and swallowed. "I was working Metro Homicide...in Nashville. I'd only had my gold shield a month when my grandmother called me."

"Must've been a shock."

"It was. Daddy ran unopposed his last three terms. He didn't have any enemies—well, obviously he had one."

"Weren't you young to make detective?"

She shrugged. "Not if a police force needs to increase its proportion of female detectives. Anyway, I came back here for the funeral and to settle his estate."

"Just a sec." He stood and walked over to the grill. He flipped the steaks and sat beside her again. "But you stayed? How'd it come about?"

She nodded and tried ignoring the smell of charcoal clinging to his hair and shirt. He certainly smelled good enough to eat.

"Right after the funeral, the county commissioner dropped by the house. He asked me to stay and serve out the rest of Daddy's term. Sounds like small-town nepotism, I guess, but it's a small county. I grew up here. Everyone knows me. I jumped at the chance since I had no intention of leaving until I found out who had Daddy killed."

"And have you?"

The pain of her father's loss knifed through her and twisted her mouth into a grimace. "No. Some detective, aren't I?"

"I'm sure you're an excellent sheriff."

Rilla bristled at his patronizing tone and lifted her chin a notch. "I am."

"I didn't mean to sound condescending."

She smiled, attempting to soften her attitude. "I don't mean to punish you for my loss. And since I've already been seduced by your sizzling..."

"Personality?" He shot her a hopeful expression and she saw a definite sparkle in his eyes.

"...steaks." Where was this headed? She brushed at her slacks. Why couldn't there be a handy speck of lint or anything so she didn't have to meet his knowing gaze. "Besides, you're way too charming for my own good."

A sly grin played about his sensual lips. "Thank you."

"It wasn't supposed to be a compliment."

"You sure?"

"Very."

"Then why don't you tell me how I'm too charming for your own good?"

"I didn't say for *my* own good."

"You did."

Good Lord, maybe she had. She took a sip of tea and pondered her next words. "I must've misspoken."

Mac's grin widened. "That must be it."

"Now see here. Your big-city boyish charm is wasted on me."

"You're not enjoying yourself?" He leaned back against the deck railing and laced his fingers behind his head. "And here I thought I was the perfect host."

"You are, but I wasn't kidding about being on duty twenty-four/seven."

"Twenty-four/seven?" His dark eyebrows drew together in a frown. "Really?"

Pointing to the cell phone she wore at the waist of her white slacks, she nodded. "Yeah, 'fraid so."

"I had no idea. I mean, don't you have deputies?"

"Of course. But being sheriff in a small county like Clinton is pretty hands-on. I try to keep one deputy for each thousand residents, but if something big happens like a car accident where someone is killed—honestly, there are a million and one reasons I can be called."

"How do you have time for a social life?"

Summer nighttime sounds of crickets grew louder. In the distance a dog howled.

She met his earnest gaze. "My social life isn't a high priority."

"There's no one special?"

"No."

There he goes again. Is he interrogating me, or is this what passes for polite conversation?

He scowled for a second and glanced over at the steaks. "Maybe I'd better hurry those babies along." He rose in a leisurely manner as if he had all night and moseyed over to the grill.

"It's been a quiet day." Not counting almost being flashed in her own office. "Maybe it'll stay that way."

"I still don't understand. I bet you've made a dozen conquests and you're too focused on your work to notice."

She laughed and shook her head. "I've known just about everyone in this county since I was a kid. Any man I'd consider spending time with is already married to someone I went to school with. The rest have spent time in my pokey. There was someone..." She hesitated. She'd be damned before she'd tell him anything about Don the Jerk.

"I knew it."

"...in Nashville, but it was over before..."

"His loss."

"Whatever." She frowned as the image of Don the Jerk screwing the blonde bitch from Vice in Rilla's own bed flashed through her mind. "Grr."

"Whoa. Sounds like a warning." Her host chuckled. "Now I *know* I'd better hurry dinner. You like your steak rare, right?"

She forced a grin and shoved the unpleasant memory as far away as she could. "As a matter of fact, I do." She jumped to her feet—anything to change the topic of conversation. "Let me help."

"Grab the meat platter off the counter, if you will." He gave her another of his killer smiles.

Dang it. A woo-woo wave of giddiness sent her mind spinning. The man's smile was a lethal weapon. Maybe she should arrest him.

Instead she sashayed inside for the platter. The table was set with a yellow linen tablecloth and place settings of heavy blue earthenware which she'd bet her badge came from Tildon's Pottery. Pricey stuff, too. "Platter coming?" Mac called from the deck.

Platter in hand, she rushed outside. "Yeah. I was admiring your table setting. Nash Tildon's work?"

"Yes, the electrician who worked on the house told me about his pottery."

"That would be Rafe Baldwin. His older sister is married to Nash."

"You really do know everybody in town, don't you?"

"Pretty much."

"I'm convinced." Mac speared the second steak and heaved it onto the platter. "Shall we eat?"

She nodded. "I'm starving." How the hell would she ever manage to eat even half of what had to be a sixteen-ounce steak?

No pair of comfortable slacks had room for all the guaranteed cholesterol-raising, heart-attack-inducing sample of sizzling, bovine protein. She'd need a doggy bag or at least a dog to take it home to.

She reached for her chair, ready to pull it out and sit down, but Mac stopped her. "Allow me."

The flush of embarrassment bloomed and heated her face. "I don't run into elegant manners very often. Around the office, I'm just one of the guys. I tend to act like one of them, too."

"You don't look like one of the guys tonight."

She smiled, and by sheer dint of will, managed to murmur a polite "Thank you" instead of bolting and heading back to the quiet safety of her office. The man before her was seriously charming, and she was in grave danger of falling for his line.

But then she saw the dessert.

Chocolate and caramel drizzled over sour cream icing. Her mouth dropped open and watered. Her taste buds twitched. Her two favorite food groups: Chocolate and caramel.

An expression of concern crossed Mac's face. "Something wrong? You're allergic to chocolate?"

"The dessert. It's..." she sighed, then continued, "my favorite."

He shot her a smug grin. "Thank you. Just a little something I whipped up this afternoon."

A sudden image of Mac emerged—he was wearing a frilly apron, covered in chocolate and hovering over a mixing bowl. She giggled and shook her head. "No, you didn't."

He chuckled. "I didn't." He scooted her chair for her. "In fact," he continued, "my neighbor on the left—"

"Sueanne English?" She should've known. The working-girl-turned-older-rich-man's wife had already been sniffing around the new guy in town, especially since Mac seemed to be rolling in the green readies.

"Yes. Mrs. English—she brought it over an hour ago."

Rilla laughed and wondered what Sueanne thought of her sinful dessert being enjoyed by another woman?

"I thought it very neighborly of her. It's one of the things I like about the South." His grin was earnest, but his eyes were unreadable.

You would. "Yes, we're very neighborly."

And some of us more than others.

"So I told Mrs. English she'd saved my life...and I had a most attractive law officer coming to dinner." He grinned. "She said she knew you, too."

"That's how small towns are."

He sat to her left rather than across from her. "I hope you don't mind. This is friendlier."

"Um, yes, it is." And his *friendly* smile sent a shiver clear through her. A good shiver which wound its way downward to her lower belly.

"So tell me, what does a sheriff do all day?"

"Well, in a highly populated county, like Davidson—you know, Nashville—my job would be mainly administrative and political."

"You mean it's not in a smaller county?"

"Yes, it's administrative and political, too, but here it's much more personal. I'm in the office from seven-thirty in the morning, and I usually end my day around seven or so. Afterwards, I'm on call. Every deputy has my home and cell phone number. And I listen to my police scanner whenever I'm in my car or at home."

"Sounds like a lot of fun." He grimaced.

Without meaning to, she let out a heavy sigh. "I don't know how my father did it all those years."

"How long was he in office?"

"Twenty years." She blinked back the tears and kept her gaze on the plate of food before her.

"Who do you think killed him?"

"Drug interests."

"In a small town like this?"

"Small towns aren't immune. Drugs are everywhere. For a long time, it was marijuana—Tennessee's biggest cash crop. And don't forget the meth labs. They're the worst. As soon as I shut one down, another springs up."

"But how does one manage to sell drugs in an area like this—where everyone knows everybody else's business?"

"Good question." Was he making conversation or was there more to his questions than mere interest...? "My theory? There's someone new in town with lots of money."

It hit her.

Like you.

But she continued, watching for his reactions. "The high school is being flooded with ecstasy. We've had a couple of overdoses this summer. One kid died."

"Sounds serious."

"It is. When my father was killed, the TBI—that's the Tennessee Bureau of Investigation—said it had the signature of a contract hit. Not long after he died..." She paused to gather her composure, her father's death as raw as a cut which refused to heal. "The party drugs started showing up. There's even a rave scene."

"Raves? Here in the middle of...?"

"...one-horse rural nowhere? Yeah. They use deserted farmhouses, barns—just about anything. They spring up on a Friday or Saturday night and move before we can catch up with them. They have first class sound and lighting, so someone with serious money is behind it."

And here, right in front of her offering a frosty glass of tea, was a stranger in town. And, to all appearances, one with a lot of money. The thought Mac might actually be behind the flood of ecstasy or her father's death shook her. Were her instincts so far off? Was she sitting at the dinner table with her father's killer?

"You know," she said, forcing a smile. "I can talk shop anytime. Why don't you tell me about yourself? Why move to a small town like Cherokee Springs?"

He gave a slightly covert glance over his shoulder, leaned forward and said in a stage whisper, "I'm writing a novel."

"How fascinating. What kind?" As if she didn't already know.

He drew back, a half grin playing about his mouth. "What kind do you think?"

"Hm, something terribly literary. Or since you're being so secretive, maybe you write mysteries?"

Mac laughed. "You're closer with the mysteries, but close only counts—"

"—in horseshoes and hand grenades. Yeah, Daddy used to say that all the time." She pretended to think a second. "Science fiction?"

"Colder."

"Okay, I've got it. You're a man masquerading behind a woman's pen name and you write romance novels."

Her dinner companion's gaze narrowed. He grinned and held up his arms and looked at them questioningly. "Am I hooked up to some kind of lie detector?"

"Was I right? I just made a wild guess." And why was he being so cagey about what he wrote?

"No. Not romance."

Something about his denial didn't ring true. A hard glint in his eyes said he was lying. She didn't care what she'd found on the Internet. Something about his story was off. If he wasn't a writer, what was he?

He was still smiling, but the smile hadn't quite reached his eyes. What was he hiding?

"So why settle here in Cherokee Springs? What *do* you write?" Her stomach growled. And why was she grilling him like he was a fat juicy steak when she could be enjoying more than dinner?

No. What was wrong with her? Why couldn't she keep her thoughts straight? Here was a perfectly good-looking, although somewhat mysterious, man, and what was she doing? Merely vacillating between being a paranoid cop and a sex-starved nympho. *Find a happy medium, Rilla.*

He drew his dark brows together in a frown. "Am I being interrogated, Sheriff Devane? Did we just switch from having dinner—which by the way, you haven't touched—to cops and robbers?"

"Force of habit." She fidgeted with a strand of hair which had fallen across her eyes. "Sorry, I guess I did sound a little official."

He leaned forward. "Okay, here's the deal. I was a reporter for one of the big New York papers, but I've been writing suspense novels for several years now. I thought I'd move to a small town for the peace and quiet and general atmosphere."

She cut her first bite of steak, then toyed with it. "I don't have a lot of spare time for reading, but I'd love to hear about your books. Are they set in the same place or in different ones?"

"Uh—" His gaze dropped. "You know, I hate talking about my work. It's so boring for someone who doesn't write."

Rilla shook her head. "Oh, come on. I think it's fascinating. I've never known a published author before. And you're right here in Cherokee Springs. At least, tell me what this new one's about."

"I'm still mulling it around..." he said slowly. "It's set in a small town...Like I said, I'm here for the atmosphere."

She darted a glance around at the old Victorian house with its top-drawer furnishings. "I didn't realize writing paid so well." If his writing paid that well, why hadn't she heard of him? She might not have much time to read, but mystery and suspense were her favorites.

Indeed, the gleaming kitchen and gracious dining room were very comfortable. Mac leaned back and gave Rilla what he hoped was his most sincere expression. "Another question, I see." He smiled, but his shoulders tightened and he resisted the urge to loosen the kinks. "No. No ill-gotten gains. Just a tidy inheritance from my grandfather's estate."

Dammit. Why was she acting so suspicious? Was something off in his manner? What had put her on the offensive? Why wasn't she buying his story?

"But why here in Tennessee? What drew you to this area?"

"Would you believe me if I told you I threw a dart at a map, and this is where it landed?" He'd seen a T.V. news reporter do the same thing once.

"I might," she replied with a smile of her own, before nailing him with, "if I thought you were telling the truth."

He did his best to appear amused. "Ouch. You're one tough lady, Rilla Devane."

Careful. He'd better handle the lady sheriff with kid gloves. He'd already made her suspicious.

"Comes with the territory." She squared her shoulders and jutted her chin at him. If he wasn't mistaken, the sheriff was a step away from getting up and leaving. And that wouldn't suit him at all.

"Don't get angry. I admire your toughness. It's very...seductive." He waited a beat, hoping she'd respond to his remark.

"I probably shouldn't have come here tonight." She let out a sigh. "By now, you must realize I'm no good at dating and making polite chit-chat. My life revolves around the job."

"You're more than the job. You're a beautiful woman—in case I haven't mentioned it before."

She brushed off his compliment with a roll of her eyes, although he noted a slight darkening of her cheeks. His never-fail charm was getting to her—he was sure of it.

"That's where you're wrong. I *am* the job. I was brought up in it. It's all I know." She stood. "I don't expect a civilian to understand. And that's the real reason tonight's a waste of time."

"Eating dinner's a waste of time?" He sprang from his seat and placed a delaying hand on her shoulder. "Don't go. Dinner's on the table. You're hungry and the dessert is beautiful." He grinned. "You said so yourself."

She paused as if considering his plea.

Dammit. He wanted her to stay. "I promise I'm one of the good guys. Besides, if you're as busy as you say, someone will call you before you can finish your dessert..." He waited a beat and shot her a look through lowered lids. "...and I can make my first move."

Before she could react to his flirting, her cell phone chirped.

No. He wanted her to stay. He hadn't lied about her air of authority being seductive.

She jerked the phone from her belt. "See what I mean? I don't have time for a life—or dinner." She flipped it open and growled, "This better be important."

She listened for a minute then shut the cell phone with a snap. "Gotta go."

"Something big?"

"'Fraid so. Another O.D. Her friends dropped her at the clinic, and she's in bad shape."

"Want me to come with you? Is there anything I can do?"

"No. I'll be gone the rest of the night. Sorry. I've ruined your dinner."

Mac shook his head. "Not at all. Are you sure I can't do anything?"

He *needed* her to stay, and just how much shook him. He couldn't risk letting his emotions get the better of him. Not again.

She hesitated, glanced at the ceiling, then back at him and shook her head. "No, thanks—for everything. Especially for listening. I know how much men hate whining."

He smiled down at her. "Not at all. You were telling me about your life—not whining." He took her hand between his, her slender fingers stiffening briefly, then relaxing. Touching her sent a jolt of heat straight to his groin. "Another time? Soon?"

Had she felt anything? Guess not, because she pulled away and continued her march to the door. Once there, she turned and faced him again, chewing the inside of her lip before she spoke.

"I don't know. Maybe—if I ever have time."

At least she hadn't told him to buzz off. No woman as confident Rilla Devane would ever have trouble telling a guy to hit the road. "You have to make time for yourself, Rilla. You know what they say. All work and—"

"Yeah, yeah, I've heard it before."

"Because it's true."

She gazed at him, her dark eyes flashing. "You have an answer for everything, don't you?"

He opened the door for her. "No, just a modicum of common sense. Sorry you have to rush off. After all, I still owe you a tour."

Just how much he wanted her to come back scared him. He wanted her to the tour the house...and damn, he wanted her in his bed. What had happened to his judgment? He couldn't bed a suspect and expect to keep his focus on the operation. Could he?

Chapter Three

Rilla's cork-soled sandals squeaked against the polished tile floor of the E.R. Good thing she had enough sense to wear them instead of stilettos.

One of her deputies stood in the hallway, shuffling his too-big feet. He was a tall, gangly, raw-boned guy—not much more than a kid. At the sight of her, his long jaw dropped. He recovered and straightened his shoulders, but didn't quite manage to wipe the smirk off his angular face. Did everyone in the department already know she'd had a date?

No, it wasn't a date. It was more in the order of a reconnaissance.

"Uh, Sheriff, I guess the dispatcher told you—"

"Yeah, Paulson. Where's the girl?"

"Didn't make it, boss." Paulson nodded to his left. "She's in there."

"Damn. Second one in a month. Tox screens back yet?"

"Nah, but her friends already told the doc they were using ecstasy."

"Where're they getting it? This isn't Nashville. Who's bringing this shit in?"

"Beats me." Paulson shrugged. "What I'm thinking is, it's gotta be somebody local. Nobody new in town."

Nobody new in town? Not quite true. Mac Callahan seemed to have a ready source of money. Again the question—was he the new dealer? But he was *too* new. The Springs' drug problems had been going on all summer. But he could've started the setup from a distance before moving to town to keep a closer eye on the operation. But why would he set up an operation in a town like the Springs? And why would he cozy up to the sheriff? She shook her head. In spite of her suspicions and the impression Mac was hiding something, she liked him. Would her job ever get any easier?

Back to business. "Where's the doc? I need to ask him a few questions."

The deputy grinned and pointed over his shoulder. "In the crapper."

She shut her eyes for a second and took a deep breath. "Too much information."

Paulson's homely face turned a deep red. "Uh, sorry, boss. The doc's takin' a break."

She sent the deputy a disapproving frown and opened the door to the exam room. God how she dreaded this. A nurse glanced up at Rilla's entrance, but continued removing the I.V. from the dead teenager's arm. "Hey, Rilla, how's it going?"

"Not good, Deb." From Rilla's position at the door, she made out two sandaled feet, but couldn't see the victim's face. "Who?"

"Barbie Soames."

No, not Barbie. A sinking sensation surged through Rilla.

"Didn't you baby-sit for her?"

"Yeah. Dammit. What were those kids thinking? Have things changed all that much since we were teenagers?"

Deb nodded. "You know it. We thought we had all the time in the world and we'd marry someone like Tom Cruise." She grimaced. "Man, were we ever wrong."

"All the promise, college, marriage—all gone. It makes me sick." In truth, as she stood gazing down at the pale blonde teenager, anger wracked every fiber of her being and shook her. All she wanted was five minutes. Five minutes alone with the culprit responsible for ending this young girl's life.

A keening wail rose in eerie crescendo then fell to a whimpering moan.

"Oh, God, Barbie's mother." Dread gathered and caught in Rilla's throat. She'd rather face down a mugger high on PCP anytime than talk to that girl's poor mother.

She turned and strode down the hall to the triage area where Sara Soames was collapsed in her husband's arms. At Rilla's approach, the devastated mother blinked and stared with an unfocused gaze. Her reddened eyes brimmed with tears.

"Rilla...Sheriff—" The woman broke off, glanced around helplessly and started sobbing.

"Sara, I'm so sorry."

Utter frustration and uselessness threatened to overwhelm Rilla. Children weren't supposed to die before their parents. The last thing in the world she wanted was to ask the grieving mother a bunch of questions. But she had a job to do.

As gently as she could, she asked, "Did they tell you what happened?"

Barbie's mother swallowed then nodded. "Yes. Dr. Logan said it was some drug...ecstasy." She looked at her husband, disbelief written across her face. "Where'd she get something like that?"

"That's what I have to find out." Emotion welled in Rilla's chest and made it difficult to speak. "We'll get to the bottom of it. I promise."

"I—I hope so...before another—" Barbie's mother stopped, clearly unable to continue.

Rilla nodded at Bill Soames. "Take her home...and take care of her."

Soames' eyes shone with unshed tears, and his face was flushed. He squared his shoulders and nodded. What else could the man do?

She had to put an end to the drugs. Clinton County had never had a big party drug problem, and she meant to keep it that way. Oh sure, there were the infrequent few who added to their incomes by growing marijuana—usually on someone else's land—but Clinton County was more of a hard-drinking, wife-beating kind of county. She was making progress on the meth labs—she'd already busted a half-dozen of the mom-and-pop operations since taking over her father's position. But until recently, ecstasy was more of a bright-lights, big-city drug. The Springs wasn't the same small town it was when she left for college. No indeed.

She turned from the Soameses and spotted three teenagers huddled in a corner of the triage area. Two boys and a girl. The Wyler brothers and Chief Deputy Barnes's daughter, Cher. There'd be hell to pay tonight. All three had tense postures, and Cher's swollen eyes and blotchy red face told the story. Both boys were pale and trying to act cool.

And failing.

The older Wyler, Rob, looked like he was a half second from skipping town while the younger hovered near a waste can like he might be ready to toss his cookies.

Double-date gone wrong? Bad wrong.

She walked over to the trio. "You all want to shed some light on what happened tonight?"

Rob Wyler flinched. "Am I under arrest?" His breath came in ragged gasps. He glanced around as if scouting for the nearest exit.

"Not yet. Are you to one who gave Barbie the X?"

He shut his mouth and clenched his jaw, but he couldn't control the muscle in his jaw which kept jumping like a nervous frog on its way to the frying pan.

"Rob?"

He shoved his hands in his pockets and studied the floor.

"*Someone* gave her the drug. *Someone's* responsible." She shot a glare at R.J.'s daughter. "Someone better start talking... Cher?"

The girl folded her arms across her chest and cast Rilla a stubborn stare. "I want my daddy."

"He's at the office," Rilla said. "And you're all coming down. You boys can call your folks after you get there."

"Shee-it." Rob looked at little brother Danny. "We're sunk. Dad's gonna lose it."

Danny rolled his eyes and swallowed hard.

A rush of quick footsteps. Mrs. Soames raced over to the group. "You killed my baby!" Before Rilla could react, Mrs. Soames grabbed the older Wyler by his shirt and shook him. "You murderer! It should've been you!"

The boy's eyes widened in shock. Rilla and Bill Soames jumped forward and pulled the heartbroken mother away from him.

Bill wrapped his arms around his wife. "Now, now," he murmured. "Enough. I'm taking you home." He half-guided, half-dragged her toward the exit, but glared over his shoulder at Rob Wyler. "You're gonna answer for this, boy. It ain't over by a long shot."

Rob cleared his throat. "Sheriff, you heard him. He threatened me."

"Can't say as I blame him." She took a deep breath. "Now. Here's how it goes down. Deputy Paulson's going to take you all to the office in his patrol car."

"Yes, ma'am." Cher's voice was scarcely above a whisper—probably already dreading what her father would say...and do.

She patted Cher's shoulder. "Go on. I'll be down shortly."

Cher chewed her lip and nodded. "Yes, ma'am."

She watched while Paulson herded the teenagers into the patrol car. The ignition cranked and the tailpipe belched smoke. *Needs a tune-up.* She watched until the tail lights turned into red pinpoints and disappeared in the distance.

She couldn't remember a worse night—not in the Springs anyway. They were all in for bad one. And like Bill Soames said, it wasn't over...not by a long shot.

Mac had waited until Rilla's Jeep was almost out of sight, then jumped into the Porsche and followed her to the hospital. What reason could he possibly give for following her—besides the real one?

His cell phone rang. He swore, but yanked it from his pocket. "Callahan."

"Progress report?" Havers said.

"How the blue hell can I make any progress when you're calling me every hour for a goddamn report?"

"I take your surly attitude to mean you haven't made any."

"You catch on fast. Now I know why you're paid the big money and I'm the DEA's errand boy."

"So how did dinner with the sheriff go? Did she even show up?"

"Yes, but as soon as we sat down, she was called away. Another teen O.D."

"Makes two in the last month."

"Yeah. I'm waiting outside the E.R. for the sheriff to come out. I'll check in when I have intel."

"Just be careful, Mac. Don't forget what happened last time."

"Yeah," Mac growled. "I know. Like I could forget?" A slim figure appeared in his peripheral vision. "Gotta go."

He watched Rilla herd the teenagers into a deputy's vehicle. She shook her head, walked to her Jeep, opened the door and climbed inside. The pale glow of the parking lot lights cast a shimmer of pale blue on her white slacks as she drew her long legs inside the vehicle.

Why couldn't she have worn a skirt? Man-oh-man. He'd give anything to see more of those long legs.

He waited for her to leave, but she didn't. Instead, she sat there staring straight ahead.

If he caught her off-guard, maybe she'd make a mistake. He eased from the Porsche Targa and ambled over to her Jeep. He tapped softly on the glass.

Rilla jumped, then rolled down the window. "What're you doing here?"

"Just wanted to see if there was anything I could do to help?"

Her forehead creased with a frown. Was she buying his helpful bit?

"Nope. Not much of anything you can do for that dead kid in there or her family."

"I'm sorry. Is there anything I can do for you? You look pretty shook up."

"I knew her—babysat for her when I was in high school. I'm distantly related to her family." She heaved a deep sigh and pounded the steering wheel with her fist. "This sucks. I'm gonna get this son of a bitch if it's the last thing I do."

"You will."

"Damn straight, I will."

She reached and turned the key. The engine cranked and caught. She glanced up at him through dark lashes and sighed. "Look, Mac. You're a nice guy—thoughtful, in fact—but you can see how complicated my job is. I just don't have time for anything else."

She's giving you the heave-ho, buddy. Gotta do something. Say something. "I'm sorry, too. Can't we be friends? Maybe it would simplify matters?"

Her expression went from frustrated to flabbergasted in a second flat. "Well?"

"I'll think about it...when I have time." She threw the gear into reverse and gunned it without so much as a backward glance.

Mac jumped back and laughed. "What a woman." He'd followed her to the hospital to see how she reacted when faced with the results of her dealing. Anger. She fairly vibrated with it. But was this the same woman who was capable of putting a hit on her own father and profiting from his drug deals now that he was dead?

No. The Agency was wrong. He'd bet his life on it.

After leaving Mac, Rilla drove straight to her office, all the while struggling to keep the questions at bay. Who was Mac Callahan? Something about him was off. Call it gut instinct or woman's intuition, everything she'd ever depended on in the field or on the job, screamed "He's too good to be true".

Was he the drug source? Whoever he was, he'd certainly bear further investigation.

Once in the office, she rang up her pal, Agent Jason Keyes at the TBI. They'd cleared a big case together when she'd worked for Metro, and he owed her a favor or two.

"Jase, I've got a mess on my hands here in Cherokee Springs. A couple of ecstasy O.D.s. in the last month. There's a new guy in town. Any chance you can check him out? See if he's ever shown up on TBI's radar?"

"Sure. Be glad to. Just give me the particulars."

Rilla told the TBI agent all she knew about Mackenzie Callahan.

"It's not much, but it's enough for a start. Any chance you can get a set of his prints?" Jason asked.

"It's not like he's done anything I can arrest him for—not yet anyway. But I can get some prints." Damn right she could. He'd leaned against the door of her Jeep. With any luck, he'd left a usable print or two behind.

"I'll push them through AFIS for you."

"Thanks, Jase." Rilla broke the connection and jumped up from her chair. She grabbed a fingerprint kit and ran outside, but stopped short. A stray dog was hiking his leg on one of her Jeep's front tires.

"Hey there, you hound. Those are my wheels, not yours."

The stray was a Chow mix, half-grown, and half-starved if she was any judge.

He jumped at the sound of her voice and barked a warning. He wagged his tail and gave her a level, but quizzical expression.

"Yes, I mean you," she told him good-naturedly.

The dog continued staring.

"You're in my way. Obstructing justice."

He whined, wagged his tail, and his expression grew hopeful.

"Okay. I'm convinced. You're cute. Now, move it." She tried a gentle nudge with her foot.

He whined again.

Such a pitiful sound.

"Are you hungry?" She reached down to feel for a collar. No collar and not an ounce of fat on him either. Just as she thought—a stray. He was probably covered in fleas and ticks, too. But he certainly had a sweet expression.

"All right, you can go home with me tonight, but you're going to the vet in the morning so he can check you out. Then someone can adopt you. I'm sure you're a very nice dog, but if I don't have time for a social life, I sure as hell don't have time for a dog."

"Sounds like you're trying to convince yourself, Sheriff. And fighting a losin' battle."

She glanced up. "Hey, R.J. Don't we have a leash law in this town?"

"You know we do."

"Well, get a leash on this mutt and—uh..."

"And what?"

"What do you think? Put him in the back of the Jeep."

"Lookee here, the sheriff's a softy," R.J. said with a snigger.

"Yes, but don't let it get out." She paused. "Damn it. Wait, bring him inside. I still have a ton of paperwork."

"Sure thang, boss."

Once Barnes had taken the dog inside, Rilla busied herself with checking for prints. She pulled out the brush and swirled it lightly in the area on the door which most likely contained Callahan's prints. She smiled and lifted them with a wide piece of tape and pressed them on a white card. "Gotcha, mystery man. Now, I'll find who you really are."

Later as she watched the interview through the two-way mirror, Rilla couldn't remember ever seeing her chief deputy so mad. Hands clenched at his sides, R.J.'s entire body vibrated with fury. He loomed over Rob Wyler, but the nonchalance with which the teenager stared back stymied her. Was the kid too stupid to realize the seriousness of what he'd done? She wanted to go inside and shake the truth out of him herself.

"What the hell were you two thinking? Giving this crap to your girlfriends... Cher's my daughter, you dip-stick."

Rob Wyler shrugged. "They're just party drugs. Everybody does 'em. How was I supposed to know Barbie was gonna drop dead?"

Rilla cringed and tamped down the rage. So, Rob had regained some of his bad-ass attitude. He'd been one pale puppy at the hospital, but now...

Now she'd like to smack the living crap out of him.

"Well," R.J. yelled, "Barbie Soames is dead—she won't be takin' anymore of 'em will she? And my Cher—could've been her who died instead of Barbie." He threw his hands in the air. "I give up. You and your brother are no damn good. He's a minor, but you're gonna take the fall for this one. Oh, yeah."

Disgust still written over his craggy features, R.J. opened the door to the hall where Rilla waited. "Gotta hold 'im," he growled. "He's eighteen. His brother and Cher are only seventeen. Think we can make it stick?"

She nodded. "Negligent homicide—it's a serious charge. D.A. shouldn't have any problems, but—"

"He needs to do hard time. Bill Soames' little gal is dead. Just as easy..." R.J. shook his head.

"You know how it is, R.J., if he flips on the dealer, he might get by with a slap on the wrist or even a suspended sentence."

"Hell, no."

"If he leads us to the dealer, and the dealer leads us to whoever's over him in the food chain..." Still, how would she ever face Bill and Sara Soames if Rob Wyler got off for turning state's evidence?

"It ain't right, Rilla, and you know it."

"I know." The urge to put her fist through the nearest wall shot through her entire body.

"Well, Cher'll talk to me, or else." He headed down to the room where his daughter waited for her turn.

"Good luck." The interviews with the Wyler boys had been a waste of time. Neither of them would talk. Thirty minutes later, not even R.J. could convince his daughter to tell where they'd bought the drugs. Alternatively he'd threatened and pleaded, but Cher only cried and shook her head.

Cher was still the weak link. But did R.J.'s daughter even know where the boys had bought the ecstasy? Usually the guys handled the drug buys.

R.J. came out of the interview room shaking his head. "I'm fit to be tied. I'm not getting anywhere with her. Stubborn as a mule...like her mama."

"Let me have a go at her. Maybe she'll talk to me. It hasn't been long since I was her age."

"Okay, but I'll tell you one thing, you never gave your daddy half the trouble this little gal of mine gives me."

She rested a comforting hand on his shoulder. "It's hard being a teenager—and it gets harder all the time. The drugs and the violence—they never stop. Too many choices and most of them are bad."

"You're too soft-hearted, Rilla."

"Maybe." She patted his shoulder. "Just tell Cher I want to talk to her for a few minutes. Then you can take her home."

R.J.'s face grew red. "Now, I don't expect no special treatment just 'cause she's mine."

"You aren't getting any." Rilla tried a smile. Her chief deputy needed to calm down. "Besides, I know where she lives."

R.J. paced back and forth in the narrow hallway, shaking his head. "This is awful. Just awful. I've tried to raise her right since Jolene ran off, but you know..."

"I know, R.J. I know." Poor guy. She'd hated seeing his pain. He'd been her father's best friend—and hers—for over twenty years.

Rilla walked into the interview room. Cher Barnes was a tall, skinny seventeen year old with long red hair and green eyes. Her normally pale complexion was as washed out as white sheets on the line. Her few freckles stood out like a field of copper polka dots. A sullen expression marred what was normally a pretty face. The girl sat chewing the cuticle on her right thumb.

Cher jumped to her feet. “You gonna yell at me, too?”

“No, hon, why don’t you have a seat. I just want to talk for you for a few minutes before you go home.”

A half sneer lifted the corner of Cher’s mouth. “Good cop, bad cop?” But the teenager shrugged and sat all the same.

“No,” Rilla said softly. Kids saw way too much police procedure on TV, but somehow, she still had to reach the basically good kid hiding behind a brash attitude. “I’m not much older than you, and I know what it’s like to be young and want to have a good time. I’ve been there.”

“Yeah, right. You were probably a narc.”

She repressed a sigh and sat opposite Cher. It wasn’t going to be easy, but a little attitude wouldn’t put her off. “You’ve had a rough night and your best friend’s dead. You owe it to Barbie to help us keep anyone else from dying.”

“I don’t know where Rob got the X. I know it’s not hard to get ’cause he can get it any time he wants. In fact, it’s better not to know.” She laughed a little self-consciously and glanced over her shoulder.

“Was tonight the first time?”

Cher shook her tangled mass of hair. “It was the first time for Barbie. I’d taken it a couple of times, and it was great. I told her she’d have a fantastic time.”

Slowly, muscle by muscle, the teen’s belligerent expression wilted to one of devastation. “It’s m-my fault. Barbie is dead and

Daddy will hate me forever. I don't know how to make it right." Tears glistened in her eyes. "I can't, can I?"

"The only thing you can do now is to help us find out who's dealing this stuff."

"If I knew, I'd tell you. I would."

"Okay." Rilla hugged the teenager and silently vowed she'd grind the dealer into dust once she got her hands on him.

"You go home now, but think about what needs to happen. You might remember something Rob or his brother might've said. Something small that didn't mean anything at the time."

"All right." Cher sniffed and ran a hand through her tangle of curls.

"Your daddy's going to take you home. You get some sleep. Later on, you might need someone to talk to about all this—to help you process it."

Cher's eyes widened. "You mean like a shrink or something?"

"Yeah, something like that."

"You think I'm crazy?"

"No, just a little confused—like most kids your age. I'll mention it to your dad."

"Great. He already thinks I'm his worst nightmare."

"No, he doesn't. He loves you and wants the best for you. That's all."

"He's gonna ground me 'til I'm thirty."

"Probably."

A ghost of a smile crossed the girl's face, a sign her usually upbeat nature was returning. Maybe there was hope for her yet.

"Can I go?" Cher stood and glanced at the door over Rilla's shoulder, obviously ready to get the hell out of Dodge.

"Sure. I'm through—for now." She escorted the teen to the outer offices where her father waited. "She's all yours, R.J."

R.J., still flushed, mumbled, "Thanks, boss."

With a mounting sense of frustration, she watched the pair leave. The younger Wyler boy had already been picked up by his parents. Giving the kids some time to think wouldn't hurt. Sooner or later, one of them would rat on the others.

Back in her office, Rilla pondered the files she'd pulled on ecstasy drug trafficking. Quickly she scanned the information. *Ecstasy, the Hug Drug—made for virtually pennies. Dangerous, can cause dehydration and the body to overheat. Can cause death. Allergies documented, too.*

An allergy? Maybe that was what happened to Barbie. Either that or it was a bad batch. Anyway the coroner would determine the actual cause of death.

Damn stuff could be bought for two dollars a pill, sold to the eager consumer for forty dollars each. A relatively small investment of one hundred thousand dollars would yield a million dollar return. And easy as hell to smuggle. One suitcase with a false bottom could carry forty thousand pills.

One hell of an investment.

But it was a lot more complicated to synthesize than methamphetamine. She'd bet money there wasn't a lab sophisticated enough within a fifty miles of Cherokee Springs, unless someone in Nashville had started up one. According to the reports, Mafia ties were needed for anyone selling ecstasy or any other drug in quantity. The reports said crime organizations were even banding together to buy and distribute the drug.

Crap. Who in Cherokee Springs had mob connections?

No matter how hard she tried not to, Rilla kept coming up with the same name: Mac Callahan. He was new in town and had plenty of money to spread around. Who else could it be? Maybe things were getting too hot for him somewhere else. Maybe he'd make sure his operation was going well and move on.

"Well, Mr. Callahan, I'll be keeping a very close eye on you from now on, and if you're the S.O.B., who's responsible, I'll see you get a nice, long prison sentence."

But she didn't want to believe it. He'd awakened long-buried desires, and once awakened, she didn't know if she could tamp them down again. And conjugal visits at Brushy Mountain State Prison weren't her idea of a relationship.

So she'd better get off her butt and clear him...or come up with the evidence to arrest him.

The dealer leaned back in his comfortable chair and chuckled as he read the headline of Cherokee Springs' weekly, *The Town Crier*. "Who's the Drug Czar?" How funny—if they only knew.

The cloned cell phone on the side table buzzed, sending the damn thing into a whirling frenzy. He snatched it and answered, "Yeah?"

"Dang it. This is going too far. Kids aren't supposed to die. We're supposed to be raking in the dough and the kids get to have a good time."

"Quit complaining. You've made more than a pocketful of the green stuff. More than your old friend, the sheriff, ever thought about with his penny-ante kickbacks to overlook Billy Bob Bass's marijuana crop. This is *real* money."

"I want out."

"That can be arranged." He broke the connection and heaved the cell phone across the room. "Damned amateurs."

Chapter Four

Sometime after midnight, Rilla made it home. So much for date night in the Springs. She looked down at her new roommate. “Hungry? Of course you are. You’re a growing puppy.”

The dog wagged his tail and looked up at her with a doggy grin.

“I hope you like roast beef sandwiches.” Rilla stood in front of the open refrigerator. She reached in and pulled out a plate of slightly dried-out roast beef. She grabbed an old take-out container, tore the roast into bite-size chunks, added slivers of Swiss cheese and set it on the floor.

“Tomorrow I’ll hit the grocery store and make sure you have some real dog food.” The dog lowered his head and wolfed down her offering. Apparently he approved.

“Don’t you get any ideas. You’re not a permanent guest. As soon as I find time, I’ll take you around to the vet and put you up for adoption. That way you’ll go to some nice family with kids who’ll have time for you…because I don’t.”

The dog collapsed on the floor with a pitiful whine.

“You’re not playing fair, mutt. You’re not.”

After the dog had eaten and taken care of his business outside, he settled down on a braided rug by the front door.

She stood with her hands on hips and informed him in her kindest and firmest tone. “Well, fine. But don’t think I’m all that impressed. I don't need a guard dog. I don't need a pet at all." Who was she trying to convince?

At one o'clock in the morning, Rilla slid between the sheets. Gran must've come by. The sheets had the clean smell of being freshly washed.

It had taken all her forceful insistence to keep Gran from setting the house to rights after Rilla'd moved in. "I'll do it in my own time—if I *ever* have the time."

Consciously she willed herself to relax, muscle by muscle.

From her bedroom, she heard the dog bark. "Hush." Another perfectly good reason she didn't need a dog. Too much noise. She was used to the peace and quiet which came with living alone...and she liked it that way.

He barked again. Now he was prancing about with his toenails clicking like castanet's on the hardwood floor.

Now what? Rilla pulled her piece from the bedside table. Automatically she checked the magazine and pulled back on the slide. "Okay, mutt, let's see what's got you so all-fired upset. And it better not be the damn cat from next door."

She inched toward the front door. Moonlight streamed in through the long windows on the east side of the house. The dog pawed and scraped at the door. The rug had been scrabbled to the side by his agitation, and the hair stood up across his back in a ridge like a Mohawk—the canine version of one anyway.

"You hear someone out there?" She eased over to the window and peeked around the blind. Her Jeep was in the deep shadow of the maple tree; she couldn't see a damn thing.

The dog kept barking. Now, that she thought about it, his barking was a reassuring sound. Maybe a dog wasn't such a bad idea after all.

The next morning Rilla turned off Green Street and pulled into the parking lot of the local home improvement store. Lloyd Bass had opened it twenty-five years ago. Luckily for Lloyd, none of the big chain home improvement stores had moved into the county, so her father's old friend had done well—very well if his recent expansion was a sign.

She jumped out of the Grand Cherokee, strode into the store and stopped at the cashier. "Hey, Allie. Where're the locks?"

Allie nodded and gave Rilla a knowing smirk. "What's the matter? Trying to lock out the most eligible man in town?"

"Huh?" Taken aback for a second, she'd forgotten how gossip traveled in small towns. "Something like that," she added with a smirk of her own.

"Don't know if I would—in your shoes." She nodded to the left. "Far end of aisle two—if you gotta."

"Thanks."

The chit chat done with, Rilla headed for aisle two, but stopped at the sound of a booming voice. "Rilla Devane, are you comin' in my store without stoppin' by to say howdy?"

Truly glad, she turned and beamed at Lloyd Bass. "No way I'd be so rude." She rushed over and hugged him.

"So how're you really doin', hon?"

His kind tone shook her from the matter-of-fact image she always tried to project. "I—" She swallowed and took a step back. "I'm doing all right. Honestly."

"Just *all right?* Listen, you need to come to supper. Katie's dying to see you. Why don't you—"

"I'd love to, Lloyd, but you know how it is. I'm pretty busy these days."

"Not too busy to see the Callahan fellow," he teased.

"Seems like you and Allie have been listening to the same grapevine. In that case, you'll already know my date was interrupted by the job. I'd hate for Katie to put herself out cooking one of her fabulous meals only to have me jump up and leave before I finished the salad course."

"Maybe when things settle down, you can get around to seeing some old friends." He said the words with a smile, but the sadness never left his eyes. Lloyd and her father had been best friends since grade school, played football together in high school and, until her father's death, went camping and fishing for a week every June on Reelfoot Lake.

"I'm sure it will. You and Katie'll be the first."

Always the salesman, Lloyd rubbed his hands together. "Now what can I do for you today?"

"New locks. I want to replace all the old ones."

Lloyd grinned and shook his gray head. "Hasn't been very long since people started locking their doors at all, but I've got some beauties here. Not to mention I've got the local contract for security system installations."

"Yeah. I was also thinking of maybe some motion detectors, too. Can't be too careful these days."

"Aw, hell, Rilla, you'll have the squirrels setting those suckers off all night long. How about some lighting which incorporates motion detectors? They'll light up, but they don't make that damn-awful noise."

She nodded. "That'll work."

"I can arrange for the new locks, the security system and the lights. Anything else while we're at it?"

She shook her head and grinned. "That's enough out of my pocketbook for today. How soon can you have it done?"

"For you, Sheriff..." Lloyd gave her a broad wink. "I'll have my installer out there today. He'll call you at the office when he's finished. That way he can give you all the instructions you'll need."

"Yeah. No rush." Old friend or not—no need letting Lloyd know she'd been spooked the night before. It'd be all over town the sheriff was a little on the nervous side.

Once her home security issues were settled, Rilla headed for the courthouse and her office. The courthouse was typical for turn-of-the-twentieth century architecture. A small town, scaled-down version of Greek Revival, the building boasted two stories of brick, with a triangular white pediment supported by four modest white columns. Her office was off the main corridor of scuffed marble floors. The marble stopped at the door to her office. No indeed. No marble, scuffed or otherwise, for the sheriff's office.

She walked through the outer office. Gina, the dispatcher, gave an absent-minded nod over her romance novel.

Rilla paused and leaned on the counter. "Must be quiet this morning." Something she already knew since the car radio hadn't squawked once on the ten minute drive from the hardware store to the courthouse.

Gina gave Rilla a minimal eye roll. "Plum dead, if you ask me." The dispatcher's gaze refocused on her book, then she snapped it shut. "Oh—speaking of dead—the coroner called."

"And?"

"I guess he might want you to call him back."

Rilla gave a mental shake. She couldn't strangle the flighty part-time dispatcher, who also worked part-time at the Curls and Cuts Emporium. The woman had been hired by Rilla's father, and rumor had it every Wednesday night the year before his death, his vehicle was parked in the driveway of her duplex on Spring Street. Presumably she'd given him some small comfort before he died, and Rilla couldn't bring herself to fire her—or strangle her either, for that matter.

"Thanks. I'll do that."

She eased down the hall to her office. The Coroner must've already determined the official cause of death. She plopped down in the chair and snatched the phone from its cradle. She punched in his number without looking at the file. She'd committed it to memory soon after taking office.

Coroner Eb Duncan was as good a coroner as a small county like Clinton warranted. He'd retired from general practice two years earlier, tired of fishing within two months and threw his hat in the ring when election time came...and to no one's surprise won. For any complicated cases, there was always the State Forensic Pathologist headquartered in Nashville.

Eb answered on the third ring.

"Got me a C.O.D yet?"

"Well, like you expected," Eb said, "it was drug-related."

"Allergy? Bad Batch? What?"

"Seems like this ecstasy causes dehydration, so it appears the little Soames gal was partying and having a good time. That caused her body to heat up, and according to R.J.'s little gal, Barbie drank a lot of water."

"So? Anyone would, but—"

"Hold on. I'm not through telling you. Another thing this drug does is cause the release of anti-diuretic hormone. I won't go into the technical physiology."

"Good. Just cut to the chase."

"All right. So the more she drank, the more water-logged her brain became until it herniated through the foramen magnum—that's a hole is the base of the skull where the spinal cord enters the brain. It depressed her respiratory center in the brain stem, and that's what killed her."

"Thanks, Eb." She replaced the handset and sat staring at the wall opposite her desk. What did it feel like, having your brain swell until you couldn't breathe?

She shook her head to erase the images from her mind. If Mac Callahan was responsible, she'd see he fried for murder—even if she had to pull the switch on Old Sparky herself.

Cherokee Springs had one funeral home. It was a long, one-story, white brick building with a wide veranda across the front. Two rows of rocking chairs flanked each side of the door looking for all the world like a Cracker Barrel General Store. Two older men sat side by side, puffing on cigars and shaking their heads, probably wondering what the world was coming to.

From her vantage point, Rilla watched teenagers file through the doors. Teenagers' funerals were the worst. And kids who once believed they were invincible were forced to face the reality they weren't. The death of a classmate brought it home like nothing else, even if only for a few hours.

Barbie Soames, cheerleader, last year's homecoming queen and all-around normal teen was dead. And while the Wyler kid might never feel responsible for giving Barbie the drug which killed her, Rilla blamed the son of a bitch who sold the drugs. Whoever he was, he was a bean counter with an adding machine in place of a heart.

She'd take him down if it was the last thing she did. And it might just be. It didn't matter a diddly-damn that the TBI had jurisdiction on drug cases. He'd already had her father killed, and now he was killing her friends and neighbors.

She couldn't put it off any longer. She opened the door and eased from the Jeep. Dread at facing Barbie's family again gathered in her stomach and slowed her pace.

Inside the funeral home, it was wall-to-wall kids, but Miss Tweedy spied Rilla right off and rushed over. "Rilla, this is the worst thing's ever happened in this town. Never saw anything like it in all my born days. You got to do something about these here drugs. We can't have our kids popping pills and killing themselves every other day."

"I'm doing my best, Miss Tweedy. The TBI is investigating the case. They'll sort it out."

"The TBI? Phooey. If your daddy were still alive, he'd set these drug dealers to rights. They'd be sitting in his jail right now. I don't mean to criticize, but your daddy was just that good. Best sheriff this town ever had. Got to find his killer. That's where you'll find your drug dealer—mark my words."

"I'm doing my best," Rilla said through gritted teeth. Miss Tweedy had a way of cutting to the quick...and all the way to the bone.

"And now little Barbie Soames is dead and the Wilkins boy last month." The old teacher tch-tched and shook her head.

She extricated her hand from Miss Tweedy's firm grip. The old gal was a lot stronger than she appeared. "Excuse me. I need to speak to the Soameses."

"Say, have you checked out the new guy I told you about? I told you he was suspicious."

"I'm keeping my eye on him. Don't worry."

She threaded her way through the standing-room-only crowd. Barbie's mom stood by the casket, holding onto the side of it for dear life with white-knuckled hands.

"I'm so sorry, Sara."

Sara looked up at Rilla. "I can't believe after tomorrow I'll never see her sweet face again. She won't come a-racing in the house to beat her baby brother to the leftover sausage biscuits."

What else could Rilla say? Certainly nothing which would be of any comfort. She slipped her arm around Sara's shoulder and shot the woman's husband a pleading look.

But the guilt lay at Rilla's door. She should've found the dealer by now, and if she had, Barbie might still be alive.

Bill Soames rushed over to his wife. She collapsed in his arms while sobs racked her body.

"I'm so sorry," Rilla managed to murmur. "We'll get the dealers—I promise you."

Soames nodded. "We know, Sheriff. Thank you for coming. It means a lot, but..." He leaned forward. "I want to know why the little bastard who gave our girl that drug isn't behind bars?"

Damn good question. "The judge let him out on bail, Bill. The D.A. asked for the judge to hold him without bond, but the judge didn't agree. The Wylers mortgaged their house and posted his bond. It's the way our justice system works."

"It's murder pure and simple, Sheriff."

"I know it must seem like it. Negligent homicide is what he's charged with. It's not a death penalty case."

"It oughta be."

"I don't disagree, but I have to follow the law." She patted him on the shoulder and turned to leave, but stopped. Mac Callahan had chosen that moment to walk into the viewing room. Anger heated her face. The man showed up everywhere she went. What the hell was he doing here...and talking to Miss Tweedy of all people?

Not like he had a valid reason. He wasn't a friend of the family. He hadn't lived in the Springs all that long. Morbid curiosity? Or checking the results of his handiwork?

She strode over to the pair. "Callahan, I didn't know you knew the Soameses. I'm sure they're touched by your concern."

Miss Tweedy spoke first. "Now, Rilla, he's just paying his respects like he ought." She pushed her wire-rimmed glasses up on her nose and nodded.

"Yes, ma'am. Miss Tweedy's right. And I do know Bill. He and his brother built the new deck on my house. Nice job, too."

Rilla forced a smile. "It's amazing. You haven't been in town very long, but you seem to know about everyone I know."

Callahan's gaze narrowed. "Small town, Sheriff. Pays to be neighborly."

"You stay here much longer and you'll sound like one of us." Quite the chameleon, he was. Another reason not to trust him.

A trace of annoyance creased his forehead, and just as quickly the expression vanished. "If you'll excuse me, I need to pay my respects to Bill and Sara."

She stopped short of allowing her mouth to drop open. Dammit. He was too nervy by half.

Miss Tweedy pursed her lips and nodded. "I might've been wrong 'bout him. Seems like a nice man, after all. Rilla, you could do a lot worse."

"Yeah," she said half-aloud. Her gaze followed Callahan across the room. He moved with the power and grace of a wolf patrolling his territory. She watched while he spoke softly with Bill Soames. Her quarry's face was grim when he turned from Barbie's parents. He nodded at Rilla, then walked out of the viewing room.

Dammit. Something about him wasn't right. How could she ever have thought he was date material? She headed out after him and caught him on the veranda.

He must've heard her rapid steps behind him. Before she could say his name, he stopped and turned. His intense blue gaze pierced her as effectively as a black talon bullet through a Kevlar vest.

"Yes, Sheriff?"

Her heart caught in her throat. Why did he have such an effect on her? She swallowed her nervousness. She wasn't a teenager, for Pete's sake.

"Uh—"

Then came his maddening—to her anyway—half-grin. That little bad boy smirk of his told her he knew exactly what she thought and felt.

"Are you going to the funeral?" she managed to stammer like a tongue-tied teenager. How could she let a suspect get to her like this? Hadn't Machine Gun Kelly had pretty blue eyes?

"No. As I said earlier, I wanted to pay my respects. I've paid them."

"I'm sure Bill and Sara appreciate it. Barbie wasn't a bad kid at all." She sighed and nailed Mac with a glance. "That's why I'll turn this county upside down to find whoever's responsible for her death."

There. That told him...and anyone else who might be listening. She turned and walked to her vehicle. Tension tightened her shoulders muscles until they weighed her down like sacks of concrete.

What she needed was a good session with the weight bag.

At home, Mac leaned back in his chair and rubbed his eyelids. He let out a heavy sigh. Time to check in with Havers. He punched in the number and hoped the boss was taking a long lunch.

"Havers."

"Listen here, Derek. You're wrong about Devane. I watched her at the funeral home. She's all torn up about these kids. She loves this town and the people."

"Maybe the sheriff's a good actress. Her old man had the town fooled for twenty years. Don't forget—her second bank account is suspicious. We're still tracking it. Large amounts in and just as quickly out. They're a dead giveaway. Chip off the old block I'd say."

"My gut tells me you're wrong."

"I'm not so sure you know what you're talking about."

"It's not like that," Mac insisted. Who was he kidding? It was exactly like that, and the boss knew it.

"See it isn't. This is your last chance. Screw up like you did last time, and you'll be riding a desk."

"I won't." Each of Havers' words hit Mac's gut like sucker punches. Leave the DEA? No family and few friends outside the agency. Undercover was all he knew. No *way* would he blow it again. No way.

"See you don't." Havers broke the connection.

Mac shook his head. Old Der wasn't a happy camper, and he'd left no room for doubt.

His assignment was to get close to the sheriff and find enough evidence to bring her and her drug contacts down.

Not exactly a difficult task—he *was* getting close to her. She was easy on the eyes. And her husky voice made him want to hit the mattress with her.

Still he'd done worse. Calling the last case a disaster was an understatement. He'd nearly blown the case and lost his life to boot.

But this time, he'd succeed—no matter who it hurt.

Rilla's basic philosophy was "when things get tough, the tough go to work". Waves of throbbing pain pounded through her head while she rummaged through the desk drawer, searching for a bottle of aspirin. An aspirin or two wouldn't be such a bad thing. Ready to abandon her fruitless search, she slid her chair back and stood, gingerly moving her head from side to side in a vain attempt to release the kinks in her neck.

Tension. Had to be. Seeing Sara and Bill Soames at the funeral home had been harder than she'd thought. Instead of graduating high school and going off to college, Barbie was lying in a box and by tomorrow evening, she'd be six feet under the hard-pack clay of Clinton County.

The drugstore was on the other side of the town square from her office. She might as well get some aspirin and some fresh air at the same time.

She sucked in a lungful of muggy air and set out for the drugstore. Her long strides quickly ate up the short distance. She opened the door and the cold blast of the A/C hit her. Whoever invented air-conditioning had changed the world. Damn if he didn't deserve a Nobel Prize or something.

At the back of the store, the pharmacist, who happened to be her old high school sweetheart, was talking to Tanya Timmons, a tall, skinny blonde with very big hair and a very small skirt. According to the local rumor mill, she was on the lookout for husband number two, since number one had run off with her little sister Tina. The Timmons matriarch, being more than a little fond of tequila, had given all her children names starting with T.

Rilla watched Tanya work Kurt and smiled. The blonde leaned across the counter. Her barely-covered butt wiggled and her shoulders twitched as she giggled. Could she be any more obvious? Tanya should consider herself luckier and wiser and take some time off from the dating game.

And maybe the same advice was good for the giver, too.

Kurt looked up at Rilla's approach and smiled.

She'd barely seen Kurt since coming back to town. They'd both been too busy taking over where their fathers left off. Was that a look of relief flashing across his chiseled features? The ten years had been more than kind. He could still pass for Brad Pitt's brother or at least a close cousin. Too bad she was more interested in a dark-haired fellow who didn't look like any movie star she'd ever seen. No, Mac had his own special...something.

"May I help you, Sheriff?"

Tanya glanced over her shoulder, frowned and cast Rilla a get-lost glare.

"Matter of fact you can. I've got a mother of a headache. Don't suppose you have bottle of aspirin somewhere in this drug store?"

Kurt nodded. "Sure thing." He handed Tanya her package. "There you go, hon. Remember my instructions."

"Of course, I will. But if I have any questions, I'll just give you a little ringy-dingy. Okay?" She turned to leave but not before she gave Rilla another look which said "eat worms and die".

"Sure, you do just that." He smiled at Rilla. "Now let me see. You want the generic or...?"

"Generic's fine." Rilla waited while Kurt rang up her purchase. "Now what's the deal calling me 'Sheriff'?"

"Just trying to be professional." He winked. "That's all."

She leaned on the counter and said in conspiratorial whisper, "Looks to me like Tanya was angling for a dinner invitation. You'd better be careful or you're going to end up as her next husband."

Kurt shook his head. "Frequent flier. She has *health* problems." He gave her a sly grin. "Speaking of dinner invitations...how 'bout it? Like to have dinner with your old steady?"

Startled, she stammered a hesitant, "Sure."

Damn. Second dinner invitation in a week. If this state of affairs kept up, she'd be too busy to do her job.

"Okay, how about tonight? Let's run into Nashville. I know some great places to eat."

Rilla shook her head. "No. Nashville's an hour away. Don't want to be so far out of contact."

"Well then, what about Uncle Billy's Catfish Paradise?" he asked with a wide grin.

"All that grease?" She hunched her shoulders in a theatrical cringe. "And those hushpuppies. Do they still—"

"—melt in your mouth like they did when we were seventeen?" he finished for her. "Yeah, they do."

She glanced down at her body. "I don't know."

"Come on, you can handle a little fried food. You don't weigh an ounce more than you did in high school." He gave her a glance of approval.

"All right. Nostalgia and fried food for two." She let out a giggle, but quickly sobered. "But you know how my job is. As long as nothing comes up."

"I know."

"Seven-thirty?"

"Yeah. See ya." Rilla whipped around and smacked into...

Chapter Five

Mac grinned down at the sheriff. Her startled expression made his day. "Hello, Sheriff. Nice day."

Her expression of surprise changed to one of annoyance. "Callahan."

"So official sounding?" How had he screwed up this time? What had happened to "Mac"?

She looked up at him—her face flushed quite nicely, too.

"Uh, Mac. Sorry, I whipped over here for some aspirin." She grabbed it from the counter. "Thanks, Kurt." She threw a couple of bills on the counter.

"That's too much," Kurt protested.

"Just credit my account," Rilla told him and high-tailed it like a perp on the lam down a dark alley.

What was her rush? Why was she in such a fizz to get away from him? He'd overheard her making a dinner date with the pharmacist. Were they an item? Was he competition? Jensen was about Rilla's age. Maybe they were merely old friends. Dammit. Why hadn't he come in time to hear more than the tail-end of their conversation?

Mac turned and watched Rilla flit down the aisle.

"Nice view. Good head on her shoulders, too," the pharmacist said.

Mac responded with a distracted, "Yeah."

"May I help you with something?" Jensen asked.

"Uh, batteries? Flashlight batteries."

Kurt smiled. "Our sheriff affects most men that way. Batteries—second aisle from the left. 'Bout half way down."

"Thanks." Mac headed for the second aisle. He had to make it look good. No point in announcing to the entire town he was dogging Sheriff Devane like a prize fox hound.

Now was as good a time as any.

Rilla parked the Jeep in R.J.'s driveway. She'd watched Cher meander home from school. Maybe she'd had time for it all to sink in. And just maybe she was ready to talk to her old friend.

She strode up the brick sidewalk to the front porch and bounded up the steps. Before she had a chance to knock, she found Cher glaring through the screen door.

"What's the matter, Rilla?" Cher stuck her bottom lip out like a petulant child. "You followed me home. Why didn't you give me a ride? Would've been more friendly-like." She frowned and opened the door. Slowly she walked outside and let it slam behind her.

"I didn't want to interfere if you had other plans. Just wanted to make sure you were coming home, so we could have a little chat. Have you had time to think about everything?"

"You mean am I ready to rat out my friends?"

"I know how it is." Dammit, she needed Cher to understand how serious the situation was. "It hasn't been long—"

Cher let out a heavy sigh. "Here we go again. Same song, second verse. Thing is, you don't understand. X is totally cool. It makes you feel so mmm...fantastic. I mean, you melt into the music. You're part of the whole scene. Your heart's in sync with the music. And the all those feelings—they don't call it the 'hug drug' for nothing."

"Cher—"

"Honestly. I don't believe it's addictive or harmful."

Frustration washed through Rilla like an acid bath. "Cher. Barbie died."

The teenager shrugged. "Well, she must've been allergic or something. I took it. And it never bothered me at all."

"Two deaths in two months. Listen here, young lady, you can keep wearing those blinders if you want to, but I'm putting you on notice. And you can tell your buddies too. I'm shutting this dealer down."

"Yeah, sure. Like you can do it all by yourself. Who do you think you are? You've been back two months and you still don't have a clue who killed your daddy." Cher set her hands on her hips and eyed Rilla with the arrogant disdain of a teenager who knew it all. "Yeah, some fine example, you are."

"You're right—for now. But I mean what I say. It may be the last thing I do, but I'll find the dealer, and when I do, I'll know who had my father killed."

"Woo hoo! Go get 'em, Sheriff Dee-vane." The girl turned, stopped and shot a smug glance over her shoulder, then sashayed inside the house.

For a moment, Rilla stood stock still. She'd lost her cool, come across exactly like an overbearing adult, and totally blown it. There had to be a way to get one of those kids to talk. Or was Cher afraid and hiding her fear behind a lot of tough talk? The drugs really had a grip on the kids in town. What Rilla needed was a weak link—but it was damn obvious the weak link wouldn't be R.J.'s daughter.

Later that evening, Rilla stood in front of the mirror and surveyed her khaki pants and navy knit top. Even with fairly sensible shoes, she was still overdressed for Uncle Billy's Catfish Paradise. She turned and checked her butt in the mirror. The slacks were definitely looser than the last time she'd worn them. If she lost anymore weight, her butt would be a memory.

All things considered, deciding what to wear to dinner with Kurt wasn't nearly the ordeal which dinner with Mac Callahan had presented.

Mac had been a date. Tonight was just dinner. Good old Kurt.

Safe. Responsible. Familiar.

At Uncle Billy's, Rilla inhaled the familiar odors of rancid cooking grease and fried onion loaves. Everything about Uncle Billy's said country and crispy-fried catfish and hush puppies. It hadn't changed a bit in the last twenty years—as long as you didn't take into account the tablecloths were now blue-and-white gingham instead of the old red-and-white.

After dinner, Kurt leaned across the table and grinned exactly the same way he had when they'd dated. "So how's it going? Being sheriff, I mean?"

"It's a lot harder than I thought. You know, Daddy made it look so easy. It's bad enough I haven't found his killer, but now two kids have died in the last month. I'm pretty discouraged."

"Have another hushpuppy. You worry too much. You'll find Ben's killer, and you'll put an end to the drug traffic. I have all the faith in the world in you, Rilla—the whole town does."

"Thanks, but sometimes I'm not sure I'm up to the job." She leaned back, shuddering at the thought of all the fat grams she'd consumed—a week's worth, at least.

"Let me give you a hand."

"How?"

"You know how it is in small towns. Sometimes I hear things. You wouldn't believe what people tell their friendly pharmacist."

She nodded. "Yeah, sure." How discouraging, when the local druggist felt he had to lend a hand because she wasn't cutting it.

"Hon, you're underwhelming me with your enthusiasm."

"Sorry. It's been a hell of a week."

"So what's with you and that guy—Caldwell?"

"Callahan. Mac Callahan. He asked me to dinner. That was the night Barbie Soames O.D.'d."

"Ah." Kurt grinned as if pleased. "I guess it put the kybosh on your date."

"To say the least."

"Ever think what our lives might have been like if we'd stayed in town and gotten married after high school?"

"Wh-what?" She knotted her napkin then tried to undo the damage. "Can't say I have. Whatever made you ask something like that?"

He grinned, removed his wire-rim glasses and studied them casually. "You have to admit we had something pretty hot going on for over a year."

Her face heated. She rolled her eyes and tried to grin. She'd lost her virginity with Kurt in the back seat of his father's old Mustang, but she wasn't interested in a repeat.

"That was a long time ago. We were kids."

Something flickered in his pale blue eyes. Did she imagine it? Whatever it was passed quickly, replaced by his usual twinkle.

"You're right," he agreed with a smile. "But a fella can't help wondering. Besides, this town is a little short on feminine charms. I haven't dated anyone since my divorce in Chicago."

Great, so he was horny.

She laughed, hoping he'd take the hint. "Wonder no more. I haven't dated anyone since I found my fiancé screwing a gal from Vice in my bed. I've had it with men. I don't have time to have my hair done much less have a life. The job is all I care about."

Shaking his head, Kurt leaned back in his chair. "That's not good for ya, darlin'."

Her phone chirped—-thank God. "Told you."

"Devane," she answered and listened to the news which would effectively interrupt the second evening out she'd had that week.

She disconnected and turned her attention back to Kurt. "Sorry, but R.J. says there's been a bad pileup on Forty-one. See what I mean?" She gave a regretful shrug. Not that she was upset at the interruption. Their conversation had wandered into uncomfortable territory. Good old memory lane.

On the other hand, if she'd been out with Mac—no, wait a minute, he was a possible suspect—not date material either.

She stood, ready to leave. "At least we had time to eat dinner."

Like the gentleman he'd always been, Kurt rose and pulled back her chair. "I'll walk you out." He threw a handful of cash at the cashier as they walked by her. "Make sure Ellie gets her tip."

"Sure thing, Kurt," the cashier said with a flirty wink. That fact she was sixty-two going on seventy didn't faze anyone.

"I'll reimburse you," Rilla offered.

"I don't believe in going Dutch. But if you want, you can buy mine next time."

"Sure, that's a promise," she agreed, anxious to be on her way.

By the time they reached her Jeep, she shifted into on-duty mode. She jerked the door open, jumped in and slammed the door.

Without a backward glance at her date, she checked over her shoulder, shoved the gear into reverse and backed out.

Long before Rilla cleared the accident scene, fatigue had taken up residence in every cell of her body. The muscles in her shoulders throbbed from one pressure point to another. Back in her office, she rolled her shoulders in a vain attempt to loosen the tension.

Two fatalities—a father of two on his way home from work and a teenager joyriding in his father's car.

Other than the years of misery and guilt, which would be a permanent visitor for the victims' families, there was nothing left for her but hours of paperwork.

The thought of those hours stretching ahead made her question her choice...her dedication. What would it be like to come home after her shift to a husband or children? Right now, all she had was one mutt dog—

"Crap." Ralphie was home alone. Quickly she gathered up the papers. "R.J., I'm taking this home."

R.J. grinned. "Gotta feed the doggie?"

Rilla gave an embarrassed laugh. "Yeah. Something like that."

"Yeah, pets're just like babies." R.J. gave a chuckle. "Next thing you know you'll have twenty cats swarming all over the house and the neighborhood kids will start avoiding your side of the street."

"Will not." But the truth was, something like that could happen. Not the twenty cats, but she could grow old and crotchety...and alone. "This is only one dog, and he's going to the vet tomorrow."

"As you said last night, if I remember correctly."

"Didn't have time."

R.J.'s broad shoulders shook with unrestrained laughter. "Just remember what I said about those cats. Meow, meow..."

Rilla wadded a scrap of paper and tossed it at her chief deputy. More nimble than most men his size, he ducked and swatted it back like a tennis pro.

"Have to put you on report for littering, boss."

She reached and caught the paper wad, then tossed it into the waste can. "Now you don't have any evidence."

"Shocking abuse of power. Obstruction of justice."

With a grin, she stood. "R.J., I'm outta here."

"Nite, boss."

Two tall maples in front of Rilla's house shaded the last third of the drive way, leaving a dark eerie appearance. She seldom used the detached garage. It was full of her grandmother's furniture which wouldn't fit into the elder Devane's new condo.

Unlocking the door, she shivered. The hair stood up on the back of her neck. Glancing around, she didn't see anything out of place. But it was dark. Damn dark. Once the new lights were installed, she'd feel better. Guess Lloyd's installer hadn't gotten around to putting them up yet. Wonder why? After all, if her father could be shot in the driveway, home wasn't safe. No place was.

The click of toenails against the hardwood floor and puppy woofs greeted her. She opened the door and Ralphie scampered around in circles.

"Happy to see me, are you?" She headed toward the back of the house. "Come on. I know you need to go outside. At least I hope you do." She opened the back door and let the dog outside. She followed to keep a watchful eye on him.

As soon as the dog had anointed every bush in sight, he ran back to her, his tail wagging and a doggy smile on his face.

"Your Prince Charming routine doesn't work with me." She knelt down beside the dog, ruffling his longish, thick black hair.

But his routine was working; the tension leached from her shoulders.

"All right. All right. You can stay. But you're still going to the vet tomorrow. He'll check you over and start you on your shots. And I don't want you to be afraid. It'll only hurt for a second. If you're going to be my guard dog, you have to stay in tip-top shape."

She hugged the animal to her chest. He was warm and alive, and she didn't have to worry about whether or not he was a drug dealer like a certain new man in town.

The memory of Mac Callahan's warmth flooded through her. She couldn't get involved with a suspect, but he was the only man she'd met in the last few months who touched her on such a deep level.

"Ralphie, let's have dinner, then I have to do a stack of paperwork. I'm afraid I'm not going to be much fun, but if you're a very good puppy, I'll let you sleep on the rug beside my bed. How's that?"

He seemed to understand. He grinned and his fluffy tail twitched with dignified enthusiasm. He trotted inside, leaving Rilla to shake her head in disbelief.

Damn smart dog.

The next day was a relief. Quiet, without a single disaster. For once, Rilla figured she might actually leave early. Maybe, just maybe, she ought to think about unpacking some of those boxes which were still sitting where the movers left them two months ago.

The telephone rang. "Damn. Suckered again." She grabbed the phone. "Devane."

Jason Keyes' deep voice boomed in her ear. "Good news, Sheriff. Your guy comes up clean."

"No match? Are you sure?"

"Absolutely. Your guy's prints aren't on file with AFIS."

"Thanks, Jase."

"Anything else I can do?"

"I know TBI has original jurisdiction on drug cases, 'cause I need all the help I can get. The son-of-a-bitch who's flooding Clinton County with ecstasy has to go down. Two teens in the last month are two too many."

"Never-ending battle, Rilla. But I assure you we're close to tracing the money trail."

"God, I sure hope so. And daddy's murder? Think it's connected?"

"I always did. It was a contract hit—we do know this much. It was too well planned. And it was set up by someone who knew your father's schedule. Someone who knew every Wednesday at noon, he'd go home to pick up his mama and take her to her bridge game."

"Hell, everyone in town knew. He'd done it for the last ten years."

"You have to hang tough, but these cases take time, sometimes a lot of time."

"Yeah, I know, but I feel so damn useless."

"Look, you have enough on your plate. Let us do our job. You know I'll keep you informed."

"I know. Thanks."

"Anytime, Rilla. I only wish we could solve this yesterday."

Common sense told her Mac Callahan was either one of the good guys, or he hadn't been caught. Unfortunately that fit the profile of his being the drug kingpin rather than a run-of-the-mill dealer.

Even if Mac Callahan wasn't a drug dealer on the side, he was definitely hiding something. She didn't need a lie detector to tell her that.

Time to do something about Rilla. Woman was too damn smart. If she kept digging away, eventually she'd come up with the right answer...or the wrong answer for her.

He considered his options. Could he scare her off? Doubtful at best. Still, for old time's sake, he could try.

He slid the cell phone from his pocket and hit the speed dial.

"Yeah, boss?"

His boss laughed, but it was an ugly sound. "Your friend—she's getting nosy. We're gonna have to do something."

"No way! Not me!"

"Who else? If not you, I have a neat solution."

"Now wait. How about a little warning? Remind her how fragile life is?"

"Don't get inventive. You'll screw it up. Make it look accidental. Don't want to put her on guard."

"I'll think of something—just not like her pa."

"I don't know what you're talking about."

Rilla scanned the grocery shelves and sighed. Okay, dog food was easy. The Any-Time-Any-Reason Market boasted at least four name brands suitable for puppies. She hoisted a forty pound bag into her cart, but the multitude of accessories was another matter. Leashes, collars—how big was the little bugger's neck anyway—doggy soap, shampoo and last, but not least, toys. Toys she hoped he would chew instead of her belongings.

"Damn. This is worse than having a baby."

"Did you say something about a baby?" a deep masculine voice asked.

She whirled around. The too-good-to-be-true, new man in town stood there, as casual as a farmer in his own field. And grinning. Dammit.

"Callahan."

"None other. Now what were you saying about having a baby?" His dark blue eyes glinted with mischief.

She huffed. "Not a baby-baby. A dog—specifically—a half-grown puppy." She made a quick grab for a leash and collar. She had to get away—before she lost her determination to resist his charm.

"I wouldn't have thought—"

"Wouldn't have thought what?"

"None of my business."

She huffed and tamped down her irritation. "But you've already started. Say it."

"Puppies take a lot of time."

"He's not a tiny puppy. He's probably six months old. More like an adolescent."

Callahan's mouth twitched. "But they say teenagers are the worst."

She gave him the old eye roll routine. "Very funny. And what's so damn funny about my having a dog?"

He straightened. "Nothing. Just trying to be funny and failing."

She reached out and grabbed a bone-shaped toy of colorful twisted twine. "I've got to go."

"Don't rush. I wondered if you'd like to try having dinner again."

Heat rushed to her face and her heart slipped into overdrive. "No, 'fraid not. You see how it is? I'm pretty busy."

She turned, ready to escape.

"I'm not giving up on your having dinner with me. And I still owe you a tour."

Why did he have to be so nice...and so damn sexy? And why did her knees go wobbly?

Hell. Why did Callahan have to be so damned high on her list of suspects?

"I-I can't promise anything. Maybe one day I'll show up for a tour—if it won't interfere with your writing schedule?"

A lazy smile spread across his face. "Interrupt me anytime, Sheriff."

Damn his lazy smile. "Well, sometime soon." She glanced at his empty basket. "Aren't you buying anything?"

The scoundrel winked. "I hear there's a special on hog jowl. Heading back to the meat department now. See you soon." He chuckled and shot her a casual salute. "Good luck with the baby."

Hog jowl?

Who did he think he was kidding? The man strolled off as if he had all the time in the blankety-blank world, leaving her with her mouth wide open and her heart beating entirely too fast.

Now why was it, everywhere she went, he turned up, too? Was he following her? The quicker she figured out Callahan's game, the better off she'd be...and her town, too.

But did he have a game plan? Maybe he really was the nice—not to mention sexy as hell—guy he seemed.

Dammit. She had to know.

Chapter Six

The sky was a clear blue and the warm summer sun beat through the window of the Jeep Cherokee. Rilla loved Tennessee in the summer and couldn't imagine living anywhere else. At the intersection with Ames Road, she braked before pulling out, but the pedal collapsed beneath the weight of her foot.

"Damn. It's not time for a brake job." She pumped the pedal until it recovered its usual position. She'd have them checked at the garage once she signed in at the office.

Her office at the courthouse was in the middle of town. Only three stoplights between her house and the office—shouldn't give her too much trouble.

Her radio crackled. "Sheriff?"

She grabbed the walky-talky. "All right. I'm on my way."

"Got a break-in out at the Deans' place. Can you take it? Charlie's busy with a traffic stop."

"What about R.J.?"

"Stayed home. Got some kind of GI bug."

Gingerly she tested the brake pedal. Not too bad. "Okay. I'll take it."

She checked the traffic flow and executed a U-turn. Bill and Martha Dean lived about five miles outside the city limits. She'd be there in no time.

She took SR 60, a twisty, winding road. Any other time she'd consider the picturesque drive a pleasant one, but with questionable brakes, she'd have to pay attention to her driving and forget about the scenery.

Stop being such a damn worry wart. The drive went well...until she topped Sullivan's Hill. At the bottom she saw a tractor pulling onto the road, a farmer heading to his next field down the road.

"Crap." She pumped the brake pedal, but her foot sank to the floorboard. She yanked on the emergency brake. Useless.

The driver of the tractor wasn't in any hurry and deserved a ticket for taking his tractor on the road, even if it was a short distance.

But writing a ticket was the least of her worries. Furiously she pumped the pedal again and again. No luck.

Adrenaline coursed through her body. Belted in. All she could do was...

Swerve and take the opposite side—

No—oncoming car.

Rilla whipped the steering wheel to the right. Her left rear fender scraped the rear tire of the tractor. The jarring shook her, but the Jeep kept moving. She bumped and careened through a ditch and landed in a corn field, her vehicle still moving.

Reaching for the key, she turned off the motor. Finally, the car shuddered and rolled to a stop.

She heaved a sigh of relief, but quickly remembered the farmer on the tractor. She opened the car door and jumped out.

The farmer had already climbed down from his tractor and rushed toward her. "You all right, Sheriff?"

"I'm fine. What about you? I clipped you when I swerved."

He glanced over his shoulder at the tractor. "Looks okay. It's pretty sturdy. Take more'n a little Jeep to upset that baby of mine."

A shiver passed through her body. "I'm sorry. My brakes were feeling mushy, but when I hit Sullivan's Hill, they gave out."

She pulled her radio off her belt. "Dispatch, Devane here. My brakes failed. I've landed in a cornfield, but someone needs to answer the Deans' call, and I need a wrecker."

"Hell, Sheriff," came the dispatcher's shocked reply. "You all right?"

"I'm fine. Just get somebody out here."

"Sure, boss."

Back in the office, Rilla drummed her fingers against the chair arm. The call to the Deans' had been a hoax. According to their nearest neighbor, Bill and Martha had gone to Dollywood for the weekend. And nothing was amiss at their place, either.

The Jeep Cherokee had been hauled to the garage for a once-over. So she waited for what she already knew.

Ring.

Finally. She grabbed the phone. "Devane," she barked, "was the brake line cut or not?"

"Well, Sheriff, emergency break was cut through, but the regular lines were nicked. Now it was a small one, but to my way of thinkin', someone did it—maybe coupla days ago. It wudn't no accident."

"Thanks, Denny. When'll it be ready?"

"'Bout five."

"Fine." She slammed the receiver. It was true, then. Someone had actually messed with her brake lines. And it had to be the first night she'd brought Ralphie home—the night he'd barked and nearly had a fit.

Someone had tried to kill her. Maybe she was lucky she hadn't been shot like her father.

Well, someone had made a mistake. She was still alive and by damn he'd have to do better if he was going to take her out. She wouldn't go easy into any kind of night.

Fingers laced behind his head, Mac reclined in his chair. Could Rilla, a verified dog lover, be dealing drugs to the entire town? Logically of course, she could. But he didn't buy it. His only problem, besides finding who the real drug dealer was, would be convincing his boss, Derrick Havers, the lovely sheriff wasn't dealing anything more dangerous than dog biscuits. Maybe someone was setting up the sheriff?

Nothing to do but to call him and get more intel.

"Havers, I want to see what else the Agency has on Rilla Devane. She strikes me as an up-front kind of person. It doesn't compute—a hot shot detective on the fast track to lieutenant abandons it all and settles down in this one-hick town to run her father's drug ring? I don't buy it. Maybe someone set up that second account to hide his dirty dealings and to make her look dirty if the bank account came under scrutiny."

"That's a possibility. But here's another. You're getting too involved with this woman. I hear it in your voice, and that's the quickest way to blow this investigation. I've a good mind to pull you off the case."

"But—"

"But nothing. You were outta commission for six months after the last case. If you blow this one, I can't save you."

"I won't. And I'd bet my left nut Devane's not our dealer. She idolized her father. And she'd be the last one he'd pull into his drug operation."

"You've been wrong before."

"But I got her in the end. The end result is what counts."

"Not before she'd shot you twice."

"Believe me, I haven't forgotten."

"Then remember this. Devane's still our main suspect, and don't let your 'nads do your thinking." Havers disconnected, but not before Mac recognized the all-out, pissed-off frustration in his boss's voice.

He didn't blame Havers. He'd been more like a father than a boss. The last fiasco still gnawed at Mac, too—even more than the punctured lung and busted femur.

Besides, Rilla Devane was nothing like Teri Chaney. Teri was the helpless female type he never fell for—except he had that one time.

She'd brought out every protective instinct still residing in a twenty-first century male. But he should've heeded the old adage about the female being deadlier than the male. She was supposed to be his informant, but she turned out a stone-cold killer, who killed her husband's business partner, her husband and nearly Mac.

While he sweated through the grueling rigors of rehab, he swore he'd never be taken in by another woman. Now, here he was falling for his prime suspect.

Rilla pulled into the driveway of Lloyd and Katie Bass's house. She'd promised Lloyd she'd come to dinner sometime soon, and sure enough, Katie had called and insisted she come tonight.

Lloyd and his much younger wife, Katie, had certainly prospered. They'd bought the largest house on North Main and completely restored it. Katie'd been born on the wrong side of the tracks—if a town the size of the Springs could have a wrong side. She grew up in a ramshackle frame house which never saw a lick of paint in all the years Rilla and Katie were friends. It was down the street from the feed mill that blew up one Wednesday afternoon, killing three of the workers. That very day, Katie vowed she'd never work in the mill. She'd marry someone with money and live in one of the big houses on North Main. Rilla hadn't discouraged her friend's dreams.

In fact, once her friend had set her mind on success, she finished high school in the top ten, went to U.T. on a partial scholarship. By the time Katie graduated with a degree in interior design, she'd developed a polish and sophistication which startled everyone who'd known her before. She'd returned to the Springs, calmly set her sights on the newly widowed Lloyd Bass.

Rilla jumped from the Jeep and strode up the brick sidewalk. The old Queen Anne Victorian was even grander than Callahan's. She shivered. Must be the thought of Callahan being so near.

"Rilla, darlin' come in here." Clad in pale blue silk, her hair smoothly styled in a sleek blond pageboy, Katie Bass ushered Rilla into the dining room. Everything about her old friend said money from her expensive clothes to her flawless makeup to her heady, pricey perfume. Her present appearance was a far cry from their high school days when the teenage Katherine Luanne Sutter came to school wearing Pricemart's cheapest jeans and sweats.

The table was set for four. It didn't take any great detecting skill to know she'd been set up. The only mystery was who?

She turned and gave her friend the evil eye. "Katie?"

A smile wreathed her friend's face. "Now, don't get upset. We invited one of our neighbors. You'll like him. He's new in town."

Oh, no. Maybe she should pray for another *date-us interruptus.*

"And here he is now," Katie said with more glee than absolutely necessary.

Yes, there he was now. Callahan stood at the front door, holding a bottle of wine, his familiar smile kicking up one corner of his mouth. He had a perfect mouth...perfect for kissing.

Dammit. Did any man have the right to be so downright tempting? How was she supposed sit still and eat dinner with a red-blooded, American version of a Greek god sitting across from her, while he watched her with those mischievous eyes of his? Something behind those blue eyes said he knew something she didn't.

And that bugged her most of all.

Her feet dragging, Rilla followed Katie to the front door.

Take deep breaths. Take several deep breaths.

"Mac, darlin', it's so good to see you again." Katie opened the door and continued, "In fact, Lloyd and I both worked with him on redoing his house...right down the block."

Rilla glanced at her watch and avoided Callahan's knowing smirk.

Katie looked from one to the other. "You two have met, haven't you?"

"Oh, yeah," Rilla muttered.

"Indeed, we have," Mac said. "It's great to see you again. I still owe you a tour."

Why couldn't the San Madrid fault hiccup? Why couldn't the floor just open and swallow her? But no, the damn oak floor stayed intact.

"It's good to see you, too," she managed. Throat dry as a stale piece of toast, she coughed. She'd pay Katie back for this piece of treachery somehow.

Mac held out the bottle of wine. Was he surprised at seeing Rilla at the Basses? No. Katie Bass had given him enough hints. "*She's single, attractive and highly placed in local law enforcement.*"

And since his suspect was easier to investigate up close and personal than at a distance, he'd accepted the invitation. Who was he fooling? Pass up a chance to have dinner with Rilla? Never.

Katie took the bottle of wine. "Aren't you just the sweetest thing. You didn't have to bring anything but your handsome self. Lloyd's on his way. He called right before Rilla got here."

"I'll—uh, check the salad," Rilla volunteered and disappeared into the kitchen.

"I think she's a little shy, don't you?" Katie offered.

"Shy? I don't know about that, but she's on the skittish side, I'd say."

Out on the pool deck, Mac watched as Lloyd took a drag on a cigarette.

"Won't let me smoke in the house, Katie won't. My house, too, but what can you do? Women."

Mac laughed. "Yeah." As if not letting a man smoke in the house was the worst one could do.

"But you don't have to worry, do you? You've got it made. Single fellow with plenty of money."

"Not a lot, but I like to invest what I have. Add to it," Mac said, hoping to draw Lloyd out. If Rilla wasn't the drug lord, someone else was. An extremely successful businessman, like good old Lloyd, might have more than one line of income.

"I've a few investments myself," Lloyd said. "I do pretty well. I could make a few suggestions if you're interested. Local things to keep an eye on. You know—with good growth potential."

"And the risk?"

"A bit, but got to spend money to make money."

"True," Mac admitted. "So...what do you have in mind?"

"The local hospital is managed by the number five hospital corporation in the nation. The stock's on the low side of thirty right now, but I'm sure it's on the way up. I have it on good authority they've leveraging to buy the fourth."

Insider trading—not what Mac had in mind. "And how do you happen to know?"

"Friend of mine sits on the board of the local hospital. Good source."

"I'll call my broker tomorrow," Mac lied. "Anything else? I'm not opposed to..." he paused, "more unconventional investments," he added with a smile and a shrug.

"Like tech stocks?" Lloyd frowned. "I'm not sure what you mean."

"Well, I'd like an excellent return on my money...quickly."

"Now, son, junk bonds are too risky. You're better off to stay with the DOW and the NASDAQ. Be careful."

Disappointed, but a little relieved, Mac hid it and laughed. "Never mind, I guess I'll have to find another way to invest my money." Lloyd Bass, if he knew anything about the drug trade, wasn't revealing it on such short acquaintance.

Lloyd's wife walked onto the deck and set her hands on her hips. "Can't leave two men together for more than five minutes, and if they're not talking the Titans, they're talking stocks and investments." She peeked over her Oakleys. "How's the salmon coming, or have you overcooked it again?"

She walked over to the grill and poked the salmon steaks with a fork. "It's a good thing we women folk are around to keep you men straight, or we wouldn't have dinner at all."

Lloyd cast his gaze downward and looked ashamed. "Sorry, Katie darlin', but—"

"Just never you mind. Bring those steaks in and give me a hand with the salad."

Through an open window the savory smell of grilled salmon wafted in while Rilla listened to Callahan and Lloyd's exchange.

Was Callahan merely shooting the breeze or trying to recruit Lloyd into some kind of drug scheme?

The oven buzzed. "Katie," she called through the window. "I'm taking the bread out of the oven."

"Be right in," her hostess replied, "as soon as I can get Lloyd to shift his lazy behind."

"I'm coming. I'm coming."

Poor Lloyd. Henpecked to death.

After pulling the hot crusty rolls from the oven, she turned and found Callahan eyeing her intently with his arms folded across his muscular chest.

"Get a good picture?" She tried softening her tone, but wasn't entirely sure she succeeded.

"Definitely."

His deep tone reverberated in her chest, setting her heart to pounding as if she were chasing a perp down a dark alley. She stepped back and stumbled.

"Watch it! I'm pretty fond of those rolls." He grabbed and caught the bread pan. "Ouch!"

"It's hot. Things right out of the oven usually are."

A wide grin softened his intense gaze. "Not as hot as you are right now." His tone was low, intimate and not heard by anyone but her.

Her knees wobbled and the blood rushed to her face. Damn. Callahan made her feel sexy and awkward at the same time. It wasn't fair.

She sighed in total exasperation. "Dinner's ready."

After dinner served on the patio, Rilla slipped off her sandals and dabbled her toes in the water. Callahan stood right behind her—too close for comfort. "Still warm, isn't it, from the sun?" His tone was warm, too. What the heck was he up to now?

"Yeah, feels good though," she admitted grudgingly. Warm water. Warm tone. It was enough to drive her batty.

"Why don't y'all go for a swim?" Katie suggested.

As tempting as it sounded, Rilla shook her head. "No suit."

Lloyd's voice boomed. "What's wrong with skinny dippin'? Or don't you do such things up North?"

"You just hush, Lloyd. We're not about to do any such thing. Rilla can borrow one of my suits, and Mac can borrow one of yours."

"Well..." Rilla hesitated. The idea of seeing Callahan in a pair of swimming trunks was more than tempting, but was it a good idea? He was still her choice for drug kingpin. And no matter how good he looked, she'd still arrest him once she proved it.

"Sounds good to me," the traitor said and winked.

She glanced away, refusing to humor him. He had no business coming to dinner with her especially after she'd warned him she didn't have time for a social life.

"Okay, that settles it." Katie nodded toward the cabana. "Come on, Rilla, I've got the perfect suit for your cute figure."

Rilla's faced heated. This hadn't been part of the dinner plans. Cavorting about in a skimpy suit...

Ten minutes later she stuck her head out of the changing room. The men hadn't appeared yet, so she ran across the slate slabs and dived into the pool. She skimmed along the bottom until she needed air and pushed for the surface.

Brushing the hair from her eyes, she found herself facing a pair of bare feet and a fine set of muscled calves. Her gaze moved higher to his thighs and to the bulge—and away from the bulge back to his right knee and thigh. Damn, if there wasn't a surgical scar at least eight inches long which started on his muscular thigh and traveled down below his knee...and what suspiciously looked like a bullet wound.

"Like what you see?" he asked, his tone amused. His blue eyes shone with good humor.

"Uh, that's a hell of a scar. Old football injury?"

Mac laughed and turned to his host. "Lloyd, call off the sheriff. She's interrogating me again."

Lloyd straightened from his pool chair. "Damn, son. I think Rilla's right. Looks like something got a-hold of you."

"Almost but not quite. I had a compound fracture. The bone came through the skin—say, you remember the old movie with Burt Reynolds where he and his pals went canoeing? That's sort of what happened to me, except I was in a car wreck last year. I've a metal plate and a bunch of screws holding this leg of mine together."

"They did a good job. I never noticed any kind of limp," Rilla said, wondering if he was telling the truth.

"I had six months of intensive rehab. I worked like an S.O.B. to get rid of the limp."

"Come on in," she said. At least if he were in the water, she wouldn't have so much trouble keeping her eyes away from his crotch.

"You're an excellent swimmer."

"Thanks." Rilla treaded water and tried to shrug, two activities she discovered weren't easily accomplished at the same time. "Come on. I doubt you'll melt." *But I might.*

He tentatively eased into the water beside her, holding to the side as if he were afraid to let go.

"What's the matter? she asked. "Don't you swim?"

He rolled his eyes. "No."

"Then you need to learn."

"Why?"

"Everybody ought to know how to swim. It's easy. Even little babies can learn." She splashed some water in his face.

Callahan shook his head. "It's been a long time since I was a baby. I've forgotten."

She laughed. "Chicken." With practiced ease, she backstroked away from him. "Come on. Come to me. I'm not far. Push off from the side, put your hands out in front like this." She stretched her arms out, hands together in a V. "And let your body float to me. I'll catch you."

He glanced toward the pool deck. "Where are Katie and Lloyd? They need a good laugh."

"If you'll just do it, you can be swimming before they come out."

His dark brows drew into a frown. "You'll let me drown."

"I assure you I won't. I was a lifeguard at the country club when I was in high school. It would be morally impossible for me to let you drown, even if you are a real pain in the behind."

"Harsh, but true." He grinned.

Did anything ever make him stop smiling?

"All right. I'm trusting you with my life."

She watched as he pushed off from the side of the pool, arms in front as she'd directed.

He reached her and snaked his arms around her, pulling her up against his chest. A thin scrap of fabric was all that separated her tensing nipples from his bare, muscular chest. Could he tell?

She felt the quick hammering of his heart against hers. Her hands splayed down his chest while his blue-as-the-pool eyes shone with merriment.

It hit her. "You *can* swim, can't you?" she murmured, strangely unwilling to let him go even if he had tricked her.

Callahan grinned. "Yeah. I knew it was the only way I was going to get you in my arms tonight."

He wanted her in his arms? A heady rush of warmth pooled in her belly. Her body molded against his—like they were made for each other—twin keys for the same lock.

She looked into his eyes, his gaze soft and warm. The heat built and shimmered between them. His muscled thigh was between hers—when did that happen? Instinctively she pressed against him and a thrill of pleasure shot to her core. She clung to him, her fingers kneading into his shoulders. Her lips parted. More than anything she wanted to taste him, rub against his hard erection and take him inside... She took a ragged breath.

"Woo hoo. Look at them, Lloyd." Katie Bass's shrill voice rang out. "I think they're already in love."

Hastily Rilla pulled away from Mac and swam for the opposite side of the pool. "Come on in, you two. The water's great."

Katie tiptoed to the edge of the pool and fluffed her hair. "No way. Just had my hair done." She wrinkled her nose, turned and sashayed back to a beach chair where she draped her body into an elegant pose.

Geez Louise. Rilla gave a mental groan. Katie's suit was basically two postage stamps and a thong. It left absolutely nothing to the imagination, and she could imagine what was running through Callahan's mind.

Why Lloyd allowed Katie to parade around in a suit like that, Rilla didn't know. Maybe he got off on it. Some men did. It made them feel like real men as if saying to the world, "Look at what I have".

And maybe it wasn't any of her business.

Mac sucked in a sharp breath. Rilla's borrowed suit was nearly transparent when wet. Her breasts were small and firm and the heat of her cunt against his thigh made him want to strip off her bikini bottom so he could feel what he already knew. Her cunt was hot and ready, but was she ready? For that matter, was he?

Her body was slender, tanned and toned. He doubted she had much time to loll around in the sun. And he couldn't see her frequenting tanning parlors either.

But somewhere, sometime she worked out. He'd bet money on it.

She braced her hands on the side of the pool and pulled herself up effortlessly, her triceps moving smoothly under tanned skin.

Yeah, she definitely worked out.

Holding her in his arms had sent a rush of blood to his dick. He couldn't haul himself out of the pool without embarrassing the two of them.

He sucked in deep breath and ducked beneath the surface. He swam along the bottom until his lungs burned, then he shot upward for a gasp of air.

She scowled at him from the side of the pool. "Show-off."

"Sorry." He grinned. "I needed a couple of minutes—some distraction."

He watched a second's confusion cross her face. Her eyes widened. She averted her gaze, but couldn't hide the twitch of her lovely full lips from his sharp eyes.

Was she pleased...or just amused?

Dammit, he wanted to fuck her, and now she knew it. And he didn't care.

Chapter Seven

The day after the Basses' dinner party, Rilla called it a day at six-thirty. All she wanted—no, needed—was a workout. She turned the Jeep around and headed for home. Earlier, Callahan had called to tell her how much he'd enjoyed the evening and remind her she still hadn't taken her house tour.

She couldn't deny the effect he had on her anymore than she could deny the effect she had on him. He'd been hard as a rock against her thigh before she pulled away from him. It was a damn good thing she'd had her own vehicle. He'd even offered to drive her home.

Hmph. Why now?

Hormones—that's all it was. And hers had to kick into high gear every time he came in range of her radar. Damned inconvenient, too.

She pulled into the driveway. A strange car was there ahead of her. A hot pink VW bug, newer model. Nobody in town drove anything like it.

She unsnapped the fastener on her holster. Too much going on to take chances.

She pulled up the Jeep and stopped behind the colorful subcompact. She jumped out of her vehicle and walked around to the driver's side. "Can I help you?"

The window glass rolled down, the motor idled. The car door opened and a pair of long, skinny legs emerged.

The female driver gave Rilla an appraising glance. “My, my, aren’t you all grown up?”

“Excuse me?”

“Don’t you recognize your own mama? You look enough like me. Leastways, like I used to look.” She stood slowly and gave the house an appraising glance. “Not much changed around here.”

A numbness settled in Rilla’s midsection. This dried-out hag was her mother? Dark hair streaked with gray, held back by a pair of hot pink sunglasses, skin which looked like she’d been left to dry in Death Valley. Tobacco-stained teeth and fingers and dark-circled eyes with reddened whites.

“Oh, yeah,” Rilla said. “I’d have known you anywhere. Where the hell have you been for the last twenty-seven years?”

“Been out in Vegas—great place, but when I heard about your daddy checking out, I rushed back here to lend you my support.”

“Daddy was murdered two months ago and you’re just now showing up?”

“Well, hon, it’s not like it made the national news. Besides, it took me a while to get back here. But I’m here now, so you can stop worrying.”

Fists clenched at her sides, Rilla paced back and forth. “You mean you’ve fallen on hard times, and you’re here for a handout.”

The woman—Rilla couldn’t bring herself to think of her as *Mother*—gave her a haughty look over an arched nose. “My, my, you may look like me, but you talk just like your daddy. May he rest in peace.”

“You need to turn around and hightail it back to Vegas. You don’t have a place here anymore.”

She set her hands on her bony hips. “We’ll see about that. Aren’t you going to invite me in?”

"No."

"Now see here, missy—"

"There's a motel at the edge of town. If the old rumors about you were true, you probably remember it quite well."

"I don't know what you think you know about me, but it's all a lie. Most of it, anyway."

Rilla took in the skin tight jeans and hot pink halter top and snakeskin boots. "I'll tell you what I know. You left your husband and little girl, ran off with one of Rickie Skaggs' roadies, and when he dumped your butt in Vegas, you started turning tricks to support your coke habit."

Her mother slammed the car door. "Vicious lies, everyone of 'em. I was a showgirl. Well, I might've dropped a line once in a while—just to be sociable. And maybe I had to depend on the kindness of strangers—so to speak—on occasion, but it wasn't anything like you tell it."

"Save it for someone who cares. What about me? I was three years old when you ran off and never looked back." She choked on the rage and pain of nearly thirty years. "I was a baby!"

"Well, you look like you did all right." The nightmare from Vegas leaned back against her car and folded her arms across her chest. "Your daddy and grandma did all right by ya."

"No thanks to you."

"Lookee here, hon, I wasn't cut out for small towns and baking cookies. I like the bright lights and winters in the desert."

"Well, you won't find either one here. The Springs hasn't changed *that* much."

"I told you. I'm here for moral support."

"And I doubt you even know the meaning of those two words."

Her mother sniffed. “Well, we’ll see about that, won’t we, missy?”

“We won’t see about *anything*. Find a room or go back to Vegas—your choice. I’ve done fine without a mother all these years...and I sure as hell don’t need one now.”

Blind-mad, Rilla walked stiff-legged into the house. Dollars to doughnuts, R.J. was responsible for her mother’s sudden appearance, and he was due for a talkin’ to. She pulled the cell phone from her pocket and punched in his number. “R.J., you have anything to do with my so-called mother turning up?”

“Now hold on. All I did was leave her a message right after your daddy passed. I thought she oughta know.”

“You didn’t suggest she ought to come back?”

“Hell no, honest. I had no idea she’d come all the way back here.”

“I don’t need a mother now.” She banged her fist on the wall. “I needed one then...” She swallowed the rage which threatened to strangle her. Better rage than tears.

“Take a deep breath, kiddo. You keep it up, and you’ll break somethin’.”

She let out a big sigh. Why was she letting her mother’s sudden appearance upset her so? Maybe it was only the latest in a list of things she couldn’t control: her father’s murder, the influx of drugs and now a skinny bag of bones showing up without a word of warning.

“Hell, Rilla, don’t let her get under your skin. She’ll get bored in a week or two and head on back to Vegas.

“She damn well better.”

“She staying at your place?”

“No! Don’t you have something to do? Now how about finding me a drug dealer instead of pushing my buttons—think you can do that?”

“Yes, boss.” he laughed. “I’ll do just that.”

After being chucked out by her daughter, Liz headed for the Any-Time-Any-Reason Market. She pulled a diet drink from the cooler and carried it to the checkout. An ancient little woman stood there, her arthritic fingers punching the keys.

It couldn't be. "Miz Tweedy, is that you?"

The old woman looked up. "Mary Elizabeth, you've come back home. Now that surprises me, and it takes a lot to surprise me. I thought you were out in Los Angeles or somewheres like that."

"Las Vegas. Say, you don't know anybody with a room to rent, do you?"

"Well, now, I have a room. It's a nice size, but you'd have to share the bathroom with me. Only got one. You have a job? A way to pay your rent?

Liz nodded. "I'm gonna check at the diner after I leave here. Used to work there for Fay's mama after school."

"It's yours as long as you can pay your rent and *no* gentlemen callers. We'll see how it goes."

"Thanks, Miz Tweedy." For the first time in two months, Liz's heart lightened. She'd come home. And home was home, even if her daughter was a bitch on wheels.

After hanging up from R.J., Rilla stripped off her uniform. Without thinking, she pulled on a sports bra and bicycle shorts. She stalked outside to the large oak tree where her weight bag hung.

"Son of a bitch!" She punched the weight bag. And followed with a sidekick. She kicked it again. After fifteen minutes of repeated kicks and punches, sweat dripped down her chest, and her damp braid hung in a clammy mass on her neck.

Her mother—just what the hell did that woman have to do with her life now? Why couldn't she have stayed in Las Vegas?

The last thing in the world she needed was a strange woman screwing up her life. As if it weren't bad enough—

Punch. Her father murdered.

Kick. Kick. Drugs flooding the county and her unable to do damn thing about it.

Spin and elbow strike. Drop back.

Over and over she went through the familiar drill.

Through her frenzied workout, she was vaguely aware of Ralphie sitting on his haunches. He watched her with a quizzical expression on his sweet face.

She stopped to drag in a deep breath. "Go chase a squirrel."

He merely cocked his head to the other side.

"You're too dignified to do that, aren't you?" She collapsed on the soft, moss-covered ground. "C'mere." She patted the spot beside her.

The dog ambled over to her. She slipped off the workout gloves and combed her fingers through the silky soft fur behind his ears.

"You're such a sweet boy. Yes, you are." Okay, so she talked baby talk to her dog. As long as her deputies didn't hear her, it was fine. She buried her face in the soft fur on the top of his head. The tension leached from her shoulders. Maybe her mother wouldn't stick her nose in her business after all. "You're a good boy. Yes, you are."

Ralphie's ears pricked. "What is it?" She hauled to her feet. Surely her so-called mother hadn't come back. She strode over to the side yard. Ralphie ran ahead of her, his deep-chested bark telling her someone was definitely out in front.

When she eased around the corner of the house... Callahan stood on the front porch, his fist raised to knock on the door.

"Callahan." She hoped her tone conveyed the disgust she felt.

A man on a mission for his boss, Havers, Mac ignored Rilla, preferring to take his time before acknowledging her and giving a damned good reason for showing up at her home unannounced. Havers had ordered him to check out where she lived and see if she were living with pricey antiques and wearing designer clothes when she was off duty.

Instead, he leaned over the porch railing and said, "Hey fella, you make a great guard dog. Where's your mama?"

"Mama?"

He grinned down at her. "Aren't you? Baby talk, the whole deal—I'd bet money on it."

"Hmph. You'd lose. My dog and I have a very dignified relationship, I'll have you know."

"You're protesting too much." He gave her a long, appraising glance up and down. Damp curls had escaped from her braid. Beads of sweat trickled down her stretchy bra-thing where he noticed the outline of her very fine set of breasts. God, she looked vibrant and totally pissed off. No way was this woman raking in drug money and spending it on clothes or high-end furnishings.

"Working out?"

Exasperated, she held out her arms. "What does it look like? Tea at the governor's mansion?"

He grinned and folded his arms across his chest. He didn't mind her short fuse a bit. "I'm sure the governor would be impressed. I am."

"Is there some reason you're on my front porch?"

"I called, but they said you weren't in the office."

"So you thought you'd pay me a little visit? I've had enough surprise visits for one day."

He raised a brow and waited for her to elaborate.

"My long-lost mother has returned to make my life a living hell."

"Are you sure ? Maybe she has another reason."

"A—out of money. B—dumped by her last boyfriend. C—fired from her job. Pick one—or all of the above."

He vaulted over the porch railing. "Okay. I wasn't expecting a multiple choice test, but I'm detecting some ill-will between you and your mother. This would be the mother who took off when you were three?"

"The one and the same."

"No chance you're in a forgiving mood."

"Hell, no." Rilla let out a huff of exasperation. "Go away. You're interrupting my workout—unless you'd rather be my punching bag." She feinted a punch in his direction.

He held up his hands in mock fear. "Please, Sheriff, ma'am. Don't hurt me. I'm a writer and a lover—not a fighter."

Apparently able to resist his charm, she heaved a sigh. "I'm sure truer words were never spoken."

He grinned down at her. "Don't you want to know why I called you at the office?"

"Not especially," she said with a pout.

Was it his imagination or did her lips beg to be kissed?

He sidled up to her and caught her hand in his. "Now, they say laughter's good for tension, too."

Her lovely mouth twitched. He'd never seen anyone so determined to stay mad.

"Oh, *they* do, do they?"

"Yeah, they do," he said. "But I'm not about to do anything you don't want."

"And why don't I believe you?"

"Because your lips already asked me to do this." He pulled her to his chest, leaned in and kissed her full on the mouth. Her body tensed in his for a second, then pressed against him—all want and hunger in his arms. Her mouth opened to him.

Quicker than anything, her arms wrapped around his neck. *God.* Her body's warmth, pressed so close, sent a burst of heat to his dick. He hardened in an instant. Aching for release, he backed Rilla against the house, his erection pressing into her belly.

Her breath came in short gasps, hot on his neck.

He slid his hand between them, desperate to feel the soft skin of her breasts.

Her writhing ceased. She shoved him away, shaking her head.

"What...?" Confused and barely in control, he took a step back.

"No. Sorry. I can't—"

Chapter Eight

Rilla shook her head and tried to control her breathing. As he peered back at her, Mac's expression was one of pure bewilderment.

"Why?"

"Just can't." How could she even consider being with someone she suspected of being a drug dealer...much less plastered against the side of her house in broad daylight?

She sucked in a deep breath. "Please, just leave."

He took another step back. In spite of the logical side of her brain telling her not to, she wanted to follow him. Hands clenched, she forced her arms to stay at her sides.

After a heated glance which left nothing unsaid, Mac nodded. "All right. Have it your way. I'll leave, but don't pretend you didn't want it as much as I did."

She let out a ragged breath. "I don't deny it."

"Then why?"

"I...we don't know each other all that well. You're a stranger..." God. She sounded like some virginal debutante. And she was anything but.

"You don't trust me—that's it." He took a step closer. "Is there anyone you *do* trust?"

She glared back. "Any reason I should trust *you?*"

"I haven't hurt you. When you said 'no', I stopped, didn't I?"

He spoke the truth, so far. She nodded. "But it's too soon to..."

"Okay, I get it. You're not easy."

Control returning, she folded her arms across her chest. "You're not exactly scoring points here."

He scowled and threw his hands in the air. "Dammit! I give up. I'm outta here."

"Good," she snapped at his retreating back.

Damn. Why couldn't she make up her mind about him? Part of her knew what she needed.

And what her body needed had already roared off in a silver Porsche, tires squealing and spraying loose gravel.

The afternoon shift at the diner hadn't been too bad, but Liz's energy ebbed as she stepped onto Miss Tweedy's low, rambling porch. Barrels cut in half were filled with petunias which spilled over the sides in a downright pretty array of pink, purple and white. Leafy ferns spaced at regular intervals hung from the porch ceiling, and the graceful fronds swayed gently in the bare breeze which had managed to find its way to the porch.

A sense of deja vu hit her. More than once she'd climbed these same steps to do makeup work with Miss Tweedy. The good woman had been her eighth grade teacher and tried to stuff all sorts of learning in Liz's head, but it hadn't helped. All too soon the lure of dating boys had taken hold, and all the geography and history in the world hadn't kept her from losing her virginity at fourteen to a high school football player.

She took a deep breath, gathered her courage and knocked on the screen door. At least it would be cooler inside.

"Hold on. Hold on. I'm a-coming." Miss Tweedy opened the door. "Come on in." She glanced down at Liz's single bag. "That it?"

"Yeah, I travel light. Best way."

"All right. The room in the back is yours. Two hundred dollars a month. You do your own laundry, your own cooking, but in the winter, I do a lot of soups and stews. Always plenty to go around, so I'm happy to share."

"Don't know if I'll be around very long." Liz stepped inside. It was clean, comfortable even, but furnished in the best of sixties' discount-store style.

"So why are you here? In town, I mean."

Liz shrugged. "Thought maybe it was time I saw what my little girl was up to."

"Humph. You'll have to try your line on someone who hasn't heard every tall tale that comes down the pike. You were always pretty inventive with excuses for not doing your homework, if I remember correctly."

"Things are kinda up in the air right now. I'll tell you sometime."

"Remember what I said at the store. No gentleman callers. You do your playing around somewheres else."

Playing around was the last thing on her mind. All she wanted was a bath and a nap. "Don't worry. That part of my life is over."

The old lady snorted. "I've heard that one before, too. Anyways, just so we're clear on one point."

"Yes, ma'am. We're clear." She set down the suitcase. The freshly made bed was calling her name.

"One more thing."

Liz repressed a groan. "Yes, ma'am?"

"I keep a shotgun readied for burglars—just in case." Miss Tweedy nodded toward the front door. "Keep it behind my settee in the front parlor."

She swallowed the giggle which threatened to break loose. "Miz Tweedy, now that I know, I feel ever so safe."

"We women-folk have to protect ourselves since there's no man about."

"Yes, ma'am. Couldn't agree more." What was the Springs coming to when an old lady thought she needed to hide a shotgun behind the couch?

Early the next morning, Rilla made a decision. It was time to have it out with her long-lost mother. The blamed woman had called and asked her to meet at Fay's Diner. So here she was, and it was time to get rid of a piece of Vegas trash.

She opened the door to the diner and spied her so-called mother sitting in the last booth and stuffing paper napkins into a napkin holder. Feet dragging, Rilla moseyed to the rear of the diner and slid into the booth.

"Thank you for coming. I wanted you to know I aim to stick around for a while." She motioned at her name tag. "Fay hired me, so I can pay my way."

"Where're you staying?" Not that she cared.

"I ran into Miz Tweedy at the grocery store. She said she'd rent me a room, if I got a job and didn't have gentleman callers."

"Well, I guess you've managed half of it."

"Now, don't be such a smart-ass. To tell the truth, I've had my fill of men. Never had much luck with'em, anyhow. How about you? You got my looks, or at least what I used to have."

"My *work's* what's important to me."

Liz nodded. "Uh-huh. Take after your daddy that way. Guess he did the best he could. O'course his mama never approved of me. It was kind of a kick watching her face go pale when we told her we'd eloped. You see, you were already on the way, but your Daddy was a gentleman."

Too much information.

“Where’re we going with all this? I’m thirty years old. I don’t need a mother anymore.” She stood. “Just stay out of my way and don’t end up in my jail.”

“I don’t blame you for—”

Unable to listen to another word, Rilla turned, ready to escape the diner. Why had she bothered to come at all? She’d wasted enough time. The woman may have given her life, but precious little else.

“Rilla!”

She stopped dead in her tracks, turned around, and faced Liz. “What?”

“Just give me a chance, will ya?” Liz held her arms out in a pleading gesture. Two dark bruises at the bends of her elbows stood out like ink blotches on white paper.

Even though Rilla was more than tired of the emotional scene, she returned to the rear booth and sat. “What’re those from?” She pointed at the discolorations.

In a nervous gesture, Liz rolled down her sleeves. “Nothing, I bruise easy. Why?”

“You’re on drugs...the hard stuff, aren’t you?”

“No way. How can you ask your mama a question like that?”

“Look, let’s get something straight. I’m the sheriff—not your little girl.”

Liz grabbed a cloth and furiously wiped the table. “You’re a hard-nosed bitch is what you are.”

“Well, maybe I wouldn’t be if I’d had a mother—”

“Order!” Fay yelled from the kitchen.”

Liz gave a quick glance over her shoulder and yelled, “Hold on a minute.” She turned back to Rilla. “I’m working. How about you cut me some slack and save your twenty questions ’til after my shift ends?”

"Sure thing, Mommie Dearest. But you're the one who wanted to see me."

Her thin lips twitching with repressed anger, Liz spun away and stomped over to the order window. She snatched up the plate of food and carried it to the waiting customer without ever giving Rilla another glance.

"Okay, fine, if that's how you want to communicate." Rilla stood. The woman who gave her birth was a waste of time and energy and skin.

Why couldn't she have kept her sorry ass in Vegas?

Much later that evening, Rilla pushed her chair back from the desk. She moved her head from side to side, trying to relieve the stiff muscles. After spending five hours with her butt glued in the chair, she was more than ready to head home.

Before she could so much as stand, the phone rang. She groaned. What now? "Devane."

"Rilla, you need to know something about your mama."

"No, Miss Tweedy. I don't."

"There's something wrong."

"Yeah, she left Vegas." She sighed. No need for her to be so rude; it wasn't Miss Tweedy's fault. "Okay, what's wrong?"

"Don't rightly know. I think you need to investigate."

"Got my hands sort of full right now."

"Rilla Devane, you listen to me. Your mama came home to make peace with you. There's only one reason people do that."

"And?"

"She's sick."

"So? She's a junky. Junkies get sick."

"Don't think so. She goes to work, comes home and falls in bed. Don't eat dinner half the time. She's a bag of bones. And now she says she's taking a second job."

"Could be anorexic."

"Don't wait too long. I'd hate to see you beat yourself up after she's gone like you did when you lost your daddy."

"There's no comparison. Daddy raised me after she took off. I don't even know her. She's a stranger. We share DNA—that's all."

"That's a load of horse pucky. And you know it. Your mama was plenty smart, but she blossomed early. Boys wouldn't leave her alone. She didn't have a good home life, either."

"You're breaking my heart. Why don't you write a book about the poor disadvantaged girl? You might sell it to somebody, but I'm not buying."

"I know you're not this heard-hearted. Wise up, gal. You're too good a person to treat her this way. Take my word for it—she's sick."

"Miss Tweedy, with all due respect—this is none of your concern."

But the old lady wouldn't give up. "She's the only parent you have left."

"I have to go."

"You may be the sheriff, Rilla Devane, but I remember when the elastic broke in your panties in third grade and fell down around your ankles. You ran home crying, so don't you get all high and mighty with me."

Rilla gritted her teeth. "Bye, now." Without waiting for her old teacher to object, she punched the disconnect button. Dammit. She had better things to do than worry about a woman who deserted her three-year-old child for a Ricky Skaggs roadie and the bright lights of Las Vegas.

Mac pulled into the town square. The sheriff's office was on the first floor of the courthouse—built in 1825, according to the brass plaque. Red brick with Tennessee limestone trim and built to last.

He followed the signs to the sheriff's office and found himself in the presence of a deputy guarding the front office. The kid had a face like an Irish wolfhound with stringy red hair. He scowled at Mac.

Was the kid even old enough to shave, much less pack heat?

Mac peered over his shades at the deputy. "Sheriff Devane here?"

The deputy stood and gave Mac a long, hard look of appraisal. "And your bid'ness with the sheriff would be?"

"Personal."

"Take it from me, pal. You don't wanna mess with her when she's in one of her moods."

He grinned. In a mood, was she? That was how he liked her best—one of the ways he liked her best. "Consider me forewarned."

Deputy Cavanaugh rolled his eyes and jerked his head toward the hallway. "Hang a left, and you're there. But ya still got time to turn around..."

"Don't worry, I won't hold you responsible for any mayhem that occurs."

The deputy snorted.

A man of few words.

Rilla's office door was closed. He rapped on it lightly.

"Yeah—"

If the raspy grate of her tone was any indication of her mood, he might as well take the deputy's advice and head for the hills.

He eased open the door.

Behind a mound of paperwork, the sheriff glared at him. Strands of her dark hair had come loose from her braid and added to her look of dishevelment. A pretty picture in his mind's eye. But she clearly wasn't thrilled with his visit. What had he done to piss her off this time?

Her eyebrows arched. "What do you want?"

"Please don't go out of your way to make me feel welcome. I was in the neighborhood."

"Yeah, I've heard the rest. I'm busy."

"You don't look busy, unless you call muttering to yourself busy...?"

"It's been a bad day."

"Not another O.D.?"

"Almost as bad. The budget's due. I'm faced with layoffs. My long-lost mother...you name it."

"Tell me about it."

"I'm *busy*."

"Dinner tonight? You can tell me about it over drinks."

Rilla nodded, anxious to get him out of her face. She couldn't deal with him right now. Too many things were whirling around in her mind. "Get outta here."

Mac shrugged. "If you say so."

"I do."

"Seven?"

"Fine."

He grinned, winked and saluted her—the cheeky devil.

She rolled her eyes as the spun on his heel and treated her to a knock-out view of his firmly muscled ass. And she knew exactly how firm it was.

"Dammit." No man should have the power to scramble her brain when she didn't want it scrambled.

Mac flicked on the turn signal and turned into the Cherokee Springs Country Club. The building was nestled in a green valley. The long, low, white-columned building formed an L with the swimming pool and tennis courts in the back.

According to Lloyd Bass, the golf course was moderately taxing and compared favorably any of those in Nashville. Based on Lloyd's sponsorship, Mac had joined. It was the only establishment in the area which served a decent steak and flew in fresh lobster...and it was the only place Mac could think of taking Rilla for a real date.

He glanced over at her. From the time he'd picked her up, she'd sat silent as a clam and just as uptight. Not a very promising start, not at all.

He bypassed the portico, pulled into a parking space and stopped. He opened his car door then ran around to open hers.

The lady scowled at him, but with a half grin tweaking the corner of her luscious mouth.

"Such nice manners. I'm honored."

"We're on a date."

"It's just dinner."

"Don't know about you, but where I come, from that's considered a date."

She swung her long legs out of the car. Good God, she was wearing the sexiest shoes he'd ever seen with sky-high heels and skinny straps. He offered his hand.

"I don't need help. I'm perfectly capable of getting out of a car on my own."

"Play nice." Damn. Not promising at all.

"I don't know why," Rilla said from beneath long dark lashes, "I ever agreed to this."

She stood and he took in her long, slender form. She wore a black dress with a high halter neck. The color and the classic lines emphasized her trim figure. His heart thudded the insistent reminder that he was a man first and a DEA agent second.

"You look damned good for a sheriff." But he wondered how she could afford a designer dress on a sheriff's salary?

"This old thing? Came from a consignment shop in Nashville patronized by the ladies of Belle Meade." She smoothed the lines of the dress along her thighs.

Damn. The woman knew she looked better than good and she was psychic, too. At this rate, things could only get worse.

"Come on." He placed a hand at her waist and pulled her close.

She tried to pull away, but he held her tight.

"What do you think you're you doing?" she asked through clenched teeth. A pretty pink flush darkened her tanned cheeks.

He leaned down and spoke softly. "I think we're having a date. Part of which means you're supposed to act like you can stand to stay in the same room with me."

She sniffed. "Just as long as you don't get any ideas."

"Being with you, madam sheriff, gives me ideas."

"Well, you can forget it if you have any notion—"

"Just dinner, Rilla. We're dating."

"No, we're not."

"Whether you like it or not, this is a real date. We can get to know each other. That's why we're here."

"How could I forget?"

Mac grinned. "I can think of several methods guaranteed to make you forget...for a while."

"And how many are illegal?"

"Not a single one."

"Right." She drew the word out. The low timbre of her husky voice sent a vibration straight to his groin.

Just dinner—hell.

Still sparring, they entered the air-conditioned comfort of the country club lobby. It was typical, not that he spent a lot of time with the country club set, but the décor was about what he'd expect if he were in the habit of frequenting them.

The maitre d' stepped forward. "Mr. Callahan, your table will be ready in about fifteen minutes. Would you and your guest prefer to wait in the bar?"

Mac nodded and guided Rilla into the dark confines of the bar and to a table for two.

She stopped and stood stock still. "No."

"What's wrong?"

She turned. Her face was pale, her body visibly trembling.

"We can't stay—I can't stay."

"Why?" Confused by her sudden about-face, he couldn't see any reason for it. "What have I done now?"

He pulled out her chair. "Sit down before you fall."

"No." She swayed and collapsed into the chair anyway. "That woman. She's everywhere I go."

"Your mother?"

"At the bar—the waitress. Her back's to us, but I know it's her. Please let's leave before she sees me. I'm not ready for another scene."

"Rilla, this is a small town. You can't run every time you bump into her."

She glared at him. "Running's a family trait. It's in my genes," she muttered, her tone bordering on sarcastic.

"Come on, bitterness isn't becoming. Put a smile on your pretty face, 'cause she's on her way to take our drink orders."

Under her breath she muttered an expletive, not that he blamed her. He wouldn't appreciate a long-lost parent's showing up and complicating his life.

Rilla's mother was tall and thin to the point of emaciation. She gave him a practiced smile. "Would you like something from the...bar?" she asked, her voice faltering as she recognized her daughter.

"Hon, are—" she started, but her daughter wasn't in the mood for small talk.

"I'm here for dinner—that's all."

"Of course. I didn't think..."

Okay, time to take control. "I'll have Jack Black, and she'll have—?" He raised an eyebrow at Rilla.

"Fruit tea."

Her mother nodded. "Back in a minute."

"Tea? Always on the job." And always in control. That was his Rilla.

His Rilla?

"Right."

He covered her shaking hand with his. "I wouldn't have brought you here if I'd known."

"It's not your fault. She must be working two jobs. Here and at the diner."

"At least she's industrious."

Rilla's lip lifted in an Elvis-like snarl. "I've seen her track marks. I'm telling you she's a junky. Can't you see how thin she is?"

"She looks ill."

"That's what Miss Tweedy says. That she's come home to die."

"How do you—" Before he could finish, Rilla's mother set their drinks on the table. She opened her mouth as if to say something, but stopped, turned away and walked back to the bar.

"—feel about that?"

"Like I need something stronger than tea." She reached across and grabbed his whiskey, took a healthy gulp and sputtered from the strength of the alcohol. She set it back in front of him.

"Better?"

"A bit."

"Want to tell me about it?"

"No." In spite of her reluctance, she continued. "She ran off and left us when I was three. I was barely old enough to remember her, and I cried myself to sleep at night for a year after she left. Daddy did his best. Grandma Devane moved in and took care of me. I'm sure I was better off with her than my real mother, but I thought she left because I was bad."

"Poor baby."

"Don't make fun."

"I'm not. Tell me about your father."

"What do you want to know?" Her mouth twisted into a wry grimace.

Mac sighed. He hated broaching another painful topic, but he needed more personal background. "Tell me what it was like growing up as the sheriff's little girl."

Her features softened as she shifted focus. "He was my hero. Everyone in the county respected him. He took me to the office for the first time when I was five. He wanted to show me off after my first day at kindergarten."

"Sounds like he loved you and was very proud of his daughter."

"Yeah. His deputies treated me like I was a princess. By the third grade, I was walking myself home from school, and I'd stop by his office every day. Other girls my age were going to Brownies and Girl Scouts, and I was hanging out with his deputies when he was busy. And if they had a call, they'd drop me at home first. I did my homework in Daddy's office…sometimes at his desk. I loved him. He was my world."

By the end of her tale, her tone no longer sounded brittle and angry. Her dark eyes glistened with unshed tears as she took a sip of iced tea.

"And your father didn't mind your hanging around all the time?"

A quick smile lifted her red lips. "Not 'til he overheard one of the younger deputies hitting on me when I was fourteen."

"What happened?"

"He fired the deputy and pulled me out of the county high school, sent me to a private school in the next county."

"That must've been different."

"I hated it, but stuck it out for a year. He must have missed me because he let me come back home to finish high school with my friends. By then, all the deputies were polite and *very* careful around me."

"I'll bet."

"He could be tough, too, but he was always fair. The only time we ever argued was when I went away to the police academy after college."

"Maybe he was afraid for you. He knew the life and he wanted more for you. That's how fathers are."

She smiled. "You know, it was R.J. who taught me how to clean and handle a weapon, and Daddy was ready to fire him for it."

"Don't blame him. How old were you?

"Six."

"Hell, you could've killed someone."

"No way. R.J. taught me all the rules first. He was careful." Without warning, she changed the subject. "What's the worst thing that ever happened to you?"

"As a kid?"

"Yeah."

"I got caught cheating on a spelling test." He loved the simple sharing of their lives. These glimpses of her youth weren't part of the DEA's dossier. Too bad his life was a lie.

"That's nothing," she said.

"Didn't you ever cheat on a test?"

Rilla shook her head. "Never."

"I can see you now. Little goody-two-shoes. Afraid to cheat on a test."

"I didn't have to cheat."

"Oh, God. I would've hated you. Smart and smug."

"I wasn't smug. Kids of law enforcement officers are either hell raisers or they're not. I wasn't. I wanted to be on the job, so walking on the dark side wasn't an option."

She picked up her napkin, unfolded it and smiled at him. "Let's don't talk about all this tonight. Tell me about your family. They can't be as dysfunctional as mine."

Mac swallowed. He hated lying to someone he was so attracted to...someone with whom, in another life, he'd want a relationship.

"Don't be too sure. My mother was a firm believer in serial marriages. I had four step-fathers by the time I left for prep school. After college, I did some graduate school, got a part-time job on a newspaper and started working on my first novel. I had a trust fund from my grandfather's estate, and I managed to live on the income until I found an agent and sold the first one. A few more books and I lived comfortably."

"Any brothers or sisters?"

"Half-brothers and sister—by my mother's third marriage, I think."

"Ever see them?"

Hating his lies, but determined to keep his cover intact, he shook his head. "She married up with each successive marriage. They're not too sure about having someone from the arts in the family. Not quite respectable, don't you know."

"But surely you spent time with them growing up?"

"We didn't have a blended family. I spent most of my time in boarding schools."

"No family's perfect, I guess."

She glanced over her shoulder and watched her mother talking to a man at the bar, who was laughing at something she'd said.

Mac saw the signs of her mother's former beauty…beauty ruined by a hard life. A long vacation and three squares a day might even restore her looks. But the sick pallor of her skin might mean she'd need more than rest.

"Why now? My life's complicated enough."

"Look, let's forget about your mother. Why don't we leave? We'll go anywhere you want."

"This is my town. She's the runaway, not me."

He reached across the table and took one of her clenched hands in his. "Let's go."

Her eyes widened. "Right now?"

"Yes, right now."

"But—"

"Who needs food? You need to let your hair down."

She fingered a strand of black hair then flipped it over her shoulder. "It already is."

"No, hon. Not literally. Figuratively. We're going dancing."

"Dancing? We can do that after dinner. Doesn't the club have a jazz band or something?"

"No, no. Stuffy jazz bands are no fun. We're going out."

"Where then?" Her expression didn't lighten with the question. Somehow he had to shake her out of her bad mood.

"Little place off the Interstate. Rusty's."

"That's a roadhouse." She glanced down at her dress. "I'm over-dressed."

"So what? Is Sheriff Devane too elegant to rub shoulders with the commoners and do a little boot-scootin' boogey?"

Her eyes widened again. "Like *you* can?"

"Texas Two-step, Cotton-eyed Joe. I'll have you know I have a very well-rounded dance education."

"Not tonight, Mac. I'm sorry. Just seeing her..." She shook her head. "Please, just take me home."

He stood, fumbled some bills from his pocket. "All right. Let's get you home."

"And don't even think you're gonna tuck me in."

"Well, if you insist." He winked to let her know he was teasing. The tired sigh which escaped her hit him like a wall of shame. "Okay, I'll cut out the bull."

"She drains me. I'm not usually like this. Honestly."

"It's all right."

Rilla remained silent during the short drive to her house. It wasn't an uncomfortable silence. To the contrary, and in spite of his teasing manner, Mac was a thoughtful man and more than capable of knowing when he'd gone too far.

He pulled into her driveway and stopped. Her new security lights flickered on, bathing the usually shaded area with light.

"Something new?"

"Yeah, I had them installed after my brake line was cut."

"Good idea. You sleep with a weapon handy?"

His protective urges amused her. "Of course."

"I'll walk you to the door."

"You're not coming in," she reminded him in her most determined tone, even though his thoughtfulness and consideration were a welcome surprise.

"I don't want to come in—no, I do, but I respect your need to take it slow. But you shouldn't be alone. You need a friend."

She cut her gaze at him. What was he trying to pull now?

"Seriously, you shouldn't be alone tonight."

"Why? You think I'm gonna eat my gun?"

"Of course not. You're upset about your mother, and I'm sorry."

"That means a lot." Her tone grew softer, in spite of her need stay in control. "Anyway, it wasn't your fault she took a job at the country club."

"Come on." For some reason, maybe lack of energy, she waited for him to come around to open the door for her. He took her hand like she was some delicate flower of a woman. She bit back a chuckle. She was no delicate flower, but strangely she didn't mind being treated like one. It made a nice change from being one of the guys.

She placed her hand in his. Together they walked to the porch, his arm wrapped around her waist. She stopped at the door. An impatient whine was a welcome reminder that Ralphie was on the other side of the door.

"You chaperone's glad you're home."

"Yeah." She touched the side of Mac's face. "You're not such a bad guy, Callahan."

"And you're a hell of a woman, Sheriff."

He backed her against the door. Her heart rate increased and left her dizzy. "Now, Mac," she warned. But did she really want him to stop?

His eyes darkened as his intense gaze seemed to pierce her heart and play hell with her emotions.

"I want to kiss you until we're both senseless. I want you naked and lying in my arms."

Images of sleeping with him rocked through her. She held back the shiver and swallowed hard. How many other women had he charmed with the same intensity? "Sweet words from a man who makes his living with words."

"No less true."

He inclined his head, clearly intending to kiss her. She tried to turn away, but couldn't. She surrendered, expecting a long, hard, knee-weakening, bone-melting kiss. But no, his lips touched hers for a brief tender moment, then he stepped back.

"G'night, Rilla."

As she watched him leave, she sagged against the door and restrained the moan building inside her. A moan borne of passion. And sheer need.

What cruel joke had brought her riveting passion and deepest suspicion in the form of one frustrating man? More than anything she wanted to screw him until her brain took a permanent holiday, but she couldn't...not until she cleared him.

Chapter Nine

Liz Downey let out a deep sigh. Thank God, the lunch rush was over. She could take a break and get off her feet. How much longer she'd be able to hold down two jobs, she didn't know, but she didn't have medical insurance, so for the time being, two jobs it was.

Seeing her daughter last night at the country club had been a shock. When she'd first seen Rilla, she'd thought maybe she'd come to make peace, but no.

She'd left coming home too late. Her daughter hated her and had made it clear there could be nothing between them.

Why bother with more chemo? Why not just give up?

The door bell jingled. Another customer. She looked up and saw Rilla's date from the country club. Was he her fiancé... a friend? She'd felt the chemistry between them, but her daughter had been so edgy it was hard to tell what was going on with them.

He walked straight toward her, his hand outstretched and a smile on his face. Hope rose in her chest. Maybe he was someone who truly cared for her daughter.

"Rilla forgot her manners last night. I'm Mac Callahan."

"Liz Downey. Mr. Callahan, I'm—" Hastily she wiped her hands on her apron.

"I know. You're Rilla's mother. And please, call me Mac."

"Well, have a seat anywhere, and I'll take your order."

"I'll take the seat, but I'm not here to eat. Take your break with me? I need a few moments of your time. I'll spring for the coffee though," he said with a wink.

After pouring two cups of coffee, Liz sat across from him.

What did he want? Might as well take the bull by the horns. "So I guess she told you what a no-good mother I was. She's right."

The corner of his mouth kicked up. "She might've mentioned something along those lines."

"So what are you doing here in the Springs...Mac?"

"Whether or not Rilla knows it, she needs you. And I think you need her as well."

His eyes were kind, but he seemed to take in everything all at once as his gaze darted from her to the diner's customers and back to her. She shrugged, then pulled a napkin from the dispenser. "Not very quick are you? She hates me—not that I blame her. I did run off when she wasn't much more than a baby."

"We all make mistakes."

"Well, I've made more than my share. And she's not going to forgive me. I won't waste my breath asking her to again."

"Given enough time, she might." He raised an eyebrow.

"That's just it." She rolled the napkin into a ball and began shredding it. "You're talking about when Hell freezes over, and I don't have that much time."

The man was a hunk and kind. Her daughter sure knew how to pick 'em. She didn't get that from her mama.

"I didn't think so. Your daughter's a good person. Tell her the truth...you're ill."

"Won't make any difference."

"It might."

Was he right? Liz shook her head. "What are you to my daughter?"

"We're friends. I care about her happiness."

"So what do you do for a living?"

"I'm a mystery writer."

"Good money in that?"

"Good enough."

"You belong to the country club set and drive a fancy sports car. I'd say that's pretty good."

"Yeah."

"You'll be around for her, after I...?"

"That's just it. I don't know if I will."

"But you can write anywhere."

"I've got wandering feet. Do a lot of traveling—research for my books."

"In other words, she's your town girl while you're here. Sweet." She tossed the remnants of the napkin into the ashtray.

His face flushed. "It's more than that. Suffice it to say, our relationship is complicated."

"Hmph. You even talk like a writer. Let me get this straight. You want me to make peace with Rilla because you're going to dump her, and she'll need somebody after you're gone. Well, the only problem is, I might be gone before you are."

Mac stood. "Don't give up on her. Give her a little more time. She'll come around."

"Buddy, time's one thing I don't have."

"She does that, too."

"What?"

He nodded at the ashtray. "The napkin. She shreds them when she's nervous."

"Then that's *all* we got in common." Liz glanced at her watch. "I gotta get back to work."

"Of course." He nodded. "It was a pleasure meeting you."

"Yeah, sure. Anytime." She watched him leave the diner then shook her head. Nice manners, but no stick-around genes. Hell. Rilla couldn't pick 'em any better than her mama.

Mac read the e-mail. Damn. Things weren't looking good for Rilla. Someone had run his prints through AFIS and triggered Havers' e-mail. It had to be her doing. He'd been investigating her for two weeks. The drug problem was no closer to being solved, and the sheriff hadn't made a single arrest. She had to be involved. But how could she? He'd bet his left nut she was truly upset at the hospital when he'd seen her after the last O.D.

The longer he knew Rilla Devane...

Damn. She simply didn't fit his personal profile of an amoral, money-hungry politico out to ruin the lives of the very people she'd sworn to protect.

The profile she did fit? The one he'd most like to crawl between the sheets with. But that was a real problem—and what the hell was he going to do about it?

Thunk. Thunk. Damn. Someone was at the door.

Irritated by the interruption, Mac paused. "What now?" Maybe whoever it was would go away.

Thunk.

No such luck. He jumped up and headed downstairs. After a glance though the sidelight, he took a quick breath.

Rilla.

Last night, he'd left her at the front door after their abbreviated dinner like he'd planned...with only a kiss. He'd barely managed to drag himself away, but the lady seemed too vulnerable for him to take advantage.

Taking it slow might just save his job...not to mention his life. In spite of the risks to his job and heart, pleasure at seeing her again tugged his mouth into a wide grin.

On the front porch, Rilla muttered, “All right. You’re investigating this man. You’re not here for a date. This is strictly business.” Somehow she had to distract Callahan long enough to get into his computer. Whether or not she could was the real question. Her computer skills were better than average, and given enough time, she could probably hack into it.

The door opened. Something deep inside flip-flopped at the sight of Mac’s deep dimples. “Am I interrupting?” she asked, a little breathless.

“Not at all.”

“Have time for a short tour of the house?” she asked with what she hoped was a seductive smile. No point in letting him know she was here to do business.

He grinned. “I’d say the tour’s overdue.”

“Mm,” Rilla replied. Why had she shown up out of the blue like this? Maybe he’d think she was one hell of a desperate woman. And he’d be right. Once and for all, she had to find out if he was the drug kingpin responsible for her father’s murder and the two dead teenagers.

“I’m glad you came. The walls were starting to close in on me.”

“Yeah? I thought writers didn’t mind spending time alone.”

“Most of the time you’d be right.”

“But not today?”

“Not today. You see, there’s this scene, and I’m having a devil of a time with it. I’m glad for a break.” He stood aside and gestured her in. “Come on in.”

Her stomach sank with dread, but she waltzed inside the old Victorian. As before, the wood paneling shone with the soft glow of beeswax, and eucalyptus branches in a waist-high urn scented the air with the sharp, clean scent she loved.

She stepped onto an oriental rug of muted blues and reds which was probably worth more than what she made in a year.

Mac motioned to the left. “Library over there. Living room, or whatever you women call them now, on the left.”

“There’re still called living rooms around here. Now in Nashville, it would be the great room or in Belle Meade, the salon,” she said, taking in the oak fireplace surrounded by pale green tiles.

“No computer in the library?” she asked. “Where do you write?”

“Uh, upstairs. I write late sometimes. More convenient.”

She smiled at him. “You know I’d love to read one of your books.”

“Would you?” His gaze darted around the room. “I’m sure a have a few extra copies around somewhere.”

“Great, May I borrow a copy? Or buy one if you have something new out right now.”

“As a matter of fact I do.” He walked to one of the bookshelves and pulled out a volume. “My latest,” he said and handed it to her.

She read the title. “*Night Sounds.* Intriguing.” She opened the book and scanned the front flap, then casually she flipped to the back cover. Would his picture be there?

Yes. Fisherman’s cable-knit sweater, glasses and all. It appeared he was legit, but if he was, *who* was her drug dealer?

“I told you. I’m a published author.”

Was she so transparent? “I never doubted you,” she protested.

“Sure, you did. Would you like a drink—or are you on duty?”

“A sip, but that’s all. It’s been a quiet day. I hope it stays that way.”

"Even the sheriff has to have a night off once in a while. From what I've read in the local paper, you've had a difficult week. I think a sip is called for." He walked over to a corner cabinet and poured a half shot of what looked like vodka. He handed it to her and she took a grateful sip before responding.

"A difficult week? It's been a difficult two months. My father, the new drugs and two O.D.s. When I saw Barbie's parents at the funeral home, I promised them I'd stop the drug trafficking." She groaned at the memory of their trusting faces. "How the hell am I going to do it?"

Not waiting for a reply, she said, "This is a small town, and I'm a failure as sheriff." She laughed. "Just look at me. I'm the big detective from Music City come home to take over where her father left off. What a joke."

Mac took her chin in his hand and raised it a notch, gazing steadily into her eyes. "Is this a private pity party or is anyone allowed?"

"You don't understand. Daddy would be so disappointed in me. I haven't found his killer. I haven't accomplished anything." She sagged into Mac's arms. His presence was so strong and comforting. At least she was *almost* certain he wasn't her drug dealer, and she could use a little comfort.

"I don't know what the hell's the matter with me," she finished with a sniff.

"You're having a weak moment. That's all. You're human and you're allowed."

Again, his comforting tone, his warm presence, enveloped her. She looked into his eyes, fighting back the tears stinging her eyes. Her lips parted in expectation of—what?

He lowered his mouth to hers and kissed her luxuriously slow. Heat suffused her body. She trembled and pulled back before molding her body to his.

Why not? He was an author, not a drug lord.

His kiss deepened. Breathing became impossible. She had to quench the raging thirst she had for his body.

He picked her up as easily as a child and carried her upstairs. Her head rested on his strong shoulder. Could anything feel more natural?

Mac tugged the shirt from Rilla's khaki pants, while she unbuckled her gun belt, turned and laid it carefully on a bedside table.

"Let me do the rest." He reached to unbutton her pants. Dark eyes glazed with desire, she nodded. They fell to her ankles, and with a nimble move, she stepped out of them.

He cupped her ass and pulled her close. A scrap of white lace was all that separated him from her hot sweetness. Who could've guessed the sheriff loved sexy underwear? He trembled with need. Soon he would taste all of her.

One button at a time, he undid her shirt. "Are you sure?"

"Yes." The word was no more than a warm, whispered breath against his neck.

Her nipples were already hard beneath a sports bra. He caressed the small mounds, eliciting a low moan from her sweet mouth.

She lifted her arms and he eased the bra over her head.

Dear God, she was beautiful. He ran his hands down her slim curves. Her head fell back, showing the elegant arch of her neck. He leaned in and kissed the hollow above her breastbone and groaned.

"Your hair... I've fantasized about it."

She smiled, reached back and slipped the fastener off her braid. She shook her head, freeing the silken strands. He ran his fingers through her hair and a hot jolt of need zapped through his groin. "Beautiful."

She bit her lip, then whispered, "Thank you," She reached out and toyed with his belt. "Now you."

No second invitation needed, he stripped down to his briefs and kicked off his shoes. There was no hiding his throbbing dick. Her effect on him was more powerful than any woman he'd ever known. He was dying to rip away the final scrap of lace and bury himself deep inside her hot pussy.

Still chewing her full bottom lip, she gazed up at him, trust evident in her eyes. God, what a liar he was...about everything but wanting her.

Carefully he hooked his thumb under the thin strip of elastic and slid her panties down to her ankles, lingering over each toned curve, kissing her hip, her calf, her ankle.

Nearly overcome with passion, he stopped at the apex of her thighs. Breathing in her musky scent, he left a quick kiss in the damp, dark curls.

She trembled against him as he flicked the swollen bud of her clit with his tongue and sampled her juices. A loud moan escaped her.

"No fair."

"You wanna play fair?" He stood, then nudged her head downward, until she knelt before him. Her hands shaking, Rilla caught her breath and slid Mac's briefs down over his ass. His penis was rock hard and jutted straight up. She teased the head with the tip of her tongue, circling...tasting the man...learning him.

He trembled at her light touch. "You're killing me." He gasped and lifted her in his arms. She wrapped her legs around his waist. Without warning, he fell onto the bed carrying her with him.

She gazed into his eyes as he knelt over her. One of his hard-muscled thighs nudged hers apart. He slipped a finger in her wet slit, and she arched against him, cupped and offered her breasts to him.

"God, you're lovely," he rasped.

He kissed and teased her nipples into taut peaks. Her head whipped back from the rush of pleasure. Never had any man ever made her feel so desirable...so needed...so precious.

She reached between them, gripped his penis and guided him to her.

"Careful," he gasped, "or I won't last another second. I want to enjoy all of you." He pulled away and began by covering the arch of her foot with tiny kisses, then her ankle, her calf, her thighs. She trembled as he drifted closer and closer to her juicy core.

Unable to wait any longer, Mac poised over her and thrust deep and hard, burying himself in her wet pussy. Together, like hand in glove, they fit. She arched to meet him, taking the full length of his dick deep within her. Her nails raked his shoulders as she met him thrust for thrust. Her loving so sweet...she gave more than she took. This soft woman in his arms...

She gasped his name and her frenzied thrusting movements beneath him pulled him along and shoved him over the edge. He filled her, each pumping wave draining him completely until he collapsed by her side.

She cried his name aloud. A rush of unfamiliar emotions surged through him. A sense of fulfillment and more contentment than he'd ever known. They were one in every way that mattered. He levered himself to his elbows.

"You all right?" He wiped away a damp strand of hair from her forehead. "Rilla?" Before she could answer, he kissed her. Once more the sweetness of her mouth sent a new surge to his groin. "Hon?"

Her eyelids fluttered, but finally her gaze focused. "Huh?"

"Are you all right?"

A smile curved her mouth. "I am *so* all right. This brings a new meaning to 'all right'."

God. She had a sense of humor, too. What more could a man want?

"You're perfect." He kissed the tip of her nose and gently moved to the side. She snuggled against him, warm and perfect, every single inch of her.

She caressed his face and sighed. "That was perfect. Just what I needed." She sat up and swung her legs over the side of the bed.

"Wait." He reached out and took her wrist in his strong grip. "Where do you think you're going?"

She grinned at him. "Don't want to wear out my welcome."

"Not likely to happen around here."

He eased her back into the bed, and she settled comfortably into the crook of his arm and shoulder. She gazed at him. "We're doing the right thing, aren't we?"

"Yes," he said with a nod. "We're definitely doing it right. Mm-hmm."

Rilla giggled and poked his six-pack abs. Who knew a writer could have such a hot body? "You know what I mean."

"Careful, don't get serious on me or I'll have to..."

"Have to what?"

"Handcuff you to the bed so you can't ever leave."

She squirmed against the bed at the idea of being under his control, powerless. "I think—"

He leaned over her and stopped her words with a quick kiss. "Then you'd better behave and do exactly as I tell you."

"I'm not very good about doing what I'm told."

"Lie still." He trapped her wrists over her head.

She bit her lip and grinned. What would he do if... "Actually I *never* do what I'm told."

"You will today."

"No. *You* will." With a twist of her wrist, she freed one hand from his grasp and feathered her fingers along his bare ribs.

"Uh-unh."

"Ticklish? Mm, fun."

He started backing away and released her other hand.

"Big mistake." She went after him with both of her hands extended.

"Now Rilla, no fair," he said with a laugh, and all the while, he scrambled to get out of bed and out of her reach.

She grasped her right wrist and pointed her finger in shooting-stance mode. "Halt! Not another step," she said in the voice guaranteed to stop any perp in his tracks.

He stopped, turned and obligingly raised his hands. "Don't shoot, me, Sheriff Ma'am. I give up."

She motioned toward the master bath with her pretend gun.

"Get movin'."

He took one step in the direction of the bathroom, then stopped. "Promise you won't tickle me, because if you do, I'll be forced to make a run for it." His tone was serious, but his glittering gaze said *fun.*

"Hush. I don't allow my prisoners to talk." She motioned at the bathroom again. "Start the shower already. And I like it hot."

She followed his slow amble into the master bath. His rear view, specifically his ass, was as superb as she'd imagined the first day in the grocery store...maybe better.

Taking in the black granite counters and white marble floors, she sighed. She wasn't used to such luxurious surroundings. True at some point, her father had installed a whirlpool tub, but he hadn't bothered with high-end tile or countertops.

"Nice."

He turned and grinned. Apparently the man was completely comfortable naked, as if he walked around in the nude all the time.

"Yeah, it's nice, but you wouldn't want to fall on the stuff. Might crack your head."

"I'll keep it in mind. Now, get busy on gettin' my water just right."

With a wide grin on his kissable lips, he turned and adjusted the rainwater shower faucets. "Hot? You like it hot? Did I hear you right?" He twisted the final knob and the water started raining down from the overhead shower.

Not that he'd actually scald or freeze her, but...

"You first."

"Yes, ma'am." Mac stepped inside the tiled shower and waited for her to follow. The water sluiced down their bodies. The temperature was just right—hot but not scalding. She closed the distance between them and stood with her body close to his, her nipples puckering as soon as they brushed his chest. She slipped her arms around his neck and rubbed her naked body against his. Her pelvic bones jutted from her taut abdomen, and her crisp black curls brushed against his dick. Damn, but she was intoxicating. Vibrant. Totally female.

His head whirled, his heart raced, and his lungs burned with the need to breathe. He cupped her ass with shaking hands and pulled her even closer.

Rilla couldn't resist teasing him. "I've never known you to be so anxious...or agreeable."

His teeth gleamed as he grinned at her. "I suppose you have evidence to support your point of view?"

"The evidence is here for all to see." She grinned and cast a glance at the topic of discussion.

"No, not for all to see. Only you." His eyes seemed to want to memorize her face, and his hands were everywhere, stroking her cheek, teasing a nipple, following the line of her waist.

"Mmm," she murmured. He pulled her toward him, wrapping her legs around his waist and bracing her back against the shower wall.

"You talk too much," he whispered, then scorched her lips with a searing kiss.

She cupped her breasts and offered them to him. First, he kissed one breast, suckled it, turning her into a pool of wanton need. Her pulse soared again, higher than ever. Never had she needed anyone so much or so often as she needed this one man. She wanted him to fill her until she couldn't take any more. Her head went back, and a moan ripped from her throat. "Now!"

He made a minuscule adjustment in position, cupped her butt and lifted her slightly. Separating her labia, he allowed her to capture his steel-hard dick and slide the head inside her slick core. Together they joined, her legs around his waist, she rode him, withdrawing and rocking with each of his savage thrusts, each one sweeter and hotter than the one before until she ignited in a blaze of desire and completion.

While Rilla dozed, Mac eased from the bed. Damn. What the hell was he thinking?

That's just it—I'm not. He'd gone too far. Technically she was still his chief suspect, but he didn't believe for one minute she was a dirty cop. He'd just spent two passionate hours with a sexy and vulnerable woman. He had to make Havers see the investigation was centered on the wrong person.

He pulled on his jeans and crept from the room and down the hall to his office. He closed the door behind him with the heel of his foot.

Damn. He'd left the computer on and there was a new e-mail from Havers waiting for him. He quickly skimmed the contents. Hell. Havers was pissed about his lack of progress. No doubt about it. He snatched up his cell phone and hit speed dial for his boss.

Rilla opened her eyes and stretched. Mac's side of the bed was empty, but the sheets were still warm from his body. She slid from the bed and wrapped the sheet around her, still able to smell his male scent on the linen. Where was he, anyway?

Just barely she heard a low murmuring. He was talking to someone? Who?

Pulling the sheet tighter around her body, she tiptoed into the hall. The door on her left was ajar, half an inch or so.

Eavesdropping? Yes, she guessed she was. Probably talking to his agent. She shouldn't listen, but as she turned around to leave, she heard, "There's not a damn thing in her file with Metro which indicates she'd turn dirty and go along with drug trafficking in her father's place."

Her file with Metro? What the hell?

"I know. And all we lacked was his source higher on the food chain."

Who was Mac talking about?

"Well, *someone* killed him. He either pissed off someone, or someone decided they wanted his place."

She eased the door open another inch.

"I'd bet my life she's clean. How many times do we have to go over this? She graduated at the top of her academy work. Gold shield at twenty-nine. She's worked vice, undercover and made grade one by the time she was thirty, numerous commendations. Admired and respected by her colleagues. She's nothing like her father."

Nothing like her father?

Why on earth was Mac discussing an investigation and her father with his agent? Okay, so it wasn't his agent, and Mac wasn't an author.

Then who the hell was he?

"I can't talk," he said softly, as she strained to hear more. "Ben Devane was crooked, that much we know. But the daughter—I'm positive she's clean."

He shook his head at the response on the phone. "No, it's not like that. Gotta go."

Drug-trafficking and her father?

She stepped back from the door. A flash of anger surged through her body. Her face burned. She bit her tongue to keep from screaming.

He snapped the cell phone shut and turned.

She kicked open the door. The crash resounded and shook the windows of the old house. "You son of a bitch," she hissed. "You're a narc and I'm one of your suspects."

Mac groaned. Damn, the door. Havers was right: he'd let his 'nads do the thinking. "Let me explain."

"You don't have to explain a damn thing. You think my father was dirty, and you think I took up right where he left off. I heard everything."

"Calm down, Rilla, we have proof your father was in control of the drug trade. As for you...I never—"

"Show me your damn proof!"

"You know I can't. But trust me—"

"Trust you?" She shifted into a fighting stance, her fists raised. "About as far as I could pick you up and throw you."

He took a step toward her.

"Damn you!" Rilla retreated a step. "You make love to me and wait for me to whisper my dirty secrets in your ear while we're in bed. Pillow talk and a little interrogation while you're at it—damn good plan, Callahan. I wish I'd thought of it first."

"Don't act like you're so innocent. You did exactly the same damned thing. You grilled me like a suspect the first night we had dinner. For all I know, you suspected *me* of being the drug dealer."

"I did!" She spun on her heel and headed for the door. "If it's the last thing I do, I'll find the dealer and prove my father was innocent."

"Come on, Rilla. It's my job. Isn't there some way we can work together on this?"

Apparently his plea was lost on her. She picked up the waste basket and threw it at his head. He dodged just in time.

"Screw your job. Screw you!" She ran across the hall. He followed, hoping she'd relent, but without ever glancing in his direction, she hurriedly pulled on her clothes, rushed by him and flew down the stairs. A second later, the front door slammed.

He sat down on the bed and groaned. Talk about the shit hitting the fan.

Chapter Ten

Early the next evening, Rilla parked the Jeep Cherokee beside the house and turned off the motor.

Damn, it sure was quiet. She climbed from the jeep and listened, but she still couldn't hear Ralphie. Normally on her return home, he yelped and whined until she opened the door and let him out. She shrugged. Maybe he was just taking a nap and chasing a dream rabbit or two.

She opened the door to the screened-in back porch which overlooked a creek and thick woods. One day when she had some free time, she might actually sit out there and enjoy the peace and quiet.

But not today.

Someone had jimmied the lock on the back door. She slid her gun from the holster and chambered a round. Using the toe of her boot, she opened the door a crack. Why hadn't her new alarm gone off? Had she already forgotten to set it?

Blood on the tile floor with a trail of dog prints leading outside.

Ralphie? The son-of-a-bitch better not have hurt him.

Carefully she worked her way through rest of the house. The entire place was a shambles, but the office was the worst. Her father's old computer was scattered in pieces all over the floor, and the hard drive was missing.

Mac's accusations came rushing back and sent a chill through her. Was it possible her father had left records about his drugs deals on his computer? No. No matter what Mac said, the DEA didn't know her father. He was a good man. Damn Mac for making her doubt her father.

"Ralphie?" she called. "Where are you?" She followed even more bloody footprints. Dog blood or human?

A snuffling sound. Gun still drawn, she whirled.

Standing on the other side of the screen door, tail wagging, was Ralphie. Relief rushed through her. "There you are."

She stepped outside and knelt beside him. "What happened here, fella? Are you all right?" She ran her fingers through his thick black fur. Nothing.

Okay, gotta preserve the scene.

"Sorry, fella, you've got to stay outside for a little while."

As if he understood, Ralphie curled up on the top step.

She pulled the cell phone from her pocket and hit speed dial for the office. "R.J., break-in. My place. I want Detective Bellows for forensics. There's blood all over the kitchen floor. I think Ralphie might've bitten the perp."

Kit Bellows stood up from collecting the blood sample. "I guess I don't need to take a pic to ID the foot prints," she said with a wide smile.

Rilla shook her head. "Don't waste the film. They're obviously Ralphie's."

"Guess he took a hunk outta someone's hide."

"Sure looks like it."

"Lot of blood. Perp might seek medical attention."

"Notify the E.R. and the local docs...and Kurt at the drug store. He might notice if someone decides to add to their first aid kit."

"Right, boss."

Rilla watched over Bellows while she took photos and dusted for prints. She didn't want any omissions on what was supposed to be a simple B&E.

"Anything?"

The detective shook her head. "Nope. Couple of smudges, but nothing usable."

"Too bad." Damn good thing Mac was intensifying his investigation and focusing on someone other than her. But if she'd been so wrong about him, who else had flown under her radar?

The day after the break-in, Rilla pored over the week's worth of TBI wanted posters she'd just pulled off the fax.

Bellows knocked and sauntered in.

"Anything from the hospital?" Rilla asked.

Bellows consulted her notebook. "Hospital, negative. Same with the clinic and the doctors' offices. I e-mailed surrounding counties sheriffs' offices. They'll check their local medical care providers, too. I haven't heard back from all of those yet."

"Good. Canvass the supermarket and all the convenience stores—anywhere someone could buy tape, bandages. My dog got him good."

"All this for a break-in? It was *your* place, but—"

"But what?"

"You're acting like you think it's more than a simple B&E."

"I do." Rilla gave an emphatic nod. "Nothing of value taken, except my computer hard drive and a shoebox of old floppy discs. I already checked all those discs when I first moved in, but someone must have thought there was something on them. So no, I don't think it was your garden variety B&E."

"It does sound fishy," Kit admitted. "So have you sounded out the drug store and hunky Kurt?" she asked with a smirk.

"You didn't?" Rilla asked surprised.

"I thought you might want to do it...personally."

Rilla frowned. Honestly nothing was private in the Springs. "Okay, since you haven't, I will."

Maybe she should interview Kurt herself. After all, he was an old friend and would probably appreciate the consideration. She picked up the telephone but put it down again. Why bother with calling when the drug store was just across the street? That way she'd be able to question his employees, too.

Five minutes later, she found Kurt at his high counter, busy with an elderly customer—none other than Miss Tweedy.

She waited and casually perused the products for feminine hygiene. On a lower shelf were rows of colorful condom boxes. Each claiming—never mind what they claimed.

Good grief. Condoms. She and Mack hadn't... Too late now, and it sure as hell wasn't going to happen again. No way she'd have the nerve to purchase them with Kurt watching. Geez, whatever happened to having vitamins near the prescription counter?

"Rilla, darlin', what can I do for you?" Kurt asked.

Her head snapped up, then she remembered Miss Tweedy stood there with raised eyebrows. Rilla's cheeks burned, but she managed to get her brain, tongue and mouth all working in the proper order. "Well, I had a little break-in, but my dog gave him a good chomp, so I'm wondering if you noticed anyone buying more than the usual amount of first aid supplies?"

The pharmacist frowned and scratched his chin. "'Fraid not, but unless your perp—that's the word you law enforcement types use, isn't it?"

"Yeah." Rilla grinned. "You've been watching too many cop shows."

"Unless he was picking up a prescription, your perp would most likely pay at the check-out up front. Why don't you ask

Donna Fay? She's here most days, and Bob Talbot—he works nights. He'll be in around three."

"Thanks, Kurt. I just wanted your permission before I did."

"Is there anything else I can do for you?" He flashed Rilla a mischievous grin. "I saw you eyeing the merchandise." His gaze cut toward the condom shelf.

She choked and coughed in spite of herself, her face heating like an open oven. "No thanks. Guess I'll be talking to Donna." She whipped around, ready to take off, but apparently Kurt wasn't through with his teasing.

"I don't guess this would be a politic time to ask you out again?"

She took a deep breath then spun back to face him. "I'm so busy right now, investigating this drug business, I'm afraid I'd be a poor date. You've already had that experience once."

"All right, you've dumped me again. I won't give you a third chance." He grabbed his chest and grinned. "My poor heart can't take it."

"Oh, go on. You know what my life is like. I never have a moment to myself."

"Yeah, yeah, you women are all the same. You might as well talk to Donna since I can't woo you away from—Mac, is it?"

"Mac?"

"New guy, now I've heard—"

She glanced over her shoulder. "You have a customer, Kurt. I'd better head up front." She nodded at the new arrival. "Hey, Mrs. Robbins, hot day isn't it?"

"Yes, Sheriff, it surely is."

Rilla seized the opening and headed to the front of the store.

Luckily the cashier wasn't busy with a customer. "Hey there, Donna. Mind if I ask you a couple of questions?"

Donna Fay closed her copy of *Soap Opera Digest.* "Sure thing. Hell of a note, isn't it—poor little Barbie Soames." She tossed her hair, but her lacquered blond hairdo didn't move a fraction of an inch. "Kids nowadays."

"This is about something else. I just need to know if you noticed anyone buying more than a box of Band Aids?"

"Is this about something important? Because I'd just love to be part of an investigation. I would. You know I always fancied I could do police work. I really—"

"I'm in a bit of a hurry. Can you just answer my question?"

"Uh—sure, Rilla—I mean, Sheriff." Donna's face flushed a dark pink. She started rearranging the breath mints. "No. The answer is no."

"You're sure?"

"Yes." The cashier's eyes widened. "Wait a minute. Bob Talbot left me a note warning me about shoplifters. He had some supplies go missing last night."

"Yeah?"

"He'll be in at three."

Rilla checked her watch—two o'clock. "What about the security tapes from last night?"

The cashier's face fell. "We use them over and over. I put it back in this morning."

"What time?"

"Nine."

"Six hour tape?"

Donna nodded.

"Let me have it. There's still an hour from last night on it."

"Sure." The cashier turned to the high shelf behind her and popped out the tape and handed it to Rilla.

"Thanks, Donna Fay. If there's nothing on it, I'll have it back to you tomorrow."

"Take your time. We have a couple extras." Donna shivered and giggled. "This is totally cool—just like on TV."

If only it were that simple. "Oh yeah, mystery solved in sixty minutes or less. See ya."

Back in her office, Rilla handed the tape over to Kit Bellows. "I know it's a long shot, but there might be something in the last hour or two of the tape."

Kit slid the tape into the VCR. "So, what am I looking for?"

"Anyone who might've stolen first aid supplies. According to the cashier, there were some first aid supplies unaccounted for this morning. Unfortunately there's already five hours of today taped over it."

"Okay." Kit shrugged. "At least I don't have to watch all six hours."

"Right. Call me if you find anything interesting. I'll be in my office working on the annual budget." Rilla let out a groan. "Now if I just knew how much money the county commission will allot me for next year's budget..."

Kit paused the tape. "Don't you just hate all the paperwork?"

"I'm getting used to it, but this budget business is beyond tense."

"Will you run when this term is up?"

"Honestly, I don't know. There's a lot more to this job than I ever knew. Daddy always made it look so easy, but I miss being a detective. It's in my blood."

And it was. She'd grown up doing her homework at sheriff's office, devoured murder mysteries like they were McDonald's fries. But what kind of detective couldn't even find out who was selling drugs in her county—much less find her father's killer?

"Okay, what's on the tape?" Rilla asked.

"Well, I fast-forwarded to the last two hours..."

"And?"

"I'm getting to it, don't rush me."

"Don't yank my chain, Bellows. Spit it out."

"Okay, nothing."

"Nothing?"

"Nothing, *nada*. Today's taping must have taped over what we're looking for."

"Crap. Are you sure?"

"Yeah. The only person who went near the first aid items was the pharmacist, and he'd hardly be stealing from his own store, now would he?"

"No, guess not." Still... "Show me that section anyway." She leaned forward and studied the not-so-great-quality tape.

"See there's the first aid aisle," Kit pointed and hit rewind. "Okay here's the date/time marker. Nine-fifteen. The cashier is busy with a customer up front."

"There's Kurt," Rilla said. "He walked into the aisle, hesitated a minute or so, before walking out again. The shelves are too high for the camera angle. I can't see what he's doing."

"Well, he's carrying something in front of him. His arms are bent at the elbow."

"Wait," Rilla said. "Right there, slow it down just as he goes behind the counter."

The detective reversed the tape and then slo-moed the scene in question.

"Yeah, he's definitely picked something up from the first aid items, but there could be a dozen reasons."

"Sure, but if you want me to, I'd be glad to go over and check out his body for dog bites."

With an eye roll, Rilla laughed. "I'm sure you would. I'll take care of it myself."

"No fair. Do you have to monopolize the only two eligible men in town?"

"Kurt's an old friend. I don't want to piss him off. He's an extra pair of eyes. Finger on the pulse of the town."

"Uh-huh. Sure. You're greedy, Rilla. Mac Callahan and Kurt Jensen." Kit shook her head. "I guess I'm going to have to move to Nashville if I'm gonna meet anyone who hasn't fallen under your spell."

"Very funny." She tossed a paper wad at her detective. "Now get out of here and find me a burglar with a dog bite."

"Yes, ma'am." Kit snapped a cheeky salute and hurried from the office.

As far as Rilla was concerned, Kit could have both men and good riddance. On second thought, she could have Kurt.

An hour later, Rilla walked into the squad room. Kit Bellows' desk was in the right corner. "Anything turned up from canvassing the doctors' offices?"

"Nothing."

"I thought sure we'd come up with someone with scratches or bites."

The only person with scratches was a Katie Bass and she said they were cat scratches."

"Katie?" Rilla grinned. "I doubt very seriously she's spending her spare time ransacking my house. Matter of fact, she does have a cat, and he's a devil with claws."

"Still we should check her out."

"Yeah, I'll run by her place…as a courtesy. We went to school together."

"Sure. Whatever you say."

Rilla shoved her hands in her pockets. "I'm bummed. I thought we had a potential lead with those missing supplies."

"Something could still turn up."

"If only it would."

Never patient, even on good days, Rilla drummed her fingers against the desk. Impulsively she snatched up the telephone and called her least favorite DEA agent. "Did you break into my house?"

"What?"

"Then where were you today while my house was burgled?"

"I have an alibi. I'm sure I do."

The playful, low timbre of his voice sent a rush of heat to her lower belly. "Uh, I need to check your body for bite marks. Ralphie bit the perp."

"I have several bite marks, but no new ones."

"I'll examine you myself," she purred. God. What had come over her? Why was she purring like a cat on the prowl? How could she lose focus so easily? This man had lied to her.

"Sheriff, will you be gentle?"

"Hell, no!"

"What time do I need this alibi for?"

"Anytime between seven-thirty this morning and noon."

"Seriously? You want me to account for my entire morning?"

"Just routine." There, that was better, more in control and getting focused.

"You're going to have to interrogate me later."

"Why?"

"I'd rather have dinner with you. We need to come up with a plan to work together, and then you can interrogate me all you want."

"That's not going to happen."

"You don't want to question me?"

"No—yes. I mean *dinner* is out."

"I didn't burgle your house."

"Fine." Rather than continue acting like a hysterical teenager, she cut the connection.

Why did she let him get to her? Why couldn't she act like a reasonable adult around that man? Why?

Shortly after her wasted phone call to Mac, Rilla strode up the brick walkway to Katie and Lloyd Bass's house. The good thing about small towns was she knew everyone...which was also the drawback. Doubly so, when dealing with someone she considered a friend.

She inhaled the rich scent of Katie's summer roses. Her friend had a real knack for growing the things, and her garden had even been featured in *Southern Living* a couple of years back.

Her own thumb was more black than green. Marigolds she could manage, and weeds, but roses—well, they required a lot more care and tending than she had time for.

She raised the ornate brass knocker and rapped it against the dark oak door and waited.

When the door wasn't answered after a second attempt to rouse someone, she moseyed around the back. Maybe Katie was in the garden or working on her tan by the pool.

Lloyd had certainly done well. Maybe he had another source of income. Could he be the drug lord? Her father's fishing buddy?

Nah.

But then she hadn't thought her father'd be involved in drug trafficking either.

The gurgle and hiss of running water reached her before she spied the pool and a newly installed water feature. Good grief. It hadn't been there two weeks ago. "Katie?"

Katie turned from the rosebush she'd been spraying. "Hey, Rilla. Like Lloyd's new toy?" She jerked her thumb toward the artful jumble of boulders where water spilled in an attractive, almost natural, display into the pool.

"Holy cow." She couldn't help wondering how much it set Lloyd back. None of her business of course, unless drug money paid for it.

"It's incredible." Truly it was. Katie's roses were in full bloom, and the air was full of their delicate scent.

"Have a seat. I'll bring you some lemonade, or would you rather have something harder?"

"Afraid I'm here on business."

Her friend's perfectly plucked eyebrows pulled together in a slight frown. "Business? *Sheriff* business?"

Rilla smiled and nodded. "Just tying up a couple of loose ends."

"Whatever I can do, you know I'll be glad to help. I just don't know what it could be.

"It's not a big deal. I'm investigating a break-in. The culprit left some blood behind so we're pretty sure the person was bitten."

"You're talking about your place, aren't you? Why on earth would you ask me about something like that?"

"I'm following up on any injuries which required medical attention. Your name came up on a list. I just came by to clear you so I can find the real culprit."

"Whew. I think I need a drink." Katie collapsed on a chair and fanned her cheeks.

"So how *did* you get those scratches on your forearm?"

"My cat. You know how temperamental he is. Guess I ought to get him fixed, but Lloyd won't hear of it. You know how men are about such things." Red-faced, Katie held her arm out for inspection. "See—cat scratches."

"I see. Sorry, I had to ask. It's just the job."

"Damn shame, that someone I've known for years comes here asking questions like I'm a common criminal." Katie gave an angry huff. “Anything else? Want to strip search me, Sheriff? I’m not hiding anything.”

Clad only in a skimpy string bikini, Katie spoke the truth, but Rilla attempted to mollify her old friend. “Now, it was just a formality. I know about the cat. I just had to follow it up. Figured you’d rather talk to me than someone else.”

“Well, it’s still insulting. Good Lord, you’ve had dinner at my house, and you’re grilling me like I’m a prime rib or something.” Katie looked away from Rilla, then back at her. “Well, anything *else* you want to know?”

“You’re blowing this out of proportion.”

“Yeah, I know. I know this, too, unless you have anything else, I’d appreciate you taking your skinny behind outta here and let me get back to my roses.”

“Okay, okay.” Puzzled by her former friend’s extreme reaction, Rilla turned and walked away. Of course, Katie’d always had a short fuse. Had she hit Katie with the questions at a bad time? Was it just a bad case of PMS or was her old friend hiding something?

The dealer drove out into the countryside well away from any spying eyes or nosy busybodies. He pulled the cell phone from his pocket. A stolen cell phone. He’d lifted it from one of his customers for this one-time use. He called the hit man’s number.

It rang twice.

“Sleep,” the accented voice said.

“Dreamless sleep,” he responded, “that knits the raveled sleeve of care.”

“Speak.”

“I have another job for you.”

“Go on.”

“The sheriff.”

"What?"

"The new one. You don't have any prejudice against killing a woman, do you?"

"No. 'Tis business. But hitting twice in the same area greatly increases my risk."

"And your price?"

"It increases as well."

"I expected that. And there's a nosy newcomer in town. I have a bad feeling about him. Take him out, too, and I'll triple the original fee."

A low, unpleasant rumble from the other end of the line raised the hair on the dealer's neck.

"Deal. Deadline?"

"ASAP, but nothing must lead back to me."

"Understood. Same arrangements as before. One half now, the rest on completion."

He wrote down the account details as quickly as the hit man read them.

"Transaction window is five minutes. Don't waste time."

"Right. I'd better get crackin'."

The line went dead. He reached for his laptop and completed the transaction. Damn, this little contract put a major hole in his retirement account.

He chuckled. Still, selling ecstasy was the most lucrative investment he'd ever made. And it would be worth it to get rid of that bitch once and for all.

No sooner had he turned on the ignition, when his private cell rang. "Yeah?"

"When can we see each other? It's been so long."

"Soon, not yet—"

"No, I'm not calling about tonight. I mean, when are we going to blow this piss-hole of a town? I'm sick of it. I'm itching for some bright lights and riches beyond belief, baby."

"Be patient. We have another six months before we can leave. You keep a low profile, hear me?"

"But why? You said..."

Her whining set his nerves on edge. "Stuff it. Something unexpected has come up. Something expensive. It'll take a little time to recoup our investment."

Careful, he warned her silently, or he'd have to take care of her, too. Why saddle himself with a whining broad anyway? Once he settled in a convenient South American country with no extradition treaty, he'd live like a king and have any woman he wanted. Yes, that settled it.

His wife was expendable.

Chapter Eleven

"Bills, ads and snail mail spam." Rilla threw the latest collection of mail on the roll top desk, then glanced down at Ralphie who was scratching the floor again—a sure sign he needed a potty break. "Want to go outside? Sure you do. You're a good doggie. Yes, you are." Geez, she was talking to the dog like he could understand her every word.

Ralphie obliged by trotting to the back door.

After watching him sprint into the back yard, she returned to her task of sorting through the mail. She slumped in the chair and sat at the desk and opened the pile of bills with a long, stainless steel letter opener. The same one her father had used for years. As sharp as the familiar implement was, the memory which knifed through her was sharper.

She'd watched her father go through his mail every weekend, dutifully writing out checks to cover his few expenses.

Shaking her head, she tried to erase the vision. This wasn't the time to get all mushy and sentimental over a mere letter opener.

A piece of metal. That's all.

Back on task, she wrote checks until Ralphie's scratching at the back door brought her out of the chair. "Okay, hound, I'm coming."

Her four-legged roommate followed her back to the office, his toenails clicking against the hardwood floor.

“Gotta trim those things, fellow. Now why can’t you just chew them off?” Did dogs chew their nails?

Nah, probably not.

Once more, she sat at the desk and stuffed each of the checks into its respective envelope. Ralphie lay down and curled up under her feet until...

“Just what do you think you’re doing? You just went out.”

The dog looked up, but continued scrabbling at the rug.

“So what is it? A bug? Or do you smell a mouse in the crawl space?” She knelt beside him and pulled up the carpet. “See? There’s nothing here.” She smoothed the rug in place.

“Hold on.” Something didn’t feel quite right. Pulling back the carpet, she ran her hand over the dark oak floorboards. Something was a little off in the surface.

A hidden compartment? She reached for the letter opener, then jimmied it under the edge and pried at the section of loose hardwood.

She held her breath and lifted a foot-long section of the floorboard. Her heart pounding, she reached in and rummaged around the secret compartment...and found a metal box. Still holding her breath, she eased it out, then shook it.

“Locked. Dammit.” Grabbing the letter opener again, she pried at the rusted lock. “Probably nothing but some old bills or love letters from the Civil War in here.”

Without warning, the lock gave, flew across the room and landed in the hallway.

Gingerly she opened the box. “So much for old love letters.” All it contained was a small, ring-bound notebook. She set the metal box aside and turned her attention to the notebook.

Her father’s handwriting.

She snapped the notebook shut. A wave of nausea roiled in her stomach. He’d obviously gone to a lot of trouble to hide it. Was Callahan right? Was her father dirty after all? Was she holding the very evidence which would forever blacken his reputation as an honest lawman?

And if it contained the name of her father's killer...

Dammit. She'd been so sure her father was honest—and just as sure Callahan and the DEA were dead wrong.

She glanced around the room. Matches. She needed matches. Should she burn it? *Could* she burn it? Tamper with evidence?

No.

And here it was. Names. Dates and details of some type of transactions. The first hint of her father's illegal money trail. And a series of numbers—a secret bank account?

She closed her eyes and willed the numbers to disappear. Why couldn't he have used invisible ink? Dammit. Here it was. Evidence against her father in his own hand.

She brushed away the tears before they could fall. How could he betray everything he stood for? It wasn't much. Half a million. Not even a whole million. Just his own version of a nicely padded 401k.

How insufferable Callahan would be when she handed the journal over to him.

And no matter how much it hurt, she would hand it over.

Across town, Mac sat hunched over his laptop, shaking his head. So Havers wanted a progress report. Progress report—hell. The telephone rang.

"Callahan."

"I have something you need to see." Rilla's voice trembled.

"What's wrong? You sound all shook up."

"Everything—in my father's own hand. He wrote some of it down in code. But I figure two heads are better than one."

"I'm sorry, Rilla. Your father..."

"It's too late for 'sorry'. We still have a dealer to take down. Get your ass over here."

"How can I resist such a charming invitation?" He replaced the phone. As much as he needed to be right, he didn't blame Rilla for her anger. Her father had betrayed her trust along with the county he served. He'd betrayed all honest lawmen.

Mac drove to the edge of town. The Springs was a picturesque little town, and he wouldn't have minded living there, but as soon as this assignment was over, the DEA would have a new one for him.

Too bad, because he loved the old house and wondered what would happen to it when he moved. In any other life, it would've been a great place to raise kids.

By the time he reached Rilla's place, the houses had turned decidedly modest with well-kept, neat yards. Hers was no different. Probably hired a neighborhood kid to mow the lawn. Sure as hell, she didn't have time to do it herself.

Mac parked beneath the branches of a large maple. After exiting his car, he ran up the front steps. Her dog barked when he raised his fist to knock on the door. The creature was loud and ready to inform everyone this was his territory.

Through the front door, he heard, "Hush, Ralphie."

An unsmiling Rilla opened the door. "Come on in. There's still a path."

Mac picked his way through the stacks of boxes and followed her into the kitchen. How could any woman look so good in a pair of hip-hugger jeans? A small green dragon peeked over the edge of her jeans in the middle of her back. "You have a tattoo?"

She turned with a shrug. "Yeah. Got it the night I graduated from the police academy."

"I don't remember seeing it when..."

"Well, we were pretty frantic."

His groin stirred. "Right. We sort of got right down to business. I didn't spend much time sightseeing."

She gave him the *look*—the one that said he was being a jerk. And he was.

"Never mind that," she said. "Want some coffee? It's fresh."

Guess not. "Growing domestic, are you?"

She rolled her eyes and shot him a look of disgust. "I make a mean cup of coffee."

He raised his hands. "I surrender. I'd kill for a cup."

"That won't be necessary," she told him in a pithy tone which was a damn sight closer to pissy. She turned and pulled a cup from the oak cabinets.

"This it?" He pointed at the notebook.

"Yeah." She nodded, but didn't face him while she poured him a cup of coffee. "Take it black?"

"Is there any other way?"

"Not as far as I'm concerned." Rilla pulled out a chair and sat across from Mac, taking care to not sit beside him. She needed the width of the table between them, more to keep from choking him than anything else. She hated his being right. Her father was dirty. She didn't have to like it, and she didn't have to kiss Mac's ass.

He picked up the notebook and ruffled the pages. "Meticulous, wasn't he? Pages of stuff here."

"It's my father's handwriting. I'd know it anywhere."

His gaze narrowed as he studied the pages. "Notations are consistent. Figuring out his system won't be too difficult."

She leaned over the table and pointed. "Look at the first column—those are dates."

"Figured as much. The initials are his customers—any of them familiar or is that too much to hope for?"

"Let me see."

Instead of turning the book over to her, he stood and moved his chair closer to hers. "I won't bite."

Her breath caught in her throat. She swallowed and made a vain attempt to lighten the mood. "I'm not afraid. You haven't bitten me yet."

He leaned in. The clean smell of soap mingled with his aftershave. His scent sent her mind reeling to the first time they'd made love. No, had sex. It was just sex with him. "Neglect on my part. Sometime, maybe I can do something about it." He stroked her cheek with his forefinger.

Chill bumps rippled across her arms and heat pooled in her lower belly and between her thighs.

She cleared her throat. "Stop it."

He dropped his hand. His expression remained solemn. "Forgive me. Sometimes I can't help myself when I'm around you." He frowned. "You'd like this to be strictly business?"

"No other way."

"Yes... I remember." His gaze was level and serious as if he regretted the pain her discovery caused.

She tore her gaze from his and bit her lip. No point in continuing something that would only leave her distraught and alone when his assignment was over. "My attitude hasn't changed."

And it won't change in the future either.

"That's a pity. Still don't trust me?"

"That's not it. Right now, I don't have a choice. I have to trust you."

"That's something."

"This is business." She shrugged just to show little he affected her.

"Okay, Sheriff Devane." He jabbed a finger at a column of initials. "Suppose you tell me if you recognize any of these."

"No one comes to mind."

"Next column. Looks like income and outgo. Totals at the bottom of each page. Making a profit. Nothing to write home about, but it added up over the years." He riffled the pages. "Oldest date is only sixteen months old. You're sure this is the only one you found?"

"Yes. Why would I hold out on you now?"

"All right, Sheriff. Calm down. I had to ask. But the drug problems have been going on a lot longer than sixteen months."

She pushed away from the table. "Just how long was my father under investigation by the DEA?"

"I've been in town since late July after your father was killed the end of June...but he'd been on the DEA's radar for about eighteen months. Over that period, drug finds and arrests dropped fifty percent—enough to set off warning bells at the agency."

"Why take so long moving someone in place?"

"They would've sent me in sooner, but—uh, my last assignment went haywire at the last minute. I spent a little time in the hospital and a lot more in rehab."

"Must've been bad. I've seen the scars...remember?"

The corner of his mouth kicked up again. "I'm trying not to...since you prefer our *business* to be all business."

He glanced away for a second before returning her gaze. "You're right. I learned my lesson the hard way."

"Is there any other?"

He shook his head. "I screwed up my last assignment because I got too close to one of my contacts."

"And yet..."

"Here I am—back to my old tricks—getting close to the person I'm supposed to be investigating."

"Investigating? Is that what you call it? All in the name of duty. Anything for the DEA? Sleep with suspects—all in a day's work?" The brittle edge that found its way into her tone shocked even her.

"Whoa!"

"That's what you were up to with me. Admit it."

"I don't deny I needed to get close to you for the investigation, but—"

"Well, you certainly succeeded at that."

"You don't understand. Undercover work—it goes on for months at a time—the lines blur. You can forget who you really are."

"How convenient." The son-of-a-bitch. She was just an assignment. That was all. An easy lay…an easy way to get close to a suspect. How could she have been so stupid and gullible? Why hadn't she listened to her gut?

"Hardly. Trust the wrong person and you end up with a couple of bullets in some inconvenient places…or you end up dead, and that's *really* inconvenient."

"Whatever, I think it's disgusting."

"I take it you didn't do much undercover work in Nashville."

"A little vice—"

"That's nothing. I mean deep undercover,"

"Nothing? I'll have you know having men grab your ass because they think you're a hooker—"

He laughed. "No, I'm afraid I've missed out on that one."

She jabbed her forefinger on the table. "Back to the notebook."

"Yes, ma'am," he said and reached for it.

She covered the notebook with her hand, ready to snatch it away. "I want to figure this out myself."

Just as quickly, he covered her hand with his. "I have to turn it over to the DEA. Their decryption geeks will scan it and have it decoded in no time."

"You can't do that! This is *my* evidence."

"Yes. I can and I am." His tone was firm and left no room for compromise. "This case is under my jurisdiction—not yours. You have a definite conflict of interest—not to mention the personal aspects which I regret more than I can say."

"Go ahead then. Take it. You feds—you're all the same."

"We don't have to be at odds over this. We both want the same thing."

In spite of herself, her anger weakened. He was right again—unforgivable trait in a man. "I know."

"Besides, it's a valuable piece of our puzzle. And if it contains a link to our dealer, it's priceless."

She shook her head and scowled. "I don't think we'll find our dealer in there. I think he had my father killed in order to take over the drug trade."

"Your father had, granted, a small operation compared to some. That's why it took as long as it did for him to hit the radar with the DEA. It was confined to the county."

"And now?"

"The party drugs are showing up in surrounding counties, but the epicenter is Clinton County."

"So who in this county has mob connections?"

"Excellent question. Because that's exactly what it takes to deal on the level this guy is."

"What makes you so sure it's a man? Doesn't fit the usual profile? That's pretty sexist."

"I've formed my own profile. Thirties to forties, respectable, last person in the world you'd suspect. Maybe friendly with the police. Has contacts with the authorities." He gazed at her steadily. "And may have accomplices within the law enforcement community."

"I don't want to believe any of my deputies were in on it. I've known most of them all my life." She shook her head. "It happens. I know."

She took a sip of coffee and swallowed the bitter brew. "If anyone knew what my father was up to, it's my chief deputy, R.J." She shook her head, hating what she suspected of a man she considered a friend. "But I'll never understand why the DEA suspected *me* of taking over my father's extracurricular activities. I had a clean jacket with Metro."

Mac looked down at the table, as if wondering how much he could tell her. "There were some—uh, questionable money transfers from your second bank account. Large amounts in and out quickly—done by computer transfer."

"My *second* account? I don't have a second account."

"Sure you do. It was set up in May with your name and social security number at the Union Farmers Bank in Franklin, Tennessee. Do you *ever* look at your bank statements? Balance your check book?"

"You're not listening! I don't *have* two bank accounts. I have one account—the one I opened in Nashville six years ago.

"You have your statements for the last year?"

"Of course, but there aren't any for the Union Farmers Bank. What's the mailing address on that account?" She stood. "I'll go get them."

When she returned, she placed the statements in front of him. "See, they're all from Third National."

"Take a look at your May statement."

"The month Daddy was murdered?" She reached for the May statement. "See there's nothing unusual. Someone must've set up a dummy with my information." She shrugged. "I'm not sure I would've noticed if it *had* been on that statement. I was pretty messed up over Daddy's death."

"That's my theory," Mac said.

"From now on, I trust no one."

"No one?"

"I don't have much choice. You're the only one who doesn't believe I'm bent."

"So from now on, everyone in your office is under suspicion?"

She agreed with a quick nod. "I hate it, but everyone."

He leaned forward and grinned. "I'm glad we have that settled."

"Yes, now you can leave." Her no-monkey-business tone should do the trick. It certainly worked with any number of her deputies.

Instead of taking her not-so-subtle hint, her unwelcome partner leaned back in his chair and laced his fingers behind his head. "What are we going to do about R.J.? We need a plan."

Finally accepting the fact her father was dirty made the rest of her staff suspect. "Not R.J. I've known *him* all my life."

"You knew your father all your life, too."

"Don't remind me. It's a lot to take in all at once. I'm not making excuses. I need time to think...and I can't think with you around."

"Two heads—remember?"

A groan of frustration ripped from her. "Not likely to forget with you around to remind me, am I?"

Rather than commit homicide, she jumped up and poured herself another cup of coffee. Mac shoved his cup across the table. "Please?"

"You're leaving."

"Not if I can help it."

"All right. I have a plan." Maybe it was just a bare nugget of a plan, and he was sure to hate it almost as much as she did.

The cheeky bastard took the coffee pot from her hand and poured his own cup.

"Let's hear it."

“First, I’ll talk to R.J. Tell him I have suspicions someone in the department is involved in the drug trade.”

“Oh, great. Warn him. Yeah, that’s a plan all right. Bound to fail, too.”

“No. Since *you’re* so convinced he’s dirty, we’ll keep an eye on him and see if he makes a mistake and leads us to his contacts...if he’s actually on the take. I don’t want to believe he is.”

“Right. He’s just going to go off and lead us right to the dealer.” He gave her a smug—bordering on smartass—grin. “Now why didn’t I think of that?”

“Sometimes, the simplest plan is the best. He’ll know the pressure is on. If he’s guilty, he’ll screw up sooner or later. It’s not that difficult to understand.”

“Okay, try it your way. But in the meantime, the teenagers in this town you’re so devoted to are still at risk.”

“Dammit, I know. That’s the only reason I’m willing to set up the man who taught me how to shoot a gun. We’ll see who’s right.”

Chapter Twelve

Now or never.

Rilla had called R.J. to come in for a sit-down, come-to-Jesus meeting. Could she pull it off without letting him know he was under suspicion along with the rest of her staff?

All too soon, R.J. stuck his head into her office. "You wanted to see me, boss?"

"Yeah, come on in and shut the door. I want to keep this on the Q.T. You're the only one I trust around here, R.J."

She watched her chief deputy closely as he sniffed and glanced down and adjusted his weapon. "What's up?"

She shook her head and sighed. He was having trouble meeting her gaze. *God, R.J., why?*

"I think someone in the department is dirty."

"Dirty? This ain't no big city police department, Rilla. What on earth gives you a wild idea like that?"

"Let's face facts. Someone is tipping off our raids on the raves. We've yet to find one in progress. Has to be someone in the know."

"Aw, hell. Those raves ain't no big deal. Just kids having a good time."

"Hold on. I'm not through. Don't forget that's where Barbie got her lethal dose of X. Whoever's responsible for the X is also promoting the raves. Someone's tipping off our drug dealer, and only someone in this office would have that information."

R.J. gave a casual nod. “Well, who do you suspect?”

“Don’t know yet. That’s why I want you to keep a sharp lookout on the younger guys. They’re more likely to have connections with the users.”

“I don’t like spying on my men, but—” R.J. stopped and swallowed hard, his Adam’s apple bobbing above the neck of his uniform. “If it’s gotta be done, then it’s gotta be done.”

“I don’t like it either, but like I said, you’re the only one I trust with this.”

“Consider it done. I’ll keep a close eye on all of ’em.”

“Thanks.” She shook her head again. “I don’t know what Daddy would have made of all these new drugs flooding the county. I hope I’m not letting him down.”

R.J.’s face flushed and his eyes grew suspiciously bright. He swiped his nose with the back of his hand. “You’re doing him proud. Don’t think you’re not.”

“Doesn’t feel that way, but thanks. It means a lot to me that you think so.”

She watched him leave. His hang-dog body language was only natural. He didn’t want to think someone in the sheriff’s office was dirty, either. R.J. was as loyal to her father’s memory as she was.

As soon as he could, R.J. made the phone call—not one he wanted to make, but one which had to be made. “She’s suspicious of someone in the office. She’s assigned me to find out who’s dirty. I told you she was smart. If you ask me, we got to cool it for a while. Lay low, until she has something else to keep her occupied.”

“I didn’t ask you. And don’t worry about the sheriff. She’s history.”

"What've you done?" R.J.'s stomach twisted. "No, you can't. It ain't right. She doesn't suspect you or me either, for that matter."

"She's in my way, and so is her nosy new boyfriend. I don't like him. There's more to him than some mystery writer soaking up local color."

"Now see here. I've known her since she was a kid."

"You knew her father, too."

"Didn't know you were gonna have him killed 'til it was too late."

"Doesn't matter. The contract's already signed, so to speak."

R.J. slammed down the phone. Stomach lurching, he stumbled from his office to his car.

Don't use the radio. The rat bastard has a police scanner. Cell phone.

"Damn little buttons," he swore, punching the buttons as the panic mounted. He started the motor, then backed out with a squeal of tires. "Answer, damn it. Answer."

"Devane."

"Sheriff, what's your twenty?"

"Sneed Road, heading—"

"You gotta turn around. Come back to the office. We gotta talk."

"What is it? I'm almost there—"

"Listen to me, Rilla. Come back."

"Is the office on fire?"

"No, but—"

"There's an accident up ahead. I'm pulling over."

"No!" But she'd already hung up. He hit redial, but this time she didn't answer. "Dammit!"

He stomped his foot on the gas pedal and floored it. He had to reach her in time. One death on his conscience was one too many.

Rilla stopped the Jeep, turned off the motor, but left on the blue and white lights while she radioed in. “Devane here. Five miles out on Sneed Road. Vehicle crossway in the road, driver slumped over the wheel. Dispatch, who called this in? I don’t see anybody but the driver.”

“Woman called it in, Sheriff. Need an ambulance?”

“Yeah, better send one. I don’t know what kind of shape this fellow’s in.”

A woman called it in? Where was she? All Rilla saw was a man with salt and pepper hair who lay slumped over the wheel. No sign or damage to the car or blood on the victim. Heart attack? As she surveyed the SUV in the shady lane, the hair rose on the back of her neck and set off alarm bells. Call for backup? R.J. was on his way, even if he did have a wild hair up his ass about something.

She eased from the Jeep, unbuttoned the snap on her holster, pulled out her weapon and chambered a round, then held it down to her side as she approached the vehicle...just in case there was something hinky going on.

“Sir? Are you all right?” She reached through the open window and gently touched his shoulder.

The man bolted upright and pointed a gun in her face. She took a step backward to give herself room.

“Not so far. I wouldn’t want to miss.” He laughed, but it was an ugly sound.

He had an accent—Scottish or Irish maybe, hard to tell.

“Whoa, fella. Ease off. I thought you were injured.”

He gave a grimace which quirked half his mouth. His pale gray eyes twinkled as if he’d pulled a great joke on someone.

"I'm fine, Sheriff Devane. How kind of ye to be askin'."

She backed another step and kept her weapon just out of his line of vision. He didn't lower his. "You have me at a disadvantage. Have we met?"

"No, that we haven't."

She eased back another step. Somehow, she had to distract him.

"I said that'll be far enough." Never taking his gun off her, he opened the car door and carefully emerged.

"I don't know what you're up to, but my deputy is only a minute or so behind me."

"Is that so? Why don't we just wait a bit and see if ye're bluffin'. Makes it excitin', doesn't it? The risk of discovery and all."

"And there's an ambulance on the way as well."

"Thoughtful, aren't ye, dear girl. I always like a thoughtful colleen, and a pretty one too. 'Tis a shame, but I can't say I'm sorry."

The twenty-two was pointed right at her and never wavered. Too well she knew the damage the small caliber bullet could do inside her skull. Making no exit wound, it would boomerang around and make Swiss cheese of her brain. She swallowed hard.

Where the hell are you, R.J.?

"Throat dry, darlin'?"

Rilla took another step back. "Something like that. Are you the son of a bitch who killed my father?" One second's distraction was all she needed.

"No...and yes."

She arched an eyebrow. Somehow she had to turn the situation to her advantage. *Keep him talking.* He liked to talk. If he would do something besides stare her down.

"Ye might say I'm just the weapon."

"And now?"

"And now, I've been hired again, this time to take care of an inquisitive young sheriff."

"Why didn't you just take me out like you did my father? Wouldn't it be a lot quicker and cleaner?"

"True, but I'm versatile. 'Tis so boring shooting from a distance all the time."

He smiled, but it didn't soften his intention. "Now then, I promise I won't make a mess of yer pretty face, just a nice neat hole in yer forehead. The undertaker won't have a problem with it. I'm sure your father was a different matter."

"Think it'll be easier to shoot me face-to-face since I'm just a woman?" She glanced over her shoulder. Where was R.J.?

"Aw, isn't he comin'? What a shame. I know what must be goin' through that pretty head of yers. 'I'm too young. Oh, why doesn't someone come and save me?'"

"I'm perfectly capable of saving myself." If she could just distract him long enough to bring her weapon into play.

"In most situations, I'm sure ye are, but I'm a professional. No one's coming to save ye, girl. And take a good look around—all ye want. This is the end of the road. Picturesque, 'tisn't it?"

"Haven't paid much attention to the scenery."

No doubt he would shoot her, but he seemed to enjoy baiting her. Her fingers tingled with the urge to bring up her weapon. *Not yet.*

In the distance, a crow circled and cawed.

The hit man's gaze flickered upward.

Now.

She brought up her weapon, dropped and rolled. Aiming for his head, she fired.

The shot went wide and nicked his ear. Damn.

He fired and gravel struck her neck. She rolled again, fired...and missed again.

"Enough! Nice moves. Ye almost made it, darlin'. Good moves. Have to give ye credit." He saluted her but the barrel of the twenty-two was still aimed at her head.

A brackish taste flooded her mouth—she'd bitten her tongue. She swallowed.

So this was how it would end. Rolling in the dirt with a bloodied lip. She'd be pissing her pants next.

She kept her gaze riveted to his trigger finger.

Then, the distinct sound of someone stepping on crushed stone at the edge of the road.

The hit man must've heard it, too. He spun on his heel and fired.

"Ugh!"

Someone hit—R.J.?

Without waiting, she sprang to her feet and fired at the hit man. He staggered a step, then whirled back to face her. She fired again. Down.

She ran over and kicked the gun out of the hit man's reach.

A groan. "Rilla."

Rounding the rear of the SUV, she found R.J. lying in the road.

Dear God. She knelt down beside R.J. A hole in his chest—the blood gushed and bubbled. Lung shot. "Dammit, R.J., why weren't you wearing your vest?"

"Too hot." He strained to sit, but talking took its toll as his chest heaved for breath.

Applying pressure to the wound with the heel of her hand, she glanced over her shoulder and noted the killer had moved. "It's gonna be all right. There's an ambulance already on the way. Just hold on."

In the distance came the wail of a siren.

The motor of the hit man's car revved, the wheels spinning and spraying loose gravel.

She jumped out of the way, but couldn't pull R.J.'s near-dead weight fast enough with her. She rolled into the ditch, firing at the driver. The vehicle bounced over R.J. and sped east down Sneed.

"God! No!" She scrambled from the ditch to R.J.'s side, then knelt on the road beside him. Frothy, red bubbles ran down the side of his mouth.

Losing too much blood. He wasn't going to make it. "Hold on, buddy. Hold on." She cradled him in her arms. "Hold on," she prayed. Hopeless.

"Cher," he managed. "Tell her...be good. I love her. My fault—" He coughed, struggling for breath. "Got greedy. Didn't know...'bout your Dad...sorry—" He coughed again, this time producing a large, dark red clot, followed by a gush of blood, and died.

No. All her fault.

Tears coursed down her cheeks. "Dammit! Why didn't you wear your vest?"

She cradled R.J.'s body until the EMTs rushed over. "He's gone. Gunshot wound to the chest, no vest. Perp ran over him with his car."

"Damn! Guy meant business, didn't he?"

"He saved my life. I was in the direct line of fire. R.J. distracted him and gave me a chance to fire. I hit the perp twice. He went down. Next thing I knew, he was jumping in his car. Bastard backed right over R.J."

The EMT scratched his head. "Perp must've been wearing a vest."

She stood and dusted off her pants. R.J.'s lifeblood was all over her shirt. Even with his confession, she still didn't want to believe he'd had anything to do with her father's death. How could he?

Money. Why was it always about money?

"I'll call the coroner... As soon as he finishes, I—I have to go tell his daughter."

She'd been where Cher was. And understood too well how devastating the news would be.

After the coroner had come and gone and Det. Bellows had collected what little evidence there was to collect, Rilla headed home to shower and change. Bad enough she had to tell R.J.'s daughter her father was dead, but she sure as hell couldn't do it covered in his blood. Would the stains ever go away—the stains his death had left on her soul and mind?

As soon as she'd changed into a fresh uniform, Rilla drove over to the high school. After conferring with the principal and guidance counselor, she watched Cher walk into the guidance counselor's office. God, but she dreaded this.

"What now?" The color leached from the girl's face. "What's wrong?"

"It's bad, hon."

"Daddy? He's been hurt in an accident?" she asked, hope apparent in her tremulous question.

"He's gone." Rilla put her arm around the teenager.

"How?"

As simply as possible, she gave Cher the details. "Who do you want me to call? You can't stay by yourself."

Tears filled the girl's green eyes. "My Aunt Betty in Franklin. She's mama's sister. We're still close. I spend a week every summer with her, more when I was a kid."

"I'll call her for you, and I'll stay with you until she comes. Is there anyone else?"

"I-I don't know. I wish my mama—somebody could call her. I know they're divorced, but—"

"You know how to reach her?"

"Yeah, she's in Nashville. She's on about her tenth boyfriend, but I want...my mama," Cher wailed, then broke into shaking sobs.

"Of course, you do, darlin'." Rilla turned to the guidance counselor. "Thank you."

"You're welcome, Sheriff. Now, Cher, you stay here with me until someone comes for you."

Numbly the girl nodded. "Yes, ma'am."

Rilla bit back her own tears. There'd be time enough to cry for her old friend, but now she had a killer to find.

And she'd never forget his cold, heartless gaze.

Never.

"Damn, Rilla." TBI agent Jason Locke, accompanied by another agent, stood in her office doorway.

"Hello, to you, too."

"Think you can describe this guy well enough for an identi-kit picture?" He nodded at the other agent.

"Hell, yeah. I'll never forget his face."

"You didn't see his gun?"

"Of course I saw the damn gun, but he was very fond of the sound of his own voice, and he got a kick out of toying with me."

She leaned over the artist's shoulder and watched while he sketched. "Arrogant and convinced of his charm. Mid-fortes, salt and pepper hair—cut short. Piercing gray eyes—dead, no life. Regular features, nothing outstanding. Complexion tan, but a weathered, ruddy tan—as if his underlying complexion is fair."

The artist nodded and kept sketching.

"No, his eyes were a shade closer together.

Short quick strokes of the artist's pencil quickly brought the hit man to life.

"Yes that's better."

The artist paused. "His eyebrows?"

"Still dark, nice arch."

The artist sketched in the brows.

So raised, they were almost Joker-like. "No, not that arched."

The artist made a quick adjustment.

"Yes, that's more like it."

"What about his mouth?"

"Lips were thin, but well-shaped. Nose, straight, narrow bridge, from the side aquiline."

"Observant, aren't you?" the artist commented with a grin and kept sketching.

"He killed my father and bragged about it. I'm not likely to forget the son-of-a-bitch."

Once he'd finished, the artist held up the completed drawing. "How's this?"

"It'll do," she said.

Jase took the photo mockup. "I'll fax this to the FBI and the DEA, but...there's something familiar about him."

Later the same evening, Rilla drummed her fingers on the desk. How long could it take to hear back from the FBI? As if reading her mind, the fax machine rang and immediately started churning out, with any luck, what she'd been waiting for all evening.

She jumped up, ready to snatch the fax as soon as it completed printing. "Kit, come in here."

"Yeah, boss?"

"We've got an I.D. on R.J.'s killer." Rilla read the details. "He's Liam O'Shaunessey, aka Ryan Malone, aka Sean Finney, ex-IRA enforcer, and now—ta-dah—freelance assassin extraordinaire. Quite a resume."

"You're lucky he didn't kill you."

"He would've, except for R.J."

"But he was mixed up in it, wasn't he?"

Rilla gritted her teeth before answering. "He was in on the drug deals. I don't think he knew I was a target, or my father, for that matter. He gave his life and saved mine."

"I can't imagine how difficult this has been for you. It must bring everything back." Kit kneaded Rilla's shoulders. "You're tense."

"That's an understatement." Rilla massaged her temples, wishing the nagging headache would go way. Gathering focus, she slapped the fax down on the desk. "I want copies of his face plastered all over town. If he's still around, I want every pair of eyes in town to know what he looks like and to stay away from him."

"Good as done, boss."

As for her helpful, newly-hired detective, she wasn't above suspicion either.

Rilla leaned back and yawned. Maybe she should call it a night, but Mac chose that moment to ease his way into her office and shut the door behind him.

"Are you all right? I heard about R.J. on the news. What really happened? " His expression was grim and concerned.

"I'm all right...I guess." She let out a sigh, then gave him a quick blow-by-blow of the day's events, concluding her tale with R.J.'s semi-confession.

"I know you wanted to believe in R.J., but you had to know how likely it was he was involved." He pulled up a chair, back to front, and straddled it, his expression turning too energetic for her liking. "I have an idea."

"Is this a new experience or do you have them often?"

"Let's do some brainstorming."

She let out a groan. “Not a good time. All I want to do is go home and cry myself to sleep. Not that it’ll actually help anyone.”

Completely ignoring her mood, he continued. “Okay, who killed your father? Someone who wanted to take over the drug trade or someone he put in jail in his thirty year career in law enforcement?”

“That’s a lot of people, Mac.”

“Someone who wanted to increase the availability of drugs? Your father was involved in marijuana, but nothing hard. Plenty of folks grow weed as a cash crop. Your father had the lowest discovery of marijuana fields in the state. That’s one of the reasons I was sent to investigate him.”

“Seems like a lot of trouble for the DEA to investigate a low priority dealer.”

“It was a low priority case, but I was coming off a period of rehab so they assigned me. Maybe the powers that be figured I couldn’t get into trouble on this one. But then your father was killed and the party drugs started up, followed by those big dollar money transfers in your account...your *second* account.”

“Murdered—not just killed. Someone hired a hit man and had a bullet put through his skull right in our driveway.”

“Who else might have a reason to kill your father?”

“Someone who wanted a larger share?”

“Who would your father have trusted? What about R.J.?”

“Remember R.J. died trying to save my life. I’ll never believe he ordered the hit on my father. Be careful. Don’t try to sully his memory in this town.” Everyone would know soon enough. Why couldn’t Mac just leave well enough alone?

“That doesn’t mean he didn’t overlook a marijuana crop now and then. Tell me about R.J.’s call when you were on the way to Sneed Road.”

"He radioed, told me I had to come back to the office right away."

"Did he say why?"

"No—wait a minute—he didn't radio me, he called on my cell phone."

"He did?"

"I'd come upon the scene. I told him there was an accident and I was stopping. I hung up and didn't answer when he called back. Instead I exited my vehicle and went over to check the man slumped over the steering wheel. You know the rest. It was a setup, and R.J. was trying to warn me off."

"Who called it in?"

"Dispatch said it was a female voice, but when I got there, no woman."

"Definitely a setup, and he has a partner. Okay, so someone unknown wants to bring in big city drugs to sleepy little Cherokee Springs, Tennessee. If our new drug dealer wants to succeed, it couldn't hurt to have the sheriff's cooperation...or if there's resistance, then the sheriff's expendable."

"Daddy must've resisted—but who?"

"Anyone new in town?"

"Just you—"

"Wrong again, Sheriff."

"I know, but you were perfect. Plenty of money, high roller for a small town."

"You wound me, but that's more or less what I wanted *you* to think. Because you were my prime suspect."

She shuddered. "Don't remind me. We must be overlooking someone. Wait a minute. Is that why you chatted up Katie Bass and her husband?"

"They run a business. Any business can be used to launder the money they make off the drugs."

"If you think Katie Bass has anything more serious on her mind than her next manicure appointment or whether or not carpet or hardwood floors are in style, you're nuts."

"I agree it might be stretching it a bit to consider Katie, but good old Lloyd is another matter."

Mac leveled his gaze on her and tried another tack. "Now, about R.J.—"

"I don't want to talk about him—not now."

"Hear me out. Your father trusted him—right?"

"They grew up together, school, played football—the whole nine yards."

"We can assume he trusted R.J. Just suppose our new drug-dealer-wannabe figures the same thing? He approaches R.J. and promises him more money than he made working with your father. Would R.J. have been tempted?"

"Obviously. He said something about being greedy, but I just can't believe he would have anything to do with killing Daddy."

"It's entirely possible R.J. didn't know the particulars of the plan until afterward. I'd say his guilt got the better of him—that's why he tried to warn you away from today's setup."

"All right. It's more than plausible. Plus, his daughter was one of the kids involved in the last O.D. I know for a fact it shook him up."

"Do you still have the contents of his desk—personal effects?"

"Yeah. Cher's supposed to come by and pick them up tomorrow. Now's the time to go through them. We might find a trace of his boss."

Rilla walked into her late deputy's office and opened his desk with the master key. "Surely he wouldn't be stupid enough to leave incriminating evidence in his desk. I hate it. I still feel like I'm betraying his memory."

“Don’t be such a girl. Leave your emotions out of it. This is an investigation and you’re doing your job—remember being a detective?”

“Jerk.” She glared at Mac, then shrugged. “But you’re right—don’t think for a minute I’m not fed up...with everything.”

She rolled her shoulders.

“Tired?” he asked.

Tired? Hell, yeah, she was. “A little.”

“After we finish this, why don’t you come home with me? We can get in the hot tub and soak all those sore muscles.”

Not on your life. I’m not making the same mistake twice.

“Um, tempting as your offer is, I have this hairy animal who needs food, and he’s waiting.”

“Okay, let’s get busy and check R.J.’s desk. Then you can get home to your companion.” He shook his head. “I can’t believe you’re dumping me for your dog.”

She laughed. The first time that day. “Believe it.”

Chapter Thirteen

With Mac hovering behind her, Rilla unlocked and opened the drawers of R.J.'s desk. Without warning, the finality of his death sucked her breath away like water down a drain. "I can do this. I have to."

Inside the middle drawer, pens, paper and paperclips were arranged with meticulous precision. R.J. had always been by-the-book in everything he did, whether it was paperwork or an arrest. His attention to detail had been admirable. How could he have had anything to do with drugs or anyone who did...unless it was her father?

Mac leaned over her shoulder. "What about an address book?"

"Don't rush me," she said, carefully removing the articles and setting them on the desktop. It was a matter of respect for R.J. and the way he'd lived most of his life.

She reached to the back of the drawer. "Here." She pulled out a small black leather notebook. Opening it, she flipped through the pages. "Looks like an ordinary address book to me."

"Could be in code. Cross-check each name and number. If there's anything off, I'll investigate further."

"Oh, *you'll* investigate? *We'll* investigate, bozo. You're not taking over my investigation"

Mac straightened. "*Your* investigation? And exactly how much progress have you made since you've been sheriff? This is an official DEA operation, and I can shut you down anytime I want."

"No way!"

"Yes, I can. You can either work with me or not. I have to knock this ring out before it gets any bigger."

"And there's finding my father's killer."

"His murder isn't under your jurisdiction, either. It belongs to the TBI, and you know it."

"All right." She gave an indignant huff. "I'm a detective. I can't stifle the impulse to solve a case which is so personal."

"You're wasted here. You need to go back to Nashville or..."

"Or what?"

"You could join the DEA."

Leave the Springs, let the people of the county down and just run off to pursue her career somewhere else? Slowly she shook her head. "No, I'm not a quitter. I can't abandon the town to the drug dealers. I owe it to the people who elected my father in good faith. I have to see this through."

"And you will. I mean *after* we clear this investigation. My gut says your father's murder and this drug investigation go hand in hand."

"My gut agrees with yours," she admitted quietly, while her mind spun with the possibilities he'd raised.

Would she be able to see Mac after this operation? Of course not. He didn't mean anything by it.

"Join the DEA?" she ventured with caution. "Are you serious?" Why did the idea of working with him seem so damned attractive?

"Or the FBI." He gave a casual shrug. "Or open your own P.I. agency. You can do any one of a million things."

"Mmm." Well, he certainly answered her real question. He could care less if he saw her once his case was cleared.

Dammit. She'd grown accustomed to his face...and his body.

"Well," she said, shrugging, "we haven't cleared either case yet, so I have some time to think about it."

"Not much time. We're closer than you think."

"Another gut feeling?"

"Yep."

Unwilling to give Mac the satisfaction of seeing her spike of curiosity, she resumed rummaging through the contents of R.J.'s desk. In the bottom drawer, she found the photograph of a woman in her late twenties with a tiny girl by her side.

"Who's that?" he asked.

"R.J.'s ex. Cher's mother ran off with some guy right after this was taken. R.J. raised Cher all by himself."

"That's another thing he and your dad had in common. Look, I know you don't want to find anything bad on R.J. But he wouldn't be the first law officer to take a bribe or look the other way when something illegal was going down."

She slammed the drawer shut. "You've made your point, dammit. I know R.J.'s guilty. He as much as admitted it before he died."

"Sorry." He grimaced, as if he regretted reminding her. "Find anything like a bank book?"

She shook her head. "No bank book."

"No problem. We can go to the bank and pull his account information."

"You'll need a warrant, and right now, I don't think you have enough evidence to support the need for one."

"I hate it when you're right."

She flipped through the last file drawer. "Here, you take these. I'll go through the other half. Maybe we'll find something."

"Don't forget the address book."

"We'll do that last."

Thirty minutes later, Mac tossed his stack of files on the desk. "Nothing in these. How 'bout you?"

"Nothing yet." She opened the last folder. "Wait a minute. Here's R.J.'s will. I guess we should turn it over to his attorney." She scanned down to the bottom of the page. "I don't recognize the name. Dylan Hiland? He's not local. Maybe he went to Franklin or Nashville... Wonder why?"

"Maybe he had something to hide."

The clatter of spiked heels against the tile floor warned her of a woman's approach. Rilla looked over her shoulder and saw Cher in the doorway. "What're you doing, pawing through my daddy's desk?"

Rilla held out the photographs to R.J.'s daughter. "I was cleaning out his personal effects. I thought you'd want these."

"What about your boyfriend?" She shot a pointed glance at Mac. "What's he doing here? He's got nothing to do with any of this."

Mac held up his hands. "Sorry. I can leave."

Cher ignored Mac's offer, snatched the pictures and started arranging them by size. She hesitated over one and sniffed. "We used to be a family. And this job—it ran my mother off and now, it's taken my daddy's life." Her face flushed with anger. "I hate everything connected with it. And I hate *you* most of all, Rilla. If it hadn't been for you, Daddy would still be alive."

"I know. And I'm so sorry." And the knowledge left a bitter taste in Rilla's mouth.

Cher spun on her heel. "You don't know anything! I got what I came for. I hope I never see this place again." She darted from the office and fled down the hall, her heels sliding as she ran.

"She's going to break her neck in those." Rilla sighed. "At least she didn't try to brain me with one."

"Gives a whole new connotation to the term 'deadly weapons'."

"She's devastated, and she'll never forgive me."

Mac hugged her to his broad chest. "Listen here, kiddo. The kid's grieving and striking out. You were just handy."

Hopefully he was right. She sagged against him and wished—God, how she wished—she could stay in his arms forever. But that wasn't part of his game plan, and she'd better get used to the idea.

"Let's deal with this tomorrow. I'm going home."

"My offer still stands," he murmured. He brushed a strand of hair away from her forehead.

She looked into his eyes. The softness of his gaze warmed and comforted her soul like no man she'd ever known. But her body heat was only a biological response and had nothing to do with happily ever after.

"No. There's too much..." She shook her head and pushed herself away from him. "I can't do this now."

"You don't have to do anything. Let me take you home and put you to bed. I'll go home...if that's what you want."

"It is." Might as well get used to saying 'no'.

She watched him leave, her jaw clenched to keep from calling after him.

Chapter Fourteen

The next four days were absolute hell. The Springs was overrun by the media, mostly from Nashville, and R.J. was hailed a hero for having saved Rilla's life by TV and print reporters alike. Rightly so. But what would the media say when the truth about his drug connections was revealed, as it surely would be?

She'd granted the vultures only one press conference and fended off most of their questions by citing the typical bullshit answer of "on-going investigation".

At R.J.'s funeral, Rilla sat with her head bowed and wondered if the service would ever end.

"Amen," the preacher said...finally.

Amen is right. Rilla raised her head, stood and smoothed the skirt of her black suit while the pallbearers filed by with R.J.'s casket. She hesitated. Custom dictated she stop and pay her respects to Cher. Had the girl calmed down enough to accept her condolences?

The skinny redhead stood next to her mother and aunt. The teenager's eyes were reddened from crying, but it appeared she was holding herself together.

"Cher?" Rilla began tentatively, "I'm so sorry."

"Thank you for coming." Cher ducked her head. "I'm real sorry about what I said...the other day. Daddy loved you."

"I know, darlin'. I'll never forget what he did for me. He saved my life. Call me anytime, if you need anything. Anything at all."

"I will. Are you coming to the cemetery?"

"Of course." Rilla hugged Cher then moved on so those behind her could pay their respects.

She found Detective Bellows pacing on the sidewalk in front of the church. "Well, I suppose this is one funeral where the killer won't show up," the detective muttered under her breath.

"Don't suppose so, since I could I.D. the son of a bitch," Rilla replied, keeping her tone low. "Still, whoever hired him is probably here."

Bellows' gaze cut from left to right and back again. "Weird, isn't it—to know someone you've probably known all your life is at the bottom of the drug trafficking and hiring hit men? Just doesn't sound like a small town anymore, does it?"

Rilla shrugged. "In one degree or another, every town is changing. I thought I'd come back to Cherokee Springs, find Daddy's killer and move back to Nashville and take up where I left off."

"Hasn't been quite so simple, has it?"

"Nope."

"What's R.J.'s daughter going to do?"

"I'm pretty sure she'll go live with her mother or her aunt in Franklin."

"R.J. sure has a big turnout. Just about everybody in town is here. There's your hunky pharmacist talking to the Basses."

Rilla turned to glance at her friends. Was Katie actually flirting with Kurt? In the space of a few seconds, she'd tossed her hair twice and touched Kurt's upper arm once. No surprise. Flirting was second nature to Katie Bass—always had been. Why Lloyd put up with it was a mystery, pure and simple.

The last of the mourners trickled by them. "You're leading the procession," Kit reminded Rilla. "I guess we'd better get in line."

Rilla walked toward her Jeep. The hair on the back of her neck rose and an eerie chill shot through her. She turned and cast her gaze on the crowd where most of the funeral goers were heading to their cars.

The younger Wyler boy walked along, shuffling his feet in the gravel drive with his head hung in a dispirited fashion. Why not? R.J. had been his girlfriend's father.

"Danny, you all right?" she called after him.

"Yeah," he muttered and slowed his pace, but his eyes darted from left to right and he never met her gaze.

"Going to the house afterward?"

"Nah, my mom's takin' some food over but..." Danny shrugged.

"Sitting around with a bunch of old folks not exactly your thing, is it?"

"Nah." He stuffed his hands in his pants pockets. "'Sides, Cher'll probably be crying and carrying on. Can't hack that." His gaze continued to dart, but he didn't seem ready to move along, either.

"I have the feeling you want to tell me something."

Danny stopped dead. His eyes widened and met hers for a second. "Who, me? Got nothing to say. You're nuts."

Right.

Better try again. "Well, if you ever do...you know where I am."

"Yeah, sure. Look, I gotta catch my brother or he'll leave me for sure." He took off in a run like a scalded dog...a scalded, *guilty* dog.

Dammit. The kid knew something and he wanted to tell her. But what? Was it his brother? Or was it something more?

At the cemetery, Rilla kept a look-out. No way would the contract killer risk his neck by attending the graveside service, but she'd bet money he was still in the area. The leaden queasiness in her gut was all the evidence she needed. He was a pro. He'd stick around until he fulfilled his contract.

Later, when she pulled up in front of R.J.'s house, an ambulance and two squad cars with blue lights blinking were parked in the driveway. "What the hell?"

Her stomach churned. She jumped out of the Jeep. "What happened?"

Detective Bellows stepped down from the front porch. "Someone broke in during the funeral. Miss Tweedy from the grocery store was keeping watch on the house. He knocked her in the head and tore up the place, looking for something."

"Is she...?" The word "dead" refused to pass Rilla's lips. Not Miss Tweedy.

Kit grinned and shook her head. "Not dead. She's conscious and mad as hell."

"I'll bet." Rilla let out a sigh. "What did he take?"

Kit shrugged. "Who knows? R.J.'s daughter is going through the mess now. He damned near ripped the place apart. Money or guns—you name it."

"Make way, please."

Rilla looked up. The EMTs were wheeling out Miss Tweedy on a stretcher. Oxygen and I.V. fluids, along with a bandage on the old woman's head, told the story.

"Dang it," the elderly woman fussed. "I need to clear up the mess that no-good rat left. People are expecting to be fed after the burying."

Rilla hid her smile. Miss Tweedy would be fine, no doubt. She turned to the deputy lingering at the end of the porch. "Paulson, call her niece in Nashville. Name's Jody Caton. If she's not at home—she's a nurse at either Centennial or Baptist—try both of them."

"Okay, boss."

Rilla strode into the house with Kit. "You weren't exaggerating." Floor boards had been ripped up and drawer contents dumped all over the floor. He'd pulled everything from the freezer, looking for drugs or money. Maybe he'd found it, too. More than likely, she'd never know for sure.

Two days after R.J.'s funeral and the break-in, Miss Tweedy was recovering nicely at home with Rilla's mother, Liz, to fetch and carry. After going through the house, R.J.'s daughter reported the only thing missing was the shotgun R.J. had used for hunting.

The town had been quiet since then. The reporters had decamped almost as soon as R.J. was buried. The office had been quiet, too. She appreciated the lull since the time for the new budget loomed. And it sure wouldn't do itself.

Rilla sat in her office and stared at her computer monitor, wishing the budget figures would miraculously conform to something close to the amount she actually needed to run the department.

Deputy Paulson rapped on the door. "Danny Wyler to see you, boss."

"Um, send him in." She'd almost given up on Danny. Now here he was.

Hands in his pockets, the younger Wyler boy wandered in, casting quick glances over his shoulder.

She stood and nodded. "Danny?"

"Sheriff, I—uh—" His face turned red and he studied the floor.

"Have a seat."

He sat down quickly on the edge of the chair as if he still might change his mind and head for the hills.

She waited. He'd come to her. He had something to say, and the longer she waited, the greater the likelihood he would finally blurt it out. No point in spooking him.

He scooted back in the chair a fraction of an inch. Good. He might actually stay...and tell her what she needed to know.

He cleared his throat. "R.J. was a drug dealer."

Rilla straightened, but her heart clutched in her chest. Another confirmation of what she already suspected. What else did Danny know? "Go on."

"Rob bought the X from R.J."

"So you couldn't give up your dealer while he was still alive?"

"That wouldn't be too smart—ya know?"

"I guess not. So who dealt to R.J.?"

"Don't know for sure, but he's local. Rob knows, but he won't tell me, much less you."

"Does he know you were coming here?"

Danny jumped up. "Hell, no. And you can't tell him."

"Settle down. Everything you tell me is in confidence." He sat down again, still on the edge of the chair.

She tried again. "You say he's local. Why?"

"Cause R.J. always had a ready supply. We all bought from him. Used to be just grass, but about three months ago, he started having a lot more stuff. 'Ludes, roofies and X. And he had a lot of 'em. He supplied lots of other places, too." Danny hung his head. "Rob was his main man at Tech. 'Fore he died, R.J. promised Rob he could have a bigger territory..." Danny's eyes bugged and his face turned white. "You can't tell him. Rob'll beat the hell outta me if he knows I ratted him out."

She shook her head. Being beat up was the least that could happen to Danny if the dealer knew the kid was spilling his guts. She stood and walked around the desk until she stood right in front of Danny. "Know anything about who broke into R.J.'s during the funeral?"

He shook his head. "Nah, don't know nothing 'bout the break-in, but might've been somebody looking for his stash." He gave her a half grin. "Wish I'd thought of it."

"You damn well better be glad you didn't," Rilla barked before she could stop. "You see where money and drugs got R.J.? Now get your sorry little ass out of here before I smack you silly. And if you ever think twice—"

"I was kidding, Sheriff. Honest."

She took in a deep breath, then let it out slowly. "All right. Don't let me ever see you in this office again for any reason."

"What if I could find out who R.J.'s source is?"

"No! You can forget that idea. You're not a narc. You're a kid. A minor. You stay away from this mess."

"But I feel bad—"

"Just think how bad you'll feel if you're dead." She snatched him by the front of his T-shirt. "Stay out of it. If I find you sniffing around where you oughtn't, I'll slam your ass in my pokey so fast, your head'll need a map to catch up. Understand?"

He nodded. "Yes, ma'am."

She let him go. "All right, now get out of here."

He straightened his back, turned around and managed a bit of a swagger as he left her office.

She sighed. Too bad he was a minor. But Rob Wyler wasn't. Maybe he could be tricked into leading her to the real dealer.

She picked up the phone to arrange a tail on Rob, but set it back down. What if R.J. wasn't the only dirty one in her office? Whom could she trust?

She picked up the phone again. "Kit, my office. Now."

Seconds later, Bellows stood in front of Rilla. "Yes, boss."

"How would you feel about an undercover mission?"

Kit's eyes widened. "Cool. I'd love it."

"I need someone to get close to Rob Wyler."

"He's just a kid."

"He's eighteen and he's our only lead to R.J.'s source. Sooner or later the source will approach Rob. Make sure he knows you want a piece of the action. If the dealer wants to continue as before, he'll need someone in my department."

Kit nodded. Her green eyes brightened. "Okay, get close to Rob and the drug dealer. Sounds like a plan to me."

"You're the only one I'm sure of in this office. The rest are my daddy's good ol' boys. Whoever the dealer is, he's dangerous. He's ordered two hits already. He won't balk at your pretty face."

"I understand. I won't blow it."

"I'd do this if I could, but—"

"He'd never buy it. No one would. Just leave it to me, boss."

"Thanks." She watched the detective leave. Had she just endangered the only person in the department she trusted, or could she even trust Kit?

A little reluctantly she unlocked the drawer which held the personnel files. Kit Bellows was her newest hire...her only hire. Her references were in perfect order. Kit had served with distinction in the Chicago Police Department for ten years before heading south.

All the more reason to keep a close watch on her.

An hour later, Rilla slid into the first booth at the diner. "Just a cup of coffee, Helen." She opened the morning newspaper.

"Oh, no." The headline couldn't have been worse. *Hero Deputy or Drug Dealer?*

She read further. “Confidential sources name deceased Chief Deputy R.J. Barnes as a drug dealer...”

Jumping up, she slammed the paper on the table. “Forget the coffee. I gotta go.”

Her exit was blocked by a red-faced Cher Barnes who was fairly vibrating with anger.

“How could you believe lies like this about my daddy?” She waved a newspaper in Rilla’s face. “He saved your stinking life. I wish he’d let that man kill you!”

“I don’t blame you for being upset, but I didn’t give that information to the paper.”

“So it’s true? You think my daddy was some kind of a drug dealer?”

Everyone in the diner turned and stared. “We can’t talk about this here. Come over to my office.”

“I’m not going anywhere with you, you ungrateful bitch. You’re a pathetic excuse for a sheriff. You can’t find your father’s killer. You can’t find my daddy’s killer. All you *can* do is spread dirt on the man who saved your useless life.”

“That’s enough. You need to settle down.” Rilla looked over at the waitress who stood wide-eyed with her lips pinched shut. “Call home and see if there’s someone who can come get her.”

“No.” Cher cried, with big tears rolling down her face. “I’ll never forgive you for trashing my father’s memory. Never.” She rushed Rilla, but slipped and lost her balance. She hit the floor sobbing as if her heart would break.

Rilla knelt beside Cher and gathered her in her arms. “I know. I know. I loved him, too. Hate me all you want. I hate this whole mess.”

And she did. Every illusion she’d had about her father and her chief deputy had evaporated like the morning dew, leaving behind pain and shattered dreams.

Ten miles from Cherokee Springs, Mac walked into Rusty's Roadhouse. The Agency had sent someone to keep a check on him. Havers had made good on his threat.

The roadhouse was a mid-size truck stop right off I-65 and frequented by truckers and the women who liked to hang around truckers. They served down-home cuisine, meaning big hunks of beef, plenty of taters and a shortage of fresh vegetables. The vegetables which made it to the plate were over-cooked and over-greased, but their chili was five-star.

He ambled toward the back, slid into a booth and waited for his contact to approach. And approach she did...ready to take his order. Roxy Quinlan...

Roxy patted her frizzy bleached hair and slinked her way over to his booth. "We got us some great specials today—great big old steak, if you're in the mood." She leaned down and put her face right in his. "Hey, bird dog."

He smiled and said, "Take a load off, darlin'." He lowered his tone. "Cut it out, Roxy."

She flashed him a wide smile. "Just makin' it look good. What do you have to report?" she asked, still smiling flirtatiously.

"I'm sure of one thing. The sheriff isn't part of any drug ring."

"Well, that's what you say, but the powers that be don't agree. What makes you so sure?"

"She cares too much about the people in her town."

"It could be a pose." She glanced down at her order pad. "You were wrong last time."

"I know...but not this time."

"Havers was right to send me down here. You've lost focus."

"I haven't. Look here, I'm on the trail of the real drug dealer. I need a little more time to flush him out."

"You've had a month, and all you've managed to do is get the hots for your main suspect. Tell me I'm wrong."

He clenched his jaw. Quinlan wasn't listening. He might as well piss in the wind. "I'd like a cup of coffee and bowl of chili with extra cheese. Think you can manage?"

Her cheeks flushed with anger, but she responded with a practiced smile. "Sure, darlin'. Be back in a jiffy."

The coffee, when she brought it, burned the tip of his tongue, but was better than he'd expected.

"Your chili'll be ready in a minute. Need any sugar or cream?"

He shook his head. "Black's fine."

"I've rented an apartment over the drug store. Be seeing you 'round." She shot him a wicked grin.

"Great. Just frigging great. I've got a babysitter."

She leaned down. "I'm many things, Mac old buddy, but a babysitter I'm not." She straightened. "And I just bet you want some extra crackers with your bowl of chili, don't ya?"

Mac scowled and watched Roxie sashay to the kitchen to pick up his order. She returned with his order quicker than the blink of an eye. But she wasn't through giving him advice.

"One more thing," she said, bowl of chili in hand. "My advice—don't screw this one up or you're going to find yourself riding herd on a desk. No more excitement. No more Mister Cloak and Dagger."

"Appreciate it, ma'am."

She set the bowl down with a thunk. "Might as well eat it," she said. "It won't kill you."

Mac looked at the steaming bowl of chili, cheese melting. His mouth watered. He shoved his spoon into the bowl and took a heaping bite.

"Ow," he gasped and grabbed a glass of water. "It's hot."

"Told you."

"You can forget the tip."

She wrinkled her nose at him, then turned to wait on another customer.

He finished the bowl of chili and left Roxy a tip anyway. She deserved it, having to work in a dump like Rusty's. In the DEA, Roxy was renowned for her chameleonic roles. She could fit in with any strata of society—high to low. Maybe she was a frustrated actress with a highly developed sense of right and wrong.

After paying for dinner, Mac was on his way out the door when someone called his name. "Callahan?"

Startled, Mac stopped and glanced around. "Lloyd—uh, fancy seeing you here." Had he heard anything of the conversation with Quinlan?

"Katie has a thing for their chili. Makes me trek over here at least twice a month just so she can have some." Lloyd raised an eyebrow. "And what are you doing here? Have a hankering for some real home cookin'?"

Mac laughed. "I heard their chili was damned good. Thought I'd try it myself."

"Cute little gal waiting on you. Wouldn't mind having her wait on me." He nudged Mack in the ribs. "But Katie would kill me."

"Can't have that."

After leaving Lloyd, Mac drove back home, but he couldn't help questioning Lloyd's showing up at the same time he had a meet with another agent. Was good old Lloyd exactly what he appeared, or was he the big dealer in Cherokee Springs? Was the businessman merely giving in to one of his wife's many whims or had he followed Mac?

More important, had his cover been compromised? After achieving a comfort level with the townspeople, he might've just blown everything.

Chapter Fifteen

One night later, Rilla sat in a booth at Rusty's with Mac, keeping a watchful eye on the door. There was genuine atmosphere, real sawdust and peanut shells on the floor. A somewhat better than mediocre band played, and several couples were already two-stepping around the dance floor.

"So tonight's the night for your detective's date with the Wyler kid?"

"Only he doesn't know it yet." She sat watching the door over Mac's shoulder. "Okay, it's show time. Kit just came in."

"She's wearing a wire?"

Rilla nodded.

He turned and gave a quick glance over his shoulder. "In *that* outfit? Where'd you put it?"

"Never you mind." She gave a huff. Where indeed? "Shut up. We're supposed to be on a date."

She nodded toward the bar. "Wyler's already here."

He wasn't a bad looking kid. About six-feet tall, he hadn't completely filled out yet and had the look of a hungry Golden Retriever. He wore his dingy blond hair in a mullet, and tonight he was decked out in a red, western-style shirt and jeans.

"Here goes nothing," Kit said into her hidden mic. "Do you copy?"

"Copy. Got your back."

Kit gave her makeup one last check and fluffed her curly hair. "Date night in Cherokee Springs," she muttered into the mic.

She sidled up beside Rob at the bar. "Hey, Robbie, glad to see you're not letting Barbie's death take you out of the game."

"What do you mean? I got a right to have a beer, don't I?"

"Not when you're only eighteen. I ought to arrest you right here and now. But I won't. Are you buying?" She tossed her hair.

"Guess you're not on duty."

She twirled around. "Do I *look* like I'm on duty?"

He took a pull on his long neck beer, then swallowed. "Nope."

Kit leaned forward. "We need to have a little chat. And come to an understanding."

"'Bout what?"

"They're playing a slow one. Ask me to dance, and I'll explain."

"Sure." He stepped back from the bar and held out his hand. "Come on."

Kit placed her hand in his. "How could I resist your charming invitation?"

He pulled the detective close. Kit backed away. Rilla figured the little jerk probably already had a hard-on.

"Don't take my offer so seriously. This is a business deal. I want the same deal R.J. had. You need someone on the force to look the other way...tip you off. Know what I mean?"

"Hell, no." He glanced around and pulled at his collar.

"R.J. didn't tell me where he was getting his supply," Kit said. "I mean to take his place, but I need the contact."

"You wearing a wire?"

She stopped dancing, glanced down at her mini skirt and halter top. "Just where the hell do you think I'd put a wire?"

Across the room, Rilla winked at Mac. “It’s a good wire.”

“Dunno. R.J. never mentioned you,” Robbie said. “And I don’t know who his contact was. I been hopin’ to hear from him myself.”

“Well, when you do, I want to know. I want a meet.”

“Don’t hold your breath.”

“I won’t.” Kit put her arms around Robbie’s neck and snuggled close.

“Say, how ’bout taking a run by the liquor store,” Robbie said. “You could buy us some booze, then you and I can take a little drive out in the country. I know a place…”

“Only in your wet dreams, Wyler.”

“I thought you liked me.”

“I like men. I don’t see one.”

“Aw, you ain’t no fun.”

“I’m a business woman. Making money is fun, not wasting time with a teenage wuss. I’m out of here. Got a date.” Her hips swaying with each step, Kit left the roadhouse, leaving poor Robbie looking like he’d been hit by a train.

“Damn. She just blew him off,” Rilla said.

Mac took a casual look over his shoulder. True enough. Detective Bellows had swiveled her hips right out the door. He didn’t like sitting with his back to the door, but neither did Rilla. He’d done the gentlemanly thing and allowed her the observer seat. “Didn’t take her long. Think it did any good?”

“She made her point.” She took a sip of her sweet tea. “The word’ll get back to whomever.”

“But will he buy her story? I don’t feel good about this.”

“Kit’s an experienced detective. She’s done undercover before.”

“Right. Here in town?”

“Chicago.”

Mac frowned. "How'd she end up here?"

"Her story is she and her boyfriend broke up and she wanted to get as far away from Chicago as she could."

"Did a damned good job of it. You checked her references, didn't you?"

"Of course. She had a great record. Did lots of undercover in drugs and narcotics."

"Sounds like you picked the right person for the job."

"Yeah. But she was very anxious to do it. She didn't show the caution I expected."

"So your gut is telling you something's off with Bellows?"

She shrugged. "Maybe. You ready to go?"

Mac grinned. "And forego the ambiance of Rusty's? What's the matter? Don't you believe I can two-step?"

"Don't be silly."

"Let's impress this crowd with our terpsichorean prowess."

She scowled and muttered, "Just because you pretend you're a writer, you don't have to talk like one around me."

"Come on." He stood and held out his hand, palm up.

"You're almost as smooth as Rob Wyler." She smirked and placed her hand in his.

Mmm. Warm and strong.

"I'll show you smooth." He pulled her to his chest and took off in an easy one-two, one-two-three swaying glide around the small dance floor.

Her body was warm against Mac's chest. "You're pretty good at this," he whispered in her ear.

"You're not so bad yourself." She gazed into his eyes. "I must say I'm surprised."

"Why? Haven't you found me skilful in other physical endeavors?"

"Have I complained?"

He laughed. “No, you haven’t at that.”

The music continued and he drew Rilla closer. Her body molded to his...and felt damned good. “Dare I say it? Your beeper hasn’t gone off once tonight.”

Her eyes widened. Placing an elegant finger to her lips, she shushed him. “You’ve done it now, but maybe not. This isn’t a real date.”

“It isn’t?” Mac nuzzled her neck. “Hmm, sure feels like one.”

She gave a small shake of her head. “No, it’s a pretend date so we could backup Kit.”

He turned to leave the dance floor “Well, that’s it. Ready to leave?”

She laughed, a low sensual growl and tugged on his hand. “Oh, no, you don’t. The music’s still playing.”

She slipped her arms around his waist and slid her hands into the back pockets of his jeans, cupped his ass and pressed against his dick.

“This is feeling less like pretend,” he said. Pretend, hell—she was teasing him and having a great time. His dick was hard as a rock, and if she kept it up...

But damn, he loved this playful side of her. He couldn’t help but wonder if they’d met under different circumstances...

Her head went back, revealing the long column of her neck. She laughed then emitted a delicious giggle which sent a searing jolt straight to his groin. Did she have any clue how she affected him? “You’re having too much fun.”

“Is that even possible?” Her eyes glittered with amusement.

Possible? He swung her around and headed for the door. “Let’s find out.”

The Porsche was parked along the side of the roadhouse in the shadows. They made it to the car.

Barely.

He backed her against the passenger door. His lips fastened on hers and she welcomed his kiss. He eased his hands under her halter top while he kissed her neck and blew a soft puff of air into her ear.

Skin—God—so soft. Her nipples hardened under his touch. She arched against him and moaned. She gazed up at him, her dark eyes glazed with heat. Could she possibly want him as much as he wanted her?

"Mac, we can't. Not here." Her breath was warm on his neck. God. He needed her so much. More than any woman he'd ever known. He pulled down her halter top and lightly raked her brown nipples with his teeth, pulled at them and sucked.

Again she moaned, a sound of desperation…for more?

"Lift your skirt." He fumbled with his zipper. His dick sprang free, ready for battle. And make no mistake about it, making love to Rilla was like a battle between two warriors.

Her skirt shielded their bodies, but if anyone saw them, there'd be no doubt what was happening. Underneath the full skirt, her slim thighs parted.

Thank God. No panty hose. She wore another one of those scraps of lace she loved. He ripped it off.

He dipped a finger between her thighs and slid into her warm, honeyed slit, rubbing her sensitive clit with his thumb.

Her body shook and trembled against his. She gasped ragged breaths against his chest, and whose pounding heart was whose? Why couldn't he have four hands? So many sweet places he wanted to touch and so little time.

His lips fastened on her mouth again. She opened to him, her hot tongue battling his for possession. He slid another finger inside her slit and she started moving against them.

"No, wait." He removed his hand and adjusted his stance for a better position and access.

"No." Her voice rasped in his ear.

"This is better," he promised and nudged the head of his cock up and down her outer lips then thrust into her wet warmth.

A low moan ripped from her.

"All right?"

"Yes," she hissed and trembled as he tried to bury himself deep within her. He cupped her ass cheeks and impaled her securely her onto his straining cock. Keeping her light weight cradled, he moved her up and down. Her inner muscles clenched around his dick so fiercely he nearly lost control.

"Easy, girl. Easy." He panted and tried to slow her bucking pace.

"No. Not easy." She clung to his jacket and wrapped her legs around his waist, forcing his cock even deeper inside. "I don't want it easy."

Exquisite pressure grew in his balls until he exploded in waves of hot release. He pumped into her over and over, unwilling to leave the blistering heat of her sweet body.

Her head whipped back as she gave a long, low moan. Her body vibrated under his hands. God. What made this woman so hot, so in tune with his needs?

Her climax took her. She stiffened and her teeth fastened on his neck, her nails digging into his shoulders as she rocked against him.

He slid a free hand under her halter and pinched her nipples, then nipped the silken skin of her neck. Another low moan, more of a groan.

Her muscles rhythmically gripped his dick even tighter as she milked him of every last drop of cum.

"Oh, God," he gasped. "Protection. We didn't..."

She raised her head from his chest. Her eyes were open but still slightly glazed. "I did."

"You did? You thought we might make love tonight? You planned for it?" Damn, the woman was full of surprises.

"I believe in being prepared, even if you don't."

She rested her head again on his chest, sending an unaccustomed rush of tenderness through him which nearly closed his throat. This woman was like no other he'd ever known. Passionate. Intelligent...yes, and reckless, too.

She gazed at him, her body still melting against his. "For some reason, I don't have much willpower when I'm around you."

"For which I'm profoundly grateful."

She heaved a sigh and gave a purr of satisfaction. "Me, too."

She looked around, eyes widened as if she'd only just realized where they were. "I—uh—"

Reluctantly, he withdrew from her warmth. "Yeah..." He straightened and managed to get his dick back in his jeans without snagging it the zipper—no mean feat under the circumstances.

"Yeah."

She jerked up her halter, hiding her naked breasts from his view. He waited while she adjusted the skirt she'd very conveniently worn. "My place or yours?"

"Haven't we been reckless enough for one night?"

"Once is never enough."

"Well, it might just have to be tonight."

"Now, even the sheriff—"

A sudden whirling hit Rilla's gut—she'd forgotten the wire. "Shit! I'm wired...remember?"

"Receiving or sending?"

"Supposed to be receiving, but I asked them to make it two-way—in case I needed to communicate with Kit."

"So, uh—"

"Yeah, the entire team...unless they packed it up as soon as she left." She scowled and pulled the tiny ear bud from her ear. How had it managed to stay in place during their lovemaking? Not a clue. She tried to put the memory of his hard thrusts out of her mind, but the dampness between her legs was an embarrassing reminder.

Mac bit his lip and tried—honestly he did—tried to hold back his laughter.

No use.

His lungs burned with the need to breathe, but all he could do was laugh until he collapsed against the side of the car.

"Not funny." She rolled her eyes at him. "This is very—"

"—entertaining for the listeners as it was for us."

Her body tensed against his. "I have to maintain the respect of my deputies. This makes it very difficult."

"Oh, I'm sure they'll respect you in the morning. I know I will."

"I'm not in the habit of—"

"I hope not." He brushed the hair away from her face as gently as he could. "Come on. It'll blow over in a few days. Things'll go back to normal and boring."

"You don't know those guys like I do. And Kit—ohmigod—do you think she heard my suspicions earlier?"

He shrugged. "She came in calm and cool. She didn't act like she overheard anything. Maybe she'll think her boss got some...and be jealous as hell."

"It's not a joke. At the very least, this was something private..."

"Not very, considering where we are." He glanced upward at the neon beer sign.

"You're not funny. Take me home." She walked around to the passenger side of the Porsche.

"That answers my previous question. But not the answer I wanted."

"I can't do this now," she said. Nervously she waved her hands back and forth. "I have responsibilities."

"All right. You've made your point. Home it is, and I'll count myself lucky to have spent all this time with you."

"And well you should," she said, her normal air of feistiness returning.

"Testy, aren't you. To hear you, no one would think you'd just been loved within an inch of your life."

Her dark lashes fluttered as the corner of her mouth twitched.

"Come on, my lady sheriff. Let's go home."

After he took Rilla home, he sat in her driveway and watched the lights come on as she went from room to room.

A bark and a door slam. She must've let the dog out.

Damn, but he had it bad. The spicy scent she wore lingered in his car. The nearness and warmth of her was like a drug. She intoxicated him, and the more time he spent with her, the more he wanted her.

Chapter Sixteen

Mac moseyed up and down the aisles of the drug store. He picked up a can of shaving cream and a pack of disposable razors. He dawdled another minute, marveling at the variety of hemorrhoid preparations. A shiver ran through him; he'd dawdled long enough. Time for a bit of research. He walked to the back of the store. "Got a minute?"

The pharmacist looked up from filling a prescription. "Just a sec."

Mac watched while the pharmacist slapped a label on the bottle and stuffed it into a small bag. As soon as Jensen stapled a receipt to the bag, he tossed it into the OUT box.

"What can I do for you, Callahan?"

"Just a matter of curiosity. 'Bout these kids overdosing on ecstasy?"

"Yeah? Bad stuff."

"I mean, what's the deal? Why isn't grass good enough? It was certainly good enough for us, wasn't it?" He winked at the pharmacist as if they were old buddies.

Jensen frowned over his wire rim glasses. "I wouldn't know."

"Oh, come on. It's pretty harmless stuff. Made for great sex."

"Well, I can tell you a bit about ecstasy—pharmacologically speaking—no personal experience with that either. It's a synthetic amphetamine."

"Simple to make? I mean these kids seem to have a steady supply. Is one of them cooking it up with his junior chemistry set?"

"No, it's a complicated compound. It requires a sophisticated set-up to manufacture." Jensen raised an eyebrow. "Aiming to set up your own little production line?"

"Who, me? No way." Mac leaned forward on the counter. "I'm a writer, not a chemist. Thought I might use it in my next book."

The druggist nodded. "Make interesting reading."

"Yeah, that was my thinking. Just doing a little preliminary research. As for setting up my own drug lab, I wouldn't know where to start. You'd have to have some pretty good contacts to start with."

"Guess so." He nodded at the items Mac held. "Can I ring those up for you?"

"Sure." He grabbed a box of condoms and set them on the counter. "These, too."

The pharmacist grinned. "Gotta stay safe," he said in a hoarse, conspiratorial whisper.

"Oh, yeah." After all, he and Rilla had taken chances more than once. Around that woman he was as randy as a teenager. Whatever "it" was, she had it in bushels. Maybe it was her dogged determination to get rid of drugs in her town. Maybe it was her long legs and the way they fit around his waist.

No, it was the intelligence and humor behind her warm, dark eyes. Or maybe it was just the whole package. Rilla Devane was a hell of a surprise in this small Tennessee town. He'd miss her when the job was over.

Yeah, a whole hell of a lot.

Rilla reviewed Kit's debrief on her initial contact with Rob Wyler. "Is he coming through or not?"

The detective wrinkled her nose and lifted her shoulders in a shrug. "I'm not sure. He knows something, but *what* I don't know...yet."

"No way would R.J. have trusted that little creep with the name of his source."

"Maybe Rob figured it out?"

"Yeah, he's a real genius."

"R.J. fooled everyone."

Kit's cell phone rang. "With any luck—" She answered, "Bellows." She nodded, signifying it was Rob Wyler.

"Yeah. Okay. No, I understand. In your dreams," she said with a snort before breaking the connection.

Rilla leaned forward. "Don't keep me in suspense."

Bellows flashed a wide grin. "Listen to this. We've got him. Rob is setting up a meet with his source for tonight."

"Okay, I'll get you wired." She reached for the telephone. "And you'll have plenty of backup."

Bellows shook her head. "No. He'll be on guard. The first thing he'll do is check me for a wire. I need to gain their confidence first. After the initial meet, I'll wear a wire."

"I want you in a vest."

"Fine. They would expect that. Just no wire or backup."

"I don't like it."

No backup. No wire. Reckless. Reckless.

"You know I'm right."

"Yeah, probably."

"See here, Rilla. I'm not a newbie when it comes to undercover. I know what makes people like this tick. I can do it."

Rilla nodded her agreement, but a plan began to form. She wasn't about to send anyone out without backup, whether her detective thought she needed it or not.

Mac watched from behind a tree as the detective pulled into the fourth parking spot at picnic area six. After hearing the details of the meet, Rilla asked him if he'd backup Bellows without her knowledge.

Bellows didn't want backup? Then she was inexperienced, stupid...or dirty.

He glanced at his watch. She was thirty minutes early. The Wyler kid would probably show up early, too, checking for any signs of a double-cross. Thirty minutes and the park would close for the night.

At nine-ten Rob Wyler tapped Kit's shoulder through the open window. She hadn't heard him approach. Dammit. She didn't like surprises.

"Wha-zup, doll? Wanna give me a blow job while we're waiting?"

She rolled her eyes. "Tempting offer—I think not." She glanced at her watch. "Let's get the show on the road."

His cell phone blared out a raucous country western tune that sounded like "The Devil Goes Down to Georgia". "Here we go..." He answered, "Okay. No, she's alone. Okay. Sorry, gotta frisk you. Gotta make sure you're not wearing a wire."

With a disgusted groan, she opened the car door and stepped from the vehicle. "Have at it." She held up her arms.

He patted her down. A little too thoroughly.

He ran his hands over her Kevlar vest. "Take this damn thing off. I gotta be sure you're not wired."

"All right. Just watch your hands, bozo...and I'm putting it back on." She unfastened the vest and waited.

"Play nice, dee-teck-tive." He ran his hands inside her sports bra while she cringed at his touch.

"Mmm. Nice rack." He tweaked her nipples. "Didn't know cops came so stacked."

"Get it over with. Unless you've got a medical license, I'm not due for a breast exam until March."

"Real funny, too."

He ran an insinuating hand between her legs. She wanted to puke. "Want me to shuck my jeans, too?" Another five minutes and she'd have to kill the sleazy little bastard.

He stepped back and grinned. "If you insist."

"Slime ball." She refastened her vest.

With a wide smirk plastered across his face, he shrugged, pulled out his cell phone and hit redial. "She's clean." He listened, nodding. "Okay, he'll meet with you."

Ten minutes later, she followed the punk into one of the park's cabins. The room was lighted by a single, feeble bulb.

Kurt emerged from the shadows. "Detective."

"Well, well, well, the friendly pharmacist. You're the source. I should've known."

"Glad you didn't. Before now, that is. You'd be arresting me instead of asking for R.J.'s share."

"Let's cut to the chase. I didn't come to the table with my hand out. You need my services to continue your operation."

Jensen turned to the kid. "Leave us." He handed Rob a plastic bag full of pills. "Bonus for tonight. Have fun."

"Cool." The shithead punk leered at Kit. Next thing, his tongue would be hanging out.

"Out!" yelled his boss.

"I'm going. I'm going."

She waited until Wyler left, then turned to Kurt.

"If it's the last thing I do, I'm gonna whack that punk-ass kid the next time he touches me."

"Be my guest. He's already a liability."

"Are you always so agreeable?" She sidled up to him.

"Only when confronted by someone of your brains and beauty."

She ripped off the vest and pulled off her sports bra. She smiled and stepped into his outstretched arms. "God. I've missed you. It's been hell."

Chapter Seventeen

The only one left in the office wing of the building, Rilla paced back and forth, her footsteps echoing against the polished tile floor. Unease settled and wrapped around her like a thick, August morning fog.

What was taking Bellows so long? The initial meet with Rob Wyler had been set for nine-thirty. Depending on where he took her to meet his source, she should be back by now, or at least calling in. Maybe the dealer was careful and meeting her outside the county. Everything could still be okay.

Was Bellows still alive? Rilla'd never forgive herself if she weren't. Why hadn't she let the TBI handle it? At least she asked Mac to provide backup, even if Kit didn't know it. But why hadn't he called?

Did everything come down to her own arrogance? She wanted to be the one who brought the dealer down...and found her father's killer.

And she'd risked her best detective to do it.

Mac eased away from the cabin window. Anger roiled in his gut.

Son of a bitch. The friendly downtown pharmacist. Who better?

And the eager undercover detective from Chi-town—his willing accomplice. He bridled his anger. He'd have to have evidence of more than just a relationship. Okay, so Detective Bellows hadn't been forthcoming about her personal relationship with the pharmacist. Unwise, given her position—but not illegal.

Too bad the windows were closed and a noisy A/C unit strained its small motor obscuring the pair's words. He hated the thought of telling Rilla.

Another betrayal. Another blot on her judgment. At least that was how she'd see it.

Technically, as a DEA agent, he wasn't required to tell her anything, but he couldn't risk not telling her. Without a doubt, Jensen was the one who'd ordered the hit on her father and the near-miss on Rilla herself.

Sweat beaded his forehead and ran into his eyes. He wiped it away and wished he could blank out the vision of the rutting couple who never made it to the sofa before they tore off their clothes.

He grimaced. Voyeurism wasn't his cup of tea. Stepping carefully, he made his way down the path behind the cabin to the motorcycle he'd rented the day before for such an eventuality. He'd better give the conspirators plenty of space before starting the motor. He didn't want them suspicious until it was too late to escape the trap.

Eleven o'clock.

And Rilla yawned, but she was ready to mount an A.P.B. for Kit and Mac. She'd worried the cuticles on her right hand and was ready to start on the left when her detective stomped into the office.

"That little scum bag!" Kit tore off the vest and threw it down on Rilla's desk.

Rilla stood. "Are you all right. Did he hurt you?"

"No." Kit shook her head. "He wasted my time—well, not exactly."

"Meaning?"

"I met him in the park as arranged." Kit paced back and forth as she debriefed. "Danny made me ride on the back of his motorcycle—blindfolded—and took me to a cabin. I think it was still in the park. But I don't have a clue how I got there."

"And?" Dammit why couldn't she spit it out?

Kit gave a satisfied smile. "I met the dealer."

"Who?"

"That's just it. I don't *know*." Kit shrugged. "The dealer stayed to the shadows with a bright light shining in my eyes. Just like an interrogation."

Rilla leaned forward. "What about his voice? Is he local?"

"Low, and he had some kind of weird accent."

"Faking an accent to disguise his voice?"

"That was my thought. So anyway, we have another meet set. First, I have to prove myself. He said he'd come up with some kind of test."

"All right. That's progress—not what I'd call a waste of time."

Kit continued her animated pacing. "He says he'll contact me in forty-eight hours. If I pass his test, he'll cut me in."

"That's when we'll wire you," Rilla said. Another two days to wait.

Kit shook her head. "No, not until after he trusts me. If he finds a wire, I'm toast. Let's take this one step at a time. We'll lose him if we move too soon."

"You may be right," Rilla agreed, albeit reluctantly, "but in the meantime, he's still selling drugs to kids in my jurisdiction."

"I know, but this is so exciting. My adrenaline level must be sky high." Kit's gaze darted toward the door. "If that's it for tonight?"

Rilla nodded. "Go on home. Get some rest if you can."

After Kit left, Rilla tried to sort out what wasn't quite right about Kit's debrief. Maybe it was an adrenaline rush... Or maybe it was something else.

After midnight, she gave up on hearing from Mac and drove home. That S.O.B.—did he think he needn't share intel with her? Had he even been able to follow Kit and Danny?

Mac waited in the deep shadows of the Rilla's front porch until she whipped into the driveway and parked the Jeep. When she stepped onto the front porch, he emerged from the shadows. "Thought you'd never come home," he drawled.

"Crap!" Her dark eyes snapped with anger. "You scared the living hell out of me. Where have you been? I waited and waited. What happened?"

She glared, but she didn't resist his touch when he brought her hand to his lips and kissed the inside of her wrist where the skin was soft and silken.

"Don't try to distract me."

He grinned and did his best to appear innocent. "Now would I do something like that?"

"In a heartbeat." She inserted her key into the lock. "Come on. Tell me we didn't waste our time tonight."

"Will you forgive me if I tell you I know who our dealer is?"

"Dammit. Why didn't you say so in the first place? Who the hell is it?"

"Inside, woman. Then I'll reveal all."

He opened the door and waited for Rilla to enter first.

"You've certainly taken your sweet time about it. I thought you'd call me."

"And I thought you'd come home as soon as you heard Bellows' version of the meet." He glanced around the box crowded living room. "Where's Ralphie?"

"He's at the vet's office. He had a little surgery this afternoon. I'll pick him up tomorrow."

"Oh, no—tell me you didn't." He cringed in spite of himself. It was one of those instant reflex deals. Emasculation was no joke for any male, human or canine.

"I did—no, the vet did. And don't change the subject."

He followed Rilla into the kitchen. She pulled out a chair and sat at the table. He sat across from her and leaned forward. "You're not going to like this."

She leaned back. Was she reluctant to get any closer? Hmm.

"Okay, spill."

He grinned—he didn't mind torturing her a bit and prolonging the reveal. "All right. When I followed Kit…yes, I saw the dealer clearly."

"After Kit left? She said he stayed in the shadows while she was there."

"Detective Bellows left out a detail or two."

Her eyes darkened. "Like what?"

"She and your local druggist have a relationship."

"Kurt?" A frown creased Rilla's forehead as she tried to puzzle out his meaning.

"Jensen is the dealer, and Kit Bellows screwed him senseless at their meet. Something tells me they're more than friends."

Her face turned beet red and she let out a string of obscenities that would've made Andy Sipowitz blush. Then, "I'm going to take her down. I'm going to grind her helpful ass—" She broke off and headed for the door.

"Hold on." Mac grabbed her wrist. "We have to play this out. What I have is circumstantial. I couldn't hear anything. All we know for sure is they're seeing each other on the sly."

"But you know...*I* know they're in this together. She was going to meet the dealer, not go on a date."

"Yes, but if we're patient a little longer, we can get the hard evidence we need."

She calmed. "You're right. And it's going to be damn satisfying when we do."

"Speaking of satisfaction..."

"Oh, no you don't." She grew rigid and jerked her wrist from his grasp. "We need to keep this strictly business. I can't afford to lose focus right now, and you can't afford to, either."

"Damn, but you're right. As much as I'd like to kiss your resistance away, I won't. This op is too close to completion."

And I'll be leaving town...no use pretending I won't.

"And you'll be heading out of town in your fancy Porsche. The town and I will be a lot better off."

Mac shoved back the chair, then stood. "You don't have to sound so happy about it."

She glanced at the table top, then raised her gaze to meet his. "I'm not...not really." She chewed the inside of her lip. Why? Surely she wasn't going to cry?

"I never meant for this to happen," he said with a rush. "I never meant to hurt you." Hurt her? Why was his gut twisting as if a boa constrictor had taken up residence?

She shrugged. "No big deal. We both knew what we were doing."

His throat ached and tried to close on him. He swallowed hard. "You know Bellows is going to set you up. She'll come up with some excuse to get you out there."

Rilla nodded. "Yeah, she will. I'll let you know when I have an idea of how and where." Her face a mask of anger, she slammed her fist on the table. "I can hardly wait to confront the two of them. Just imagine. The high school jock I used to date is responsible for ordering the hit on my father and for the deaths of those two teenagers." She leaned forward with her elbows on the table and massaged her temples. "My department is riddled with deceit and I'm a piss-poor judge of character."

"Hold on here. I—*we* are going to take them down—no doubt about it. And you've known these people all your life. It's not easy to see betrayal everywhere when you've just lost your father—basically had your life turned upside down."

With deliberation he walked around behind Rilla and placed his hands on her shoulders. "We've made a lot of progress tonight on our case. You deserve some time off."

Her shoulders went rigid under his hands. "Not while there's someone still selling X in my county."

"Babe, your shoulders are like steel bands." He worked his thumbs in a circular motion across the tight muscles. "I can give a pretty mean massage. Now," he added quickly, "I know what you're thinking. I'm just trying to get in your pants again. That's not it. You need to relax."

Rilla shook her head. "I don't want your hands on me again. I can't take it."

"Damn...all right, Rilla, I won't argue with you." Reluctantly he headed for the door. "Call me tomorrow. I don't think they'll waste any time."

"Sure." She stood and followed him. "Um, drive safe."

His throat nearly closed again. He pulled at his collar—not that it did any good. "Yes, ma'am. And you lock this door behind me, hear?" *God.* He didn't want to leave...not like this.

But he did.

The next afternoon, Mac climbed the outer staircase—one of those wrought iron jobs—to Roxy's apartment which was situated over the drug store. Wouldn't Jensen be surprised to know he had a DEA undercover agent living right over his store? A line of rusting trash cans rested against the side of the brick building at the end of a row of restored structures. Colorful awnings, fresh paint, window boxes of flowers and an energetic senior citizen leaving the drug store made the small downtown street picturesque. He was leaving all this—for what?

Without answering his question, he shrugged off the fleeting sense of loss and knocked.

Roxy Quinlan opened the door, a frown ingrained in her usually attractive face. "'Bout time you showed up. Get your ass in here. We've got work to do."

Oh, yeah. She was in a hell of a mood. "How could I resist your gracious invitation?"

She snorted. "My feet hurt, and it's all your fault."

He looked around the room that served as her living room and bedroom. A tired sofa with a faded cover made up the living room and a half-made bed occupied the back corner. A sink, a two-burner stove and an ancient fridge along one wall made up the rest. Hell. He'd lived in a lot worse. "I see you brought in a decorator."

Her upper lip curled into a sneer. "Enough with the compliments. How's your investigation going? Still convinced the sheriff's on the up and up?"

He eased his too-long frame into a sagging chair, barely managing to keep from banging his shin on a rickety, coffee-ringed table.

"Sheriff Devane has been quite helpful and forthcoming with information."

Quinlan's brows rose halfway to her hairline. "She knows who you are?"

"Yes, and it's made a tremendous difference."

"How so?"

"She's turned over her father's notebook—the one I'm handing over to you now. It's in code, so get the decryption geeks on it."

"How do we know it's any good?"

"Gut feeling." He leaned forward, desperate to convince her of his progress...and Rilla's innocence. The last thing he wanted was more interference. "I've fingered the local pharmacist as the dealer. I just need to dig up some solid proof."

"The one downstairs?" A wicked grin flashed across Roxy's face. "So, what makes you think he's the perp if you don't have anything solid?"

"Nothing admissible...yet." He gave her a quick rundown of the detective and Jensen's cabin tryst.

"You're right. All it proves is they have a relationship. What do you need me to do? Surveillance?"

"Backup."

"You got it. Let me know where and when." She smiled and stretched her long legs, slipped off her shoes, then wiggled her toes. "I'll be more than glad to give up my job at Rusty's. My feet are killing me."

"Won't you miss this place?"

"*This* place?" Roxy glanced around and chuckled. "Hell, no. I'm ready for a vacation."

"Think you'll actually take one when this assignment is over?"

"Of course. Time to decompress and let my feet heal."

"That's so female...whining about your dogs."

Quinlan shot him a drop-dead expression, then shrugged. "I'm parched. Want some iced tea?"

He nodded. "Yeah."

Barefoot, she walked to the fridge and quickly poured two glasses. She took a long drink from hers, then smiled. "Now that's better. She handed him the other glass before heading back to the sofa. She sat and tucked her legs underneath. A cagey expression crossed her face. "So, what're your plans for your next break between cases?"

He hesitated. What *were* his plans? He didn't want to think about leaving Rilla.

Slow it down, bud. She's getting to you. And that isn't good.

"Earth to Mac?"

"Haven't given it much thought." He shrugged as if nothing mattered, but it did. Damn, it did. He drummed his fingers on the scarred end table.

"Yeah right." Roxy smiled knowingly. "Looks like *something* tied of up those few brain cells of yours."

"Uh..."

She leaned forward, her expression way too serious for his liking. "Listen to me. If you're smart, you'll pull out of here as soon as the case is made and the dealer's in custody. Doesn't pay to get too friendly with the locals."

"Now wait a damned minute—the whole point of an undercover—"

"Yeah, I know you have to get close, but not *that* close. The job's stressful. You need to unwind—sort out your feelings. Decide if you want—or should—continue."

"What else is there? It's all I've ever wanted since I joined the Agency."

"As good as you are, maybe you need to do something else. You're thirty-six. No close ties. No real family." Quinlan took a sip of tea, but her gaze never left his.

"Which makes me ideal for deep undercover." What the hell was going on? Was the Agency ready to kick him to the curb?

Quinlan smiled, but it didn't reassure him. "I'm saying maybe you want more out of life."

He straightened. "Are you talking white picket fence and two-point-five-kids territory? Me? Are you nuts?"

"You're human. Why not a family...kids?" Roxy shrugged. "It wouldn't be a bad life."

"Look at me. You know my history. I grew up in foster homes. No real father figure. What kind of father and husband would I make?" Mac took a long swallow of tea. This conversation was not what he expected, or wanted.

"You're a good man, basically. Stands to reason you'd be a good husband and father."

"Hell, no!" He shook his head. "Sometimes, I don't even know who I am. When I was a kid, I pretended to be whatever I thought the new foster family wanted. And now I'm still doing the same—only this time it's for the government. I'm a shadow. I live and work in a world of lies. It's all I know."

"Now who's whining?"

Mac leaned forward. "Roxy, I'm not whining. This is my life. I'm not going to let it go without a fight."

"You may not have a choice."

"What're you saying? You telling me I'm no good at this? Is that it?"

She straightened, then said, "Mac, part of my assignment is to evaluate your performance. After the last—"

He met her level gaze. "Go ahead, say it—fiasco."

"All right after the last fiasco, there were grave concerns, but you were given another chance."

He nodded. "I know."

"I think you need to consider other options. What if this isn't settled all clean and tidy? What will you do?"

What she actually meant was, if Rilla was arrested. "I don't want to do anything else. This is what I know. And I'm damned good at it."

"I may be wrong, Mac." Her tone and expression softened. "But you strike me as man who needs more from life than shadows and lies."

He shook his head, not wanting to believe his life as an agent was over. "No." But why not? Could he have Rilla? Children? Was he too old and damaged to change?

"You deserve happiness—as much as anyone else, Mac." There was that soft tone again. Did she think he was someone to be pitied?

He shot her a long look. "What about you?"

She leveled her gaze at him. "*My* performance isn't under scrutiny."

He banged the table with his fist. "I'll show you and Havers and everyone else at the Agency. This mission is on the verge of success. It'll only take another couple of weeks at most."

"You'd better be right." She leaned back casually, as if she hadn't just threatened him with the loss of his job, and grinned. "Like I said, my feet hurt."

Rilla wrestled a fifty pound bag of dog food off the shelf and into the basket. With any luck, her Ralphie would be thrilled to see her when she picked him up from the vet. Surely he wouldn't hold the surgery against her.

She rolled the cart into Miss Tweedy's checkout lane.

Her former teacher's wrinkled face creased with a wide smile and a wink. "I just want you to know I'm helping you keep an eye on that new feller."

"Callahan?" It wouldn't matter if Mac stayed in town for twenty years. To Miss Tweedy, he would always be the *new feller.*

"Of course that's who I mean. I think you need to keep a close eye on him. Did you know he's seeing some trashy gal who just moved in over the drug store?"

A quick rush of blood heated Rilla's face. "What?"

"Yes, ma'am. I was coming out of the drug store with my prescriptions—you know, I have the bad arthritis—and I saw him go right up to her apartment and knock on the door. Went inside. Stayed a while, too."

"Go on. Make your point."

"Not that I'm a nosy busybody or anything like. I had to go to the bank and then to the Wash 'n' Curl. That fancy car of his was still there when I headed home."

"Good job, Miss Tweedy." Rilla quickly paid for the dog food and rushed from the store. When she reached the Jeep she slowed down and took a deep breath. Had she jumped to the wrong conclusion? Maybe the trashy waitress was a DEA contact. Maybe not.

Without warning, a hazy vision of Mac in bed with the other woman flashed through her mind.

Dammit. He had no right to screw around with her emotions like this. He wasn't any better than Don the Jerk. Men!

Finally home and seething with jealousy, Rilla snatched the phone and punched in Mac's number. Luckily the dog was oblivious to her insanity. He, the fortunate creature, was sleeping off his sedation in the corner of her office.

As soon as Mac answered, she barked, "My house—now." Before he could protest, and with great satisfaction, she disconnected him.

By the time he arrived, she'd managed to regain her cool, or at least a semblance of it. She'd be calm. Yes, she would.

Even though alerted and a little alarmed by the urgency of her summons, Mac ambled up the porch steps to Rilla's house.

She whipped open the door with his first step onto the porch. "Took you long enough."

"I'm here. What's the big deal? Miss me?"

She stopped pacing in the narrow aisle between packing boxes and whirled to face him. “Not that I care, mind you, but who’s the broad living over the drug store?”

Shit. Damned small towns. Everybody knew everybody’s business. “Roxy? She’s a waitress at Rusty’s. She served us—don’t you remember?”

“And the reason you dropped in on her?”

If he said business, it would be a giveaway. If he said personal, she’d have his ass in a sling. What to do?

“No comment?” She turned away from him and threaded her way to the room she used as an office.

“Been following me, Sheriff?” Attack rather than admit the truth. Just because he’d blown his cover with Rilla, he wasn’t about to blow Roxy’s.

Face red, she huffed. “No. Miss Tweedy ratted you out.”

“Great! Maybe we could use *her* in surveillance. She has a real flare for it.”

She tapped her foot, while her pretty face pulled into a not-so-pretty scowl. “Don’t think I haven’t noticed you didn’t answer my question.”

“What’s your point?”

“Is she a DEA contact?”

“If she were, I couldn’t tell you.”

“And if she’s not, then you’re a low-down horny toad. Is that pointed enough for you?”

He started laughing. Probably a mistake, especially with a woman as pissed-off as this one. “You’re jealous.”

Her elegant, arched nose tilted up an inch or so. “Am not.”

“C’mere.” He caught her wrist. “It’s all right. It was business. Okay?”

She shrugged, making a show of nonchalance. “I knew that.”

But she quit resisting and allowed him to pull her up close...and guide her into the bedroom. The fresh scent of citrus-scented soap or shampoo filled his nostrils and sent a rush of blood to his dick. She was all woman, with soft breasts yielding against his chest, her long slender fingers caressing the back of his neck, and her pelvis pressing against his erection, driving him absolutely nuts.

"You're in serious danger," he warned. God. He wanted her like he'd never wanted a woman. She'd found her way into his heart without his knowledge or will. Of course, he wanted her. Who wouldn't?

But the warmth and contentment that wove through him when she melted into his arms was a quantum leap beyond anything he'd ever experienced. No other woman had made him feel like he could leap over mountains or fly without wings.

She raised her head and peered at him, her dark eyes already glazed with passion. "How so?"

"You're in serious danger of being fucked within an inch of your life."

Her dark gaze pinned him with its intensity. "Maybe you're the one in danger..."

He stepped back. "Maybe I am."

Rilla advanced, selfishly relishing the heat in his blue eyes as they darkened to slate. "If it's even possible..."

His bad boy grin widened, sending a shimmer of heat to her lower belly. Damn the man, but she couldn't resist teasing him. "Want to find out?"

"I thought you were pissed off."

She took another step forward and pointed her finger at him. "Shut up. You've been bad. Very, very bad."

"Yes, I have. What're you going to do about it?"

"I have half a mind to have my way with you."

"How quaint." He laughed, his eyes crinkling at the corners.

How much longer would she be able to look into his eyes? Not long at all. Soon he'd leave town and her in the dust.

"We'll see who has his or her way with whom." His broad shoulders lifted in a shrug. "Did I say that right?" he asked with a mischievous grin.

"*You're* supposed to be the published author. I'm just a lowly public servant."

"Public servant, maybe. But lowly—never."

With one finger, she flipped open his top button, then another. The man was never at a loss for words, was he?

"Woman, don't play with me." His heavy-lidded gaze smoldered with an intensity that sent a flood of heat to her lower belly and weakened her knees.

"I intend to do more than play with you." She reached down and unsnapped his jeans, unzipped his pants, then insinuated her hand into the opening. His dick was already hard as a gun barrel. When she freed his erection, he gasped. "Careful, babe. You have me at a disadvantage, and I'm 'bout ready to shoot my wad."

She grinned up at him. "Oh, my." Kneeling in front of him on a thick throw rug, she breathed in his male musk. Wait. He still wore his jeans. She desperately wanted to feel his naked body to hers. She slid his jeans and underwear down to his ankles. He nimbly stepped out of them and kicked them to the side. His dick jutted hard and hot. She moistened her lips, then circled the head of his penis with her tongue. "Mm. Like?"

His knees trembled, and he grasped her shoulders as if to steady himself. "What's not to like?" His breaths came in ragged gasps.

A pearl of cum glistened, and she flicked it with her tongue, tasting the slightly salty liquid. His cock jumped in response. She loved the way he reacted to her slightest touch.

"God, you're killing me."

He released her shoulders, backed against the bed. Resting against the edge of the mattress, his hard-muscled thighs clenched as he wound his fingers through her hair. She took more of his shaft into her mouth and sucked rhythmically, cupping his balls with her free hand.

"Aw, baby, baby..." he said with a near groan.

His penis jerked and warm cum shot into her mouth. His thighs trembled and a groan ripped from his throat, but she swallowed his cum over and over and teased his long length with her tongue until his climax finished.

He fell down on his knees in front of her, gazing into her eyes. "My God, woman. You don't play around."

He unbuttoned her blouse and slowly pulled it from her pants. His long fingers slid inside her sports bra and cupped her breasts. "Now it's my turn."

She sucked in a ragged breath, then slowly let it out. "I-I—"

"What? You don't like this?" He tweaked a nipple between his thumb and forefinger.

"Mm." She bit her lips and held back the moan which raged to rip from her throat. She gave what had to be a feeble grin. "Like you said, 'what's not to like?'"

"We have time. Be patient." Slowly and methodically, he pulled off her sports bra and eased it over her head and nipped her shoulder as he did. A chill shuddered through her, tightening her nipples into tiny nubs.

"Beautiful." He kissed and licked each nipple, then pulled lightly with his teeth, sending a shocking zap of electricity straight to her core.

He slid her khakis down over her hips and helped her wiggle out of them. Her heart hammered in a staccato beat. The more he touched her, the more pronounced and erratic the rhythm. Then his mouth was on hers and he cupped her breasts, then her ass.

Damn the man. He touch caused havoc with her nervous system. Something still wasn't right, but for the life of her, she couldn't think what it was. His mouth devoured hers. His tongue swept and battled with hers, for her very life, or so it seemed.

"Now," she urged.

Finally, no more barriers, they were skin to skin...and heart to heart.

He parted her thighs with his knee. With his fingers, he separated her labia and thrust two fingers inside her already wet slit. Immediately she grabbed his fingers with her inner muscles and moved as he finger-fucked her and massaged her clitoris with his thumb.

God. The heat in her body gathered and centered in her feminine core.

No, not this way. She wanted him inside her right now. "Now," she urged.

Instead of removing his fingers, he substituted his tongue for his thumb, nipping, licking and pulling at her clit until she thought she'd explode from the intense waves of pleasure building in her core.

It seemed as if the entire world was centered in her cunt. Every nerve ending cried for him to fill her. "Damn you, fuck me. I can't wait."

Her body was on fire and only he could douse the flames. His tongue trailed a fiery path up and down her labia, then back to her clit. Each stroke sent her closer and closer to the edge.

Then mercifully, he laid her down on the floor, then lifted her legs over his shoulders and thrust deeply into her core, grinding and rotating her hips on his cock. Her inner walls gripped his rigid cock, but she was completely under his control.

It was a torturous and wondrous blending of male and female, yin and yang, night and day. From the most primal expression to the most spiritual of pleasures, she experienced them as they wrestled, thrust and loved. Sensation after sensation banished her cares and memories until she lost all sense of time and place. Every slamming stroke set her on fire. And the growing blaze he built in her made every cell of her body ignite and go up in flames.

Faraway, someone shrieked Mac's name.

Chapter Eighteen

Somehow the next morning Rilla made it to work. Damn the budget. She shook her head in disgust at the figures on the spreadsheet. No matter how she tried, she couldn't get the numbers to come out right. No wonder. She couldn't get her thoughts in order enough to do the budget.

Mac had left her bed entirely too soon. She'd hoped to wake up with him lying by her side. Instead, sometime during the early morning hours, he'd sneaked out without waking her.

Damn him. No, he was right. No point in her getting used to his company. He'd be leaving town as soon as the case against Kurt and Bellows was completed.

Back to the damn budget. She had to cut expenses. The state was giving the county less money than last year and expenses were higher. Her proposed budget was a joke. How had her daddy ever waded his way through this ordeal year after year? There wasn't even enough money in the county coffers to hire a part-time accountant.

Well, at least she knew one position about to be cut. About time, too. The one person she'd hoped she could trust—the bitch.

R.J.'s loss was an even bigger one. She'd have to replace him as soon as possible.

Before she could throw her hands up in utter disgust, there was a knock at the office door.

Cheeks pink with obvious excitement, Detective-*Traitor* Bellows literally bounced into Rilla's office.

"Sheriff, I've heard from him. The next meet is on for tonight. He says we can come to terms."

"You still don't recognize his voice?"

"No, he used one of those voice altering mechanisms."

Sure he did. "How do you suggest we proceed?"

"What I suggest is we go in early, set up surveillance. We can retrieve it tomorrow after the meet. That way we'll know who he is without his being the wiser."

"I thought you were blindfolded," Rilla said.

"This time, he left me directions."

Instead of jumping across her desk and strangling the detective, Rilla clenched her jaw and fists then followed with a deep breath. "You think we can gain access to the cabin without his knowledge?"

"He doesn't live there. The cabin was almost empty, and the furniture was covered in dust. All we have to do is go in early, and we'll have him on tape. Just think of it!"

As soon as Bellows sashayed out, Rilla snatched the telephone and punched in Mac's number. "Come on. Come on."

As soon as Rilla could sneak away from the office without Kit's noticing, she drove home. Now she perched on an unpacked box in her living room as far away as she could get from Mac. Wisely he'd chosen another box by the window. In spite of the distance between them, his mere presence in the same room had her body twitching in places it had no business twitching...not when it when the end of the case was so close at hand.

"Bellows has set up a meet with our dealer for tonight. She and I are supposed to go in early and set up surveillance."

Mac frowned. “Tonight? That doesn’t give us much time. So you’re just supposed to walk into her trap?”

“As far as I can tell, that’s her plan.”

“See here. You can’t do it.”

“You’ll be there as backup, and I’m guessing your friend, Roxy, the so-called waitress, will be there, too. That’s plenty. I’ll be fine.”

“Jensen isn’t likely to do his own dirty work. He’s hired a hit man twice.”

As much as she hated to admit it, Mac was right, and an image of the hit man’s face swam before her eyes.

Focus. “Bellows’ll be his hitter this time. I can’t believe I bought her act. She’s always around, always helpful. Too helpful. This plan has been in place for a long time. She had the right credentials. I trusted her—the bitch.”

“You’re right. He’ll use *her* to take you out, but don’t forget his hit man. I wouldn’t put it past him to stick around and finish his job. Those guys like to earn their fees. Their reputations depend on it.”

A chill crawled up her back. “There’s been no sign of him. He’s probably in Canada or under some rock by now. Besides, there haven’t been any more attempts.”

“Bellows’ trap is the perfect opportunity. One way or another, they don’t expect you to leave the cabin alive.”

A burst of adrenaline surged through her, shoving her heartbeat over the speed limit. “So we form our plan. And take them all.”

“Who do you trust?”

“In my office? No one.”

Mac shook his head. “I don’t like it. We need more backup.”

“We don’t have time. Wait—I’ll call Jase. He’s with the TBI I trust him.”

"TBI doesn't need to get involved at this point." He shook his head and sneered.

"Mac, TBI has jurisdiction on drug cases."

"Not in *my* investigation. And they'll be pissed we've waited until the last minute to notify them."

"That's nothing new. Look, Jason Keyes is an old pal of mine. I'll call him and—" She reached for her cell phone.

"No. This is my case."

She set her hands on her hips. "I can't believe this territorial crap is coming from you. Besides, you've forgotten something."

"And that would be?" Mac couldn't keep the ice from his tone. Damn. She pushed his buttons like no one else.

"Part of being a good agent is knowing when to ask for help or backup, as the case may be."

He averted his gaze from Rilla, stood and started pacing. Damn. Right again. They did need backup, and he was risking everything—not only the case but her, too.

He turned and faced her. "Suit yourself. Go on. Call your pal."

"You know I'm right."

"I have to say it?"

"No, the tortured expression on your face says it for me." She laughed and opened her cell. "I have him on speed dial," she said with a wide grin.

After calling Jase and giving him the details on the meet, she turned her attention to Mac. "Are you going to tell me what's going on in that devious mind of yours?"

Fists clenched, he sucked in a deep breath. "Now you're my shrink?"

"You need one?"

"Look, I'm on shaky ground with the Agency after my last screw-up. I can't afford to blow the case...for any reason."

Furthermore, he didn't have a right to risk their lives in an undermanned mission. His arrogance didn't reach that far. Might as well fess up.

"You're right."

"That didn't hurt, now did it?" She hid the smile tweaking the corner of her mouth.

"You wouldn't understand. It's a guy thing."

"I guess not, being a gal."

A few hours later, from her living room window, Rilla watched Jason Keyes haul his lanky body from a gray Ford Taurus. She opened the front door, stepped onto the porch and called to him. "Thanks for meeting here instead of my office. The third team member will be here any minute."

"Anything for a comrade-in-arms, Sheriff Devane," he drawled.

"In fact, she's pulling in right behind you." Roxy Quinlan's black Camry pulled into the driveway and parked.

Jase stepped onto the porch. "Good deal, hon. You think the three of us are enough backup? I would've been glad to call in more."

"It's Mac's jurisdiction—his call."

"Not necessarily. TBI has jurisdiction in drug cases." He folded his arms and leaned against a porch column.

"Don't nitpick. You know DEA trumps TBI and the locals."

Her old pal grinned and shrugged.

Before she could fire back with a smart-ass answer, Roxy Quinlan joined them on the porch and wasted no time giving the TBI agent a long, appraising look.

"Introductions," Rilla said. "Mac Callahan and Roxy Quinlan, DEA. Jason Keyes, TBI."

"Now we know the players, what's the score?" Jase asked.

Mac spoke first. "Sheriff's department has a dirty detective in league with the local drug connection. Rilla's supposed to go with her to plant a surveillance camera to trap the dealer. But we're pretty damned sure it's a trap. Rilla will go in first with the detective. We're her backup. We'll take down the dealer and the detective. And this town will be minus two players."

"Sounds like a plan." Jason turned to Rilla. "This okay with you? Being bait?"

"Damn straight." Rilla nodded. "The way I see it, Bellows will take me to the meet, then she'll take me out—or try to. Her dealer will be there to make it look good, but he'll let her do the dirty work."

"Not a hands-on kind of guy?"

"No. Even though we can't prove it conclusively yet, we're sure he's the one who hired Daddy's shooter."

"Some proof would be nice. It would certainly clear some cases, wouldn't it?" Jase said with a wry grin. "So who is our drug connection?"

"Bear this in mind," Mac said. "What we know is part circumstantial...and gut instinct. Detective Bellows tells us she met someone in a cabin in the state park, but he supposedly used a voice-altering device."

"I take it you didn't believe her."

Mac laughed. "Not unless she was looking for the device with her tongue down Kurt Jensen's throat."

"You followed her?" Jase raised an eyebrow.

"At the last minute, Bellows refused backup. Said it might compromise the mission." Mac winked at Rilla. "The sheriff and I decided a little backup never hurt anyone."

"Okay, let's get you wired." Jason shot Rilla a wicked grin. He dangled the tiny receiver and transmitter in her face.

"I'll take that, thank you very much." She snatched the surveillance equipment and turned to Agent Quinlan. "Mind doing the honors?"

"Are we going to stand around jacking our jaws all night, or are we gonna take down a drug dealer?" Mac asked.

Quinlan grinned. "I'm always ready."

Rilla jerked her head in the direction of her bedroom. "In here."

Jase's mocking laughter followed her. "Didn't know you were so modest."

Inside the bedroom, the agent quickly had Rilla wired up for the mission. "So what's with you and Agent Keyes?"

"We're worked on a big case together when I worked for Metro. Just friends, but Jase is a tease."

"I can tell. Are you sure it isn't more for him?"

"No way. His wife would kill me. She's six-feet tall and a body builder. Believe me, Jase doesn't stray."

Roxy laughed. "Well, I still think your Agent Keyes is disappointed."

Mac walked into the bedroom with a scowl. "Agent Keyes'll get over it…or he'd better."

Roxy let out a hoot of laughter. "You've got it bad, Mac. I haven't seen you like this since—" She broke off.

Since what? His last mission, the one he screwed up? Rilla shrugged it off. This wasn't the time for a stroll down memory lane.

After leaving her backup team, Rilla met Bellows at the office where they collected their surveillance equipment for the cabin. They drove to the state park, and after scouting the area around the cabin for any of the dealer's lookouts, Rilla took a deep breath and glanced over at Bellows. "You ready?"

"Ready as I'll ever be." Bellows rubbed her hands together. The detective was fairly vibrating with anticipation...the bitch.

"You're sure this is the right one? There's a couple dozen of these old cabins in the park, and they all look alike."

"The one thing I remembered seeing when Wyler took off the blindfold was the sign I tripped over in the path to the door. 'Hummingbird Lane', it said. I checked on line with the Parks Service and found the location on the campsite map."

"Good thinking."

Yeah, right. Old Kurt gave good directions. "But I don't remember your mentioning anything about the sign in your report."

Bellow's mouth formed an O. "Damn. Didn't I? Sorry, guess I should have. It must've slipped my mind."

Rilla shrugged away her rage. Just a little longer, and Kit Bellows would be bunking with some big bruiser of a woman named Hilda. "Anyway, let's get in there, wire the place and get the hell out."

"Sounds like a plan, boss."

Rilla nodded. Bellows had a plan all right, but the surprise would be on her.

Bellows' movements were antsy as she continued to yammer. "All we have to do is sit back and wait for our drug dealer to show his face at our next meet. We'll have him."

"You're sure he'll use the same place again?"

"Positive. Like I said, he already set it for here."

"Well, I'll feel a lot better once we're finished. Let's get a move on."

Because I can't wait to take you down, you no-good bitch.

She unsnapped her gun holster. The temptation to pull the weapon was so strong, her fingers curled in the palm of her hand. She sucked in a breath, let it out and forced her fingers to relax.

"What's the matter, Sheriff? This is a piece of cake. Five minutes in and out."

"Must be going soft out here in the sticks." Rilla forced a casual laugh through a throat almost closed with tension. In spite of backup, too many things could still go wrong.

"That's more like it."

Bellows' enthusiasm was plain, from the sparkle in her pale green eyes to the tip of tongue showing through her teeth. Well, just see if she was thrilled after it all went down.

"Let's do it." Rilla crouched and headed for the door. "I'll go in the front. Cover me, just in case."

"Got it."

Here goes nothing. As long as Bellows or Kurt didn't shoot her the second she opened the door, everything should go as planned.

As soon as Rilla and Bellows stepped inside the cabin, Mac motioned his team to advance. Rilla was coming in loud and clear, and so was the Bellows bitch. How Rilla was keeping her cool, he had no idea. Strangling the dirty cop was too good for her. There had to be a special place in Hell for officers who betrayed their own.

As planned, Quinlan moved to cover the rear of the cabin while he and Keyes moved in low from opposite sides of the small clearing in front of the cabin.

Whether or not Kurt would show up for the ambush, Mac wasn't sure, but somehow he doubted the drug dealer could resist the chance to rub Rilla's nose it in before killing her.

"Damn. It's dark in here." Rilla held her breath and waited for her eyes to adjust. Kit was so close behind she felt the detective's hot breath on her neck. She wanted to whirl around and put an end to the charade, but she needed to play dumb a little longer.

Her hand hovered near her weapon. Was she wrong about Bellows? No. Mac had seen her with Kurt. They had to be in it together.

"Come on, Kit. Let's get this over with."

"Just a sec. I'm looking for the light switch."

On cue, a light flashed in Rilla's eyes. No time for her eyes to adjust again—she averted her gaze from the glare.

It begins.

"Good evening, Sheriff. I'm glad you dropped in. It saves me a lot of trouble." Kurt's familiar voice came from the shadow behind the flashlight.

Play dumb and dumber...a little longer. Mac and Jase needed time to get into position.

She shaded her eyes from the glare. "Kurt? Is that you? What's going on?"

Behind Rilla, Bellows laughed, a sick gleeful sound which raised the hair on Rilla's neck.

"You're too stupid to live, much less be the almighty sheriff," Kurt said.

Rilla's hand settled on her gun butt.

"No you don't." The detective snatched the semi-automatic from Rilla's holster and held it up in the light. "Nice. Good taste in guns, but not much else."

She glanced at Kit and tried to appear as dumbfounded as her detective obviously thought she was. "I don't—I mean—"

Bellows laughed again. "I told you she'd never guess in a million years. It's the end of the book, and she's still on page one."

"Enough. Take the light. I want a little quality time with my old girl friend."

The flashlight bobbled as Kurt handed it to his accomplice.

Gun in hand, he stepped into the light. “So, have you figured it out yet?”

“Yeah.” Rilla swallowed hard. What was taking Mac so long? She’d have to assume they were covering her ass and draw it out until they had all they needed on tape.

“A little longer,” came Mac’s voice in her ear.

Keep Kurt talking.

“Why? Why would you do this?”

“Do what?”

“Sell drugs?”

“I’ve always been a drug dealer, girl. It’s merely a progression of my career plan.”

“And my father?”

“Your daddy didn’t want to share the wealth. Kind of backward that way. He didn’t mind looking the other way and taking payoffs on marijuana, but he drew the line at the more sophisticated offerings I had in mind.”

“You’re pond scum! I can’t believe—”

“To be fair, I offered him a cut, but his ethics—” He broke off and laughed. “Wouldn’t allow him to take more risk. Fortunately, his chief deputy wasn’t nearly as ethical—not in the beginning, anyway.”

“Where does Bellows fit into your deal?”

“Kit and I met in Chicago. I wouldn’t have been able to set up this operation without her help...my wife’s help, I should say. Her family is in the *distribution* end of the business. She followed me to town. *You* hired her. And now, you know it all.”

Outside the cabin, Mac nodded. They had almost everything they needed on tape. He spoke softly. “Keyes?”

“On mark.”

“Rox?”

“On mark.”

Roxy spoke next. "I'm ready at the back door."

"No line of site here," Keyes said. "Curtains are closed."

"Damn. Another minute. Let's get all we can."

Rilla stood stock still during Bellows' frisk, hoping the traitor would miss the backup piece under her vest. No such luck.

"Oh, Sheriff, you're a bad girl." Bellows ripped the Smith and Wesson 642 from Rilla's second holster, then waved it in the air before tossing the weapon aside.

"Good thing you found that, darlin'." Kurt moved closer to Rilla. "Now that you're unarmed, I think I'd like one last taste of your sweetness before my darlin' wife shoots you."

Rilla backed up and snarled, "Like hell."

"Kurt! Stop fooling around."

"I'm not fooling around, sugar. Did I never tell you how sweet she was at seventeen...? And hot. Lordy, she was hot as a pistol. Couldn't wait to give it up, could you?"

"Careful. You're making your wife jealous. Better not piss her off, Kurt. She's got a gun, too."

He shoved a gun barrel under her chin. She flinched away from the cold steel.

With his other hand, he unbuttoned the top button of her uniform shirt. She gritted her teeth. Every muscle tensed as the urge to puke twisted her gut. If she didn't have enough evidence on tape by now, she never would. Where the hell was her backup?

Kurt undid another button and grinned. "Lovely." Using the barrel, he flipped back her lapels. "Just a small taste. Cover me, doll. Kill her if she moves." He licked his lips and bent forward.

"Dammit, Kurt!" Kit yelled from the corner of the room.

He glanced away. "Shut up!"

An opening. She cupped her hands and delivered simultaneous blows to his ears while she jammed her knee into his balls.

Kurt went down with a loud roar. Seizing her chance, Rilla dived and rolled for cover. A bullet struck the log wall behind her, followed by quick spits of a silenced revolver—Bellows'?

Rilla pulled herself forward with one elbow and tried to find where Kit had tossed the revolver—no luck.

"Bitch!" Bellows screamed, "You're dead now." She dropped the flashlight and fired wildly.

Rilla counted the shots. Five or was it six? Kit still had Rilla's primary weapon—it held eleven rounds including the one she'd chambered.

Kurt rolled around on the floor, still grabbing his balls, and yelled, "Kill *her!* Not me! Damn it."

"Quit whining like a kid!" Kit yelled back.

A glint of metal. God! Kurt's gun lay at the shadow's perimeter. Rilla inched her hand from beneath the table where she could make out the shape of the weapon.

The door burst open.

About damned time.

"Rilla?" Mac called.

The beams from three flashlights played around the room. "I'm fine." She grabbed Kurt's gun and emerged from her hiding spot.

"That's what you think, bitch!"

A beam of light caught Kit in its glare. Rilla sucked in a breath. The detective had Rilla's weapon aimed at her head. "Stay back or she's dead."

"Go ahead," Rilla said with a calmness which hadn't quite made its way to her heart. "Shit, Bellows. It'll make a mess, but don't worry about cleaning it up. You won't be around."

The woman's face turned red. The gun trembled in her hand. Indecision was written clearly across her face as her gaze darted from the agents covering her to Kurt on the floor. Finally she held out the weapon, butt first. Rilla stepped forward and snatched it from her.

"You fucking loser!" Kit screamed at Kurt. "This is your fault." Then she turned a cool face to the agents. "I want a deal. I'll tell you everything."

Chapter Nineteen

Rilla wrestled Kurt's hands and arms behind him and snapped on the handcuffs none too gently. "You bastard." From his spot on the ground, Kurt groaned and glared at Roxy who'd already cuffed and shoved Kit into the back of Rilla's Jeep.

All the lives wrecked. Anger frothed in Rilla's throat. "*You.* A trusted businessman and an old friend. All this time, it was you. You killed my father. Tried to have me killed. Barbie Soames, R.J., all of them. You're responsible."

Kurt shrugged as if he didn't have a care in the world. "You surely don't expect me to confess like some felon on T.V.?"

"And you thought I'd walk into your trap without a wire? You don't have to confess. We already have you on tape. You won't see the outside of a prison cell as long as you live."

He sat up, raised an eyebrow and shrugged. "Win some. Lose some."

"Sorry son of a—" She grabbed Kurt by the shirt and jerked him to his feet. Her breath came in gasps. Rage shot through her. This was the man responsible for killing her father. Anger shook her body as hard as if she were firing an Uzi. "I'd kill you myself if there weren't so many witnesses. Then again..." She smiled and shoved him to the ground...slowly pulled her weapon.

"Rilla!" Mac jerked her elbow, reached around, and pried the gun from her hand. "Come on. You don't want to do that."

It would take someone smarter than the local constabulary to pierce his disguise. The buggers had plastered pictures of him all over town. He couldn't walk ten steps without coming face-to-face with one of the bloody things. He'd almost turned and walked out of the grocery when he'd seen the first one. But his disguise held. The little scrawny cashier had stared at him a second longer than necessary and nearly talked his ear off about the sheriff's being a good law enforcement officer as well as her good friend.

He'd made a big mistake in not killing the sheriff when he'd had the chance. No. He'd grown too bloody fond of the sound of his own voice. And the yokel of a deputy had come along at the wrong time.

Now he had unfinished business. All he had to do was what he'd failed to do the last time. And do it up close and personal just to prove to his employer he could do the job...even though up close hadn't worked out so well the last time. He'd underestimated the sheriff, but this time he wouldn't. And what better lure than a little old lady who was her friend?

Mildred Tweedy glared at the stranger. A stranger with a knife. "It won't do you any good to point a gun at me. I'm an old lady and ready to meet my Maker. He'll take me in his arms..."

"Stop yer blather."

"Tell me something. Are you stupid?"

"Don't call me stupid."

"You must be. We're not alone. My boarder is in bed asleep, but if you keep makin' all this noise, he'll wake up. He's a very big man with a gun." The Lord would surely forgive her for telling such whoppers.

"Wake him."

"No. See, you don't want to mess with him. He's known for his mean ways. Probably not much worse than you are. Though

I doubt he's ever hog-tied an old lady and threatened her with a knife."

"Is that so? What if I think yer bluffin'?"

"Don't care what *you* think."

"Shut yer mouth. I'm tired of yer white trash accent."

"I talk like everbody else around here. You're the one with the accent. You're some kind of furriner. Not only that, I just bet you're the no-good scallywag who conked me—"

"Shut up!" He held the knife to her throat. "Now make the phone call. Call the sheriff."

Hours later, after all her reports were entered and filed, Rilla clasped her hands behind her neck and stretched the kinks from her shoulders and back.

"All done?" Mac asked from the doorway, his long, lean body looking too damn good for words. But he'd be leaving now. His assignment was over. No point in her getting all worked up over his body or his sexy smile.

"Yeah." She repressed a yawn, which begged for release. Pushing back her chair, she stood. "I'm heading home. You through, too?"

"For now. Want to go back to my place?" He took a step toward her, slid his arms around her waist and pulled her to him. As much as she wanted him, her muscles were limp as over-cooked spaghetti.

"Unh-uh. Right now, I want a bath. Have to wash—" she glanced toward lockup "—their filth off me...and outta my head."

"Been a long day. I'll walk you to your car. Or I *could* drive you home," he suggested, the hope apparent in his tone.

"I'd be poor company." Might as well let him go and get it over with.

When they reached the Jeep, he opened the door, leaned forward and kissed the tip of her nose. He was so sweet. Why shouldn't she simply go home with him and enjoy what time there was left? No. It would hurt even more than it did now.

"I have a lot to sort out, Mac."

"It's over, hon." His mouth descended on hers, his kiss heated yet tender. He pulled back. "Call me before you go to bed…to say goodnight, will you?"

She smiled. *Goodnight, not good-bye?* Well, it would come soon enough. "I will. Thanks for understanding."

"I mean it. Call me."

She nodded and climbed into the Jeep. "I will."

Liam took a bite of pizza and glanced over at his elderly hostage. She sat and struggled against her bonds. He chewed and swallowed. "I do appreciate ye lettin' me have a piece of your dinner."

The old biddy managed a muffled, "Mnf."

"That's it. Soon enough, I'll be letting ye speak. Mind ye, only what suits me…if ye want to live, tha 'tis."

His words brought a renewed struggle. "Never mind, me darlin', 'tis sorry I am for puttin' ye through this ordeal. Ye almost remind me of me own ma. Almost. Hellcat temper she had. Best ye be calm and not risk mine."

He glanced around at his hostage's comfortable furnishings and lace curtains. Nothing worth taking, but nothing lacking, either. His old mother would've thought herself fortunate to have the comfort of the tidy house instead of the coldwater flat where she'd died of consumption.

"In a few minutes, I'll have ye make a phone call to yer lovely sheriff. Convince her someone be breaking into yer house. Indeed, ye have." He smiled. "Can ye do it? Without spilling the secret of me presence?"

The old woman glared back at him. Defiant to the end, she was.

He pulled the hunting knife from his belt, allowing the light to glint along the well-honed edge.

His hostage's eyes widened and her shoulders twitched. He laughed. "Now this is a beauty, 'tis. So sharp, I could slice yer throat so easy and quick, ye'd never notice 'til yer little apron was awash with blood. More's the pity."

Her eyes grew round like saucers. Fear did that. And heaven knew the poor old thing had reason aplenty to be afraid.

"But we can't have that now, can we? The sheriff might get suspicious if ye answer the door with a cut throat." He sniggered at his joke. "No, I want the sheriff to hurry over here to reassure her old teacher the boogey man isn't hiding in the closet... Except he is."

He leaned down, but she averted her face, refusing to look at the knife. Carefully he laid the flat of the blade against her wrinkled neck.

A muffled sob shook her wiry body.

"Now, now, Grandma. 'Twon't be long."

Rilla drove homeward, stifled a yawn while she rubbed the sleep from her eyes. Going twenty-four hours without sleep wasn't high on her list of favorite things. True, she'd done it more than once, but tonight had taken an emotional toll as well as physical.

She had incontrovertible proof Kit Bellows had betrayed her badge. Bellows had been the closest thing to a girlfriend Rilla'd had since coming home.

A squawk emitted from her comm unit, snapping her wide awake.

"Sheriff?"

"Yeah?"

"I know you're on your way home, but Miz Tweedy says she's in a bad way. Needs you to come right now."

After a mental groan, she asked, "What's her problem this time?"

"Says she hears a noise. Hit man or someone in her attic."

"Probably a squirrel. Okay, she's on my way. I'll swing by and reassure her." Damn, the twenty-four/seven crap was getting old.

She gunned the accelerator and whipped the steering wheel into a sharp left turn.

Without warning, the prickles started crawling on her neck. She took her foot off the gas. Mac's words about the hit man sticking around to finish the job echoed in her mind. Call it gut instinct. Maybe Miss Tweedy *wasn't* crying wolf this time. How did Miss Tweedy even know about a hit man? Okay, maybe she'd seen the posters. The thought of an innocent like her old school teacher in the hands of a cold-blooded contract killer sent a wave of nausea roiling through her stomach. Her throat dry as cotton, she swallowed.

She hadn't felt this on-edge and uneasy since she and her last partner had nearly waltzed into an undercover drug buy which was meant to be an ambush. Their gut instincts had warned them in time and put them on guard.

Like she was now.

"Son of a bitch better not hurt her."

If she wasn't imagining it all. But what if she was wrong? Well, Mac would have a good laugh at her expense. So what?

She grabbed her cell phone and punched in Mac's number.

Damn. Voice mail.

"I hope you get this damn soon, undercover boy, 'cause I'm in serious need of some backup. Just got a nuisance call from Miss Tweedy. I know it's a wild hunch, and don't ask questions, but I think our hit man is holding Miss Tweedy... Anyway I'm heading over there right now. Approaching on foot from the rear. Hope I'm wrong. Hope to see you soon."

She pulled the Jeep into the convenience store parking lot a half block from Miss Tweedy's, then parked behind the store. Easing from the vehicle, she closed the door, pulled her weapon and chambered a round. In a crouched run, she headed down the alley which ran behind Miss Tweedy's property.

Gun drawn, she eased around to the back porch. After making a full circuit of the two story frame house, she still couldn't banish the elephants now doing a Texas Two-step in her stomach. The shades were drawn. All was quiet.

Too quiet for someone who'd called for help.

She stepped up on the back porch and held her breath. It didn't creak. She tested the screen door.

Open.

The kitchen was dark. If she could get inside without alerting anyone, including Miss Tweedy who might just decide to let loose with both barrels of her shotgun...

She walked through the darkened kitchen, slowly, one step at a time. After each step, she stopped, waited and listened.

Nothing. Not a single sound. *Nada.*

She paused at the doorway into the dining room. It too was dark, but a dim light was visible from the living room.

Why wasn't Miss Tweedy hovering anxiously at the front door, peeking out through the white lace curtains?

She eased to the doorway of the living room. The top of the old woman's gray head was barely visible over the top of her rocking chair. All seemed quiet, but something was off because the two-stepping elephants had just segued from a jitter-bug into a vigorous flamenco.

The hair stood on her nape. Too late to turn back.

Behind her, the click of a hammer drawn.

She froze.

Chapter Twenty

"Excellent choice, Sheriff," came the familiar Irish brogue. "I'll be takin' yer weapon. No fast moves or they'll be yer last."

"Miss Tweedy, are you all right?"

The good woman turned to Rilla. Her mouth was taped, but she nodded.

The Irish assassin would kill both of them unless she came up with a plan damn fast. He hadn't come for a piece of Miss Tweedy's apple pie—he was here because of a loose end.

Slowly she turned around. In the darkness she could make out his tall form against the drawn shade on the far side of the room.

Her heart slammed in her chest, and it took every ounce of self control to control the burst of adrenaline surging through her body. No sudden moves. No risky maneuvers against a man who out-weighed and out-meaned her.

"Very bright of ye, Sheriff. I wouldn't be makin' any desperate attempts to save yerself or the old lady."

"Let her go. She's served her purpose. I'm here."

"Sorry, she's seen me face. I can't be lettin' her describe me to whatever will be left of law enforcement in this pig patch of a town."

"Describe you? She's half blind. You have no idea how much money the grocery store's lost since she started working as a cashier."

“Clever, aren’t ya? ’Fraid I can’t take the chance. If I could, I’d not be here now. Ye’re a loose end and so’s the darlin’ old girl in the front parlor.”

“You haven’t hurt her?”

"“Not yet. I haven’t quite made up my mind about her manner of dying...”

“You son of a bitch. How can you stand there and talk about killing her like that? She can hear you.”

He laughed. “No, I be thinkin’ maybe she be half deaf, too. Now I need your weapon.”

She wrinkled her nose. “I’d rather not.”

He laughed again. And it didn’t lighten the atmosphere any better than his last attempt.

“’Tis a pity we don’t have more time. I find yer humor in the face of certain death charming. And brave. That’s why I’m here. After our last meetin’, I wanted to see ye again. Didn’t want to take ye out from a distance, even if ’tis the easier way.”

“Yeah, we might have a real mutual admiration society going here if you weren’t in such a damn hurry to kill me.” She waited a beat. “Why?”

“Why what?”

“I don’t understand how you can spend your life this way. There are plenty of causes, but you do it for the money. You kill people for money.”

“That’s the easy thing to explain. I’m one of those fortunate people who was born without a conscience. Need an outlet for me energy now that the Peace Movement has the upper hand on the old sod.”

“Glad to know you’re happy with your career choice.” *Okay, Mac, anytime now would be good.*

“I’m satisfied and I’m the best at what I do.” He began to move behind the round oak table.

Now or never.

Rilla threw her full weight and shoved the table into him.

Something hard and metallic clanged against the china cabinet. Glass shattered.

She dropped to the floor, scrambled beneath the table and grabbed for his ankles. He kicked her hand away.

"Bitch!"

Desperate, she felt the floor for his gun. Dammit, she'd heard it hit somewhere.

He heaved the table over her head. It crashed to the side, blocking the way to the kitchen.

Her cover gone, she rolled to her feet.

He landed a backhand blow to her cheek. Sharp needles of pain shot through her jaw and cheek bones. She staggered, but recovered her balance. She jammed her knee into his groin with a satisfying jar when her knee struck his pubic bone.

Groaning, he clutched his testicles and sank to his knees, a flood of Gaelic mingled with obscenities filled the room.

Her foe temporarily disabled, she scrambled for her weapon.

There. She snatched it and pulled back the hammer. "Hold it!"

More obscenities.

"Hey, mind your mouth. Miss Tweedy is a lady of gentle upbringing."

Aiming the weapon at his head, she reached with one hand for her cuffs.

His foot snaked out and swept her off her feet—her gun sailed across the room.

And landed somewhere behind her.

She rolled and scrambled to her knees, but he grabbed her braid and jerked her head back.

Then his hands were around her throat, cutting off her air. She forced herself to ignore the ever-tightening fingers digging into her throat. Her lungs burned. *Air.*

With all her strength, she rammed her elbow into his ribcage, pulled her knees under her body and forced her body back with the momentum of her kick.

His grip loosened. She sucked in the oxygen her brain needed and jumped to her feet.

Damn. He'd already regained his feet, if somewhat off-balance. He grabbed the corner of the china cabinet for support. She spun and kicked high to his head. The kick glanced off, but he paused long enough to shake his head.

"Bitch," he hissed and lunged, his long arms grappling for her. She dodged. No way could she let him get hold of her again.

Her fingers inched along the wall until she found the light switch. She flicked it on.

Nothing.

Her breath came in ragged gasps. She had to end this fight and soon. He was too experienced and too quick.

The front door of the house opened. "What the hell's going on here?"

At the sound of her mother's voice, Rilla spun around. And paid for that moment's distraction.

Without warning, the hit man was in her face again. He slammed her against the wall, his forearm shoved under her chin, cutting off her breath. "Who's that?" he growled.

"She's a renter."

"The old bird told me her renter was a man asleep in his room."

He relaxed his hold on her neck a bit. "So? She lied," Rilla said, then gasped for air.

"Rilla, honey, who—? Hey! What d'you think you're doing to my baby?"

Crap.

"The renter's yer ma?" The amusement in his tone didn't bode well for her outcome, either.

"Yes," she hissed.

He released his hold, and swung her body around, positioning her between him and her mother with his forearm still around Rilla's neck.

"Pay attention, dear. If you want yer daughter to live, ye'll keep your bony arse in the living room with the old girl."

Carefully Liz set her purse on the floor and leaned against the door jam. "What're you gonna do with her?"

Who knew her mother would show such presence of mind in the face of a stone-cold killer? Clearly knock-down, drag-out fights were common everyday occurrences in her life away from the Springs.

"She's taking a little ride with me, and if ye call anyone, I'll come back and slit yer scrawny neck for sure."

Rilla hiked her knee and jammed her heel on his instep. The hit man's hold loosened. She slipped from his grasp, whirled and front-punched his throat.

He gagged from the blow and staggered. "Bleedin' bitch. I've had enough o' this." He pulled a blade from the leather holder on his belt. He went in to a low crouch, the knife in his right hand waving in a wide menacing arc.

His arms longer than hers, his reach greater. She dipped and dodged to keep out of his grasp.

After Mac surrendered his prisoners to the U.S. Marshals, he jumped in his car and drove to Rilla's house.

The small frame house stood dark and deserted, nor was her Jeep in the driveway.

Damn. She should've been home by now.

He pulled into the driveway to make sure she hadn't pulled around to the back.

A low, moaning howl rose and echoed eerily though the night air. The dog.

Mac jumped out and tried the backdoor. Locked.

Fierce barking and growls erupted from the animal locked inside. Poor creature probably needed to take a piss in the worst way.

"Hey, Ralphie, it's me," he said through the door, hoping the dog would recognize his voice and calm down. If the dog kept scratching at the door, Rilla wouldn't have one by the time she returned.

Where the hell is she, anyway?

"Sorry, buddy, your mistress's alarm will kill your ears if I set the damn thing off. She oughta be home soon."

Hell. Here he was talking to her dog like it could understand every word he said. He must be losing it.

Ralphie let go with another low rising yowl.

What was that? Another sound—this one shriller than the dog's howl. His cell phone?

"Hush, Ralphie." Mac listened again, then sprinted for the car. He grabbed the phone, but not in time to keep it from going to voice mail. He waited, then listened to Rilla's hurried message.

"Damn!"

Rilla eased into the living room where she'd have more space to maneuver. Never taking her eyes from the blade, she said, "Mama, you and Miss Tweedy get out of here—if you can. Move her—chair and all."

A quizzical frown furrowed his brow. "Bloody hell! Do ye think yer gettin' out o' this?"

"Give it up. My backup will be here any second. You'll be surrounded."

He laughed, but it was a harsh sound. Good. She wanted him in an over-confident mood. Anything to give Mac time... Her mother and Miss Tweedy were moving around behind her, but they weren't out of harm's way—not yet.

"Girl, dear, if ye weren't such a pain in me arse, I believe I'd kiss ye. Yer the most entertainin' contract I've ever had."

He feinted with the knife, but she evaded the honed blade...barely.

"Close," he said, with an evil grin. "I'll get ye next time."

"Close doesn't count." Where were they? "Get down behind something," she ordered the women, not daring to take her eyes off her opponent.

Click-clack. The unmistakable sound of a shotgun readied for action.

The hit man's eyes widened. He shook his head. "Can't do it, can ye?"

Not willing to turn away from the hit man, Rilla held her breath. Which one of them had the shotgun? How good was her aim?

His gaze narrowed. His smile took on an ugly bent. "Takes a special—"

Boom!

He dropped. Blood sprayed in a glistening red arc along with a spate of pellets. She jumped aside, but the fiery stinging in her left arm and ribs told her she hadn't dodged quickly enough.

Her mother walked over to Liam's body and gave an indignant sniff. "I told him he'd better not mess with my baby."

My baby. Her mother's maternal nature may have kicked in late, but better late than dead.

The front door opened with a crash, and Mac peered inside. “Dammit, Rilla. Are you all right?” His gaze traveled from Rilla to the body on the floor. “I guess I’m a little late.”

“You got that right,” her mother said, then laid the shotgun on the sofa.

Rilla allowed Mac to pull her into his arms. Warm and safe against his chest, she took a deep breath. Liz was already at work, cutting away Miss Tweedy’s bindings. They had a bit of blood spatter on the front of their clothes. Nothing major there. Thank God.

“Rilla, hon,” he said gently. “Are you all right?”

She nodded rapidly. “I’m fine. Just a few pellets,” she said, brushing away her injuries with a shrug.

But she couldn’t control her trembling body.

“You’re one tough lady, but I’m taking you to the hospital. Those pellets have to come out.”

As much as she wanted to take him up on his offer, she shook her head. “Not now. After all this is cleared.”

“Paperwork’ll be there in the morning.”

“But I have to wait for the medical examiner. Have to turn the shotgun over for ballistics.” She shook her head, struggling to bring the details of a officer-related shooting to mind, but her brain whirled with having almost been killed. Her mother had killed the hit man. Her mother had saved her life and Miss Tweedy’s, too.

“Department policy. Jason will interview me here at the scene as well.” She sighed. “And I need to call the D.A.”

“You’re hurt. You need a doctor.”

“It’s just a little buckshot.” She waved away his objections. “It can wait a while. I need to straighten out some things here, too.”

Liz stepped forward. “No, you don’t. You need medical treatment.”

Mac grinned. "Ms. Downey, why don't you and Miss Tweedy go upstairs away from this." He glanced at the body on the floor. "I'll make the calls. Agent Keyes probably hasn't made it home yet. And I'm calling a doctor, too."

Liz removed the last bit of tape from Miss Tweedy's mouth. "Lord a-mercy, Rilla. Never been so scared in all my born days," Miss Tweedy said. "And, Mary Elizabeth, you're a hell of a shot. For the life of me, I can't imagine where you learned to handle a gun like that."

"You don't want to know, Miss Tweedy," Liz said with a wink and ducked her head.

What *had* her mother been up to in the last twenty-seven or so years?

"Get the first aid kit out of the bathroom cabinet," Miss Tweedy said. "Likely Rilla here's gonna bleed to death while we chew the fat."

Rilla snorted. Nothing could keep that old woman down—not even being terrorized by a hit man.

Liz ran for the kit. Why wasn't Liz upset either? The more she got to know the woman who gave her birth, the more confused Rilla was.

Liz returned and handed Mac the first aid kit. "Don't you let her out of here until you at least wash off those places with some soap." She turned to Miss Tweedy. "Let's you and me get ourselves upstairs. Don't know about you, but I'm sick of lookin' at that dead body."

"We'll get your statements in the morning," Rilla called after her mother.

He leaned over Rilla shoulder. "Now I know where you inherited your stubbornness."

Chapter Twenty-one

Hours later, Rilla dragged herself home. All she wanted was a hot bath and a couple of hours sleep. Once the Jacuzzi had filled, she added the scented bath oil. Suddenly, the clean scent of citrus filled the bathroom. She intensified the scent by lighting the candles which came with the bath set her grandmother had left on her last visit.

She looped her braid into a figure-eight and pinned it on top of her head. Then she eased her overused body into the fragrant, bubbling water. “Ah, wonderful.” She couldn’t keep from sighing as the warmth began to soothe her aching muscles. A plastic bandage sealed her wounds from the moisture of the bath.

Her father’s installing the whirlpool tub was one of the few upgrades he’d made to the house while she was living in Nashville. Probably bought with drug money. But maybe not. Anyway, it was here and she was going to enjoy it.

She folded a towel into a roll, placed it behind her neck and rested her head on it. The warmth and the pounding jets of the Jacuzzi could now do their work. Drifting on a pleasant plane of memory, she felt a hand at her breast.

She opened her eyes. “What are you doing here? How did you get in? Why didn’t Ralphie—”

Mac stopped her with a light kiss on her forehead. "Hush, I gave him a treat. Did you think you would be able to sneak away from the office and from me?"

He flipped down the commode lid and sat. With a broad smile, he leaned back against the tank and watched her. "Besides, Ralphie likes me almost as much as you do."

"Yeah?" She took the sponge and squeezed it, letting the fragrant, steamy water trickle down her back. "You sound pretty sure of yourself."

His brows drew together in a frown, but somehow his dark blue eyes still glimmered with amusement. "Are you saying you *don't* like me?"

"No." She smiled. Like him? Hell, she loved him—for all the good it would do. Why bother to explain when he'd be gone in another twenty-four hours?

"Being cryptic doesn't suit you."

"How so?"

"Well, maybe it's just me, but we have something...together, I mean."

She giggled. "What we've had are some good times."

"More than good times." Mac leaned forward and rested his elbows on his knees. His expression was earnest as if what she thought really mattered. "We worked as a team, and we took some bad guys off the street."

"It's true. We did." She smiled and sponged more water over her breasts. She sank down to her neck again. "Mm."

"And your mother?" Mac said with a grin. "Maybe you should hire her on as a deputy."

She did the eye roll. "Hm. I'm thinking that's not one of your better ideas."

"How's this for an idea? We could be a good team."

She sighed. The tension was melting away. “You mean in the twenty-four hours you have left in town?” She held out her arm. “Hand me a towel.”

He shook his head. “I have a better idea.”

She shot him her skeptical smile. “Really?”

“Really,” he said with a grin. He quickly slipped out of his clothes, his gaze darkening into slate as he nimbly he stepped into the Jacuzzi, sat behind her and started kneading the muscles in her neck and shoulders.

His hands were magic...even better than the whirlpool. He was gentle but strong, and he seemed to know exactly which muscles needed his attention before she knew herself. She relaxed back in his arms, her head resting on his chest. With one hand, he reached forward and cupped one of her breasts. With the other hand, he found her clit. She rocked against his fingers and retaliated by running her nails up his inner thigh. There was an immediate response—his dick hardened and poked at her butt.

“Hmm, did I do that? I must say, I’ve never known you to be so, so—what’s the word I’m looking for? Oh yes, excitable.” She loved the effect she had on him. What woman wouldn’t?

“Excitable? You think I’m the excitable type?” His tone dropped into a soft, seductive range that gave her twitches all over.

“Yes.” She squirmed, rubbing her bottom against his hard dick. She’d never...ever. But curiosity, and desire, too, nudged her ass closer to his dick. He was so large...how could he fit?

He groaned and pulled her closer, spread her ass cheeks and rubbed his dick up and down her crack. “Careful,” he breathed in her ear. “You’re tempting me to do something...”

His long fingers slithered from her clit to her ass. Her breath caught in her throat. “Uh—”

"I'll be easy. You're wet." He reached for the bath oil and poured it into his palm. "This'll help. But stop me if... Oh, hell, get over on your knees and elbows," he said, his tone a low rasp.

Thighs shaking with anticipation, she complied and propped her elbows on the ledge. He slathered the oil on his dick and then on her ass and deeply into her crack. With one long finger he probed her asshole. That wasn't so bad, but the disparity between the size of his finger and his dick. Oh, God, what was she about to let him do?

She tensed as his finger was withdrawn. His dick bobbed at her rear opening, sending twinges from her back passage to her core. God. She wanted him to do something, anything.

"Don't tense up," he breathed into her ear and kept massaging her clit. Threads of warmth and desire wove through her body and centered between her legs. Without conscious thought, she wiggled her bottom closer to his hard cock.

The next sensation was his oil-slick penis rubbing at her anal entrance. "Take a slow, deep breath," he said, and followed by inserting one, then two fingers, preparing her.

She nodded, then the head of his dick breached her opening while he continued to massage her clit...harder and harder. He pushed inside, filling her. "Okay?"

Her breaths came hot and rapid, but she managed to nod. Sensations of stretching and filling, along with his constant attentions to her clit, had every nerve ending in her body on fire. Unable to resist the urge, she moved her hips against his pressing dick. In response, he grasped her breasts and slid deeper inside. Her body burned and begged for release. She thrust backwards, tightly gripping his cock with her muscles.

Slippery with bath oil, their bodies smacked together in wet slaps as they moved together and apart. With one hand supporting herself, she massaged her clit with the other as he drove into her over and over until...

Her vision grew dim, and a kaleidoscope of color burst along with the pulsing of her inner walls. She cried his name and nearly collapsed, gasping as waves of release swept through her entire body.

No man had ever...ever done anything like this to her. Why him? Why had she let this man, one who would soon be leaving town, do something so extreme—extremely satisfying, that is?

Mac watched Rilla sleep. She slept deeply and soundly like a child, molded to his side. He wished he could express the love he felt for her. The words had never been spoken between them. He wasn't free to say them, and she deserved so much more than his love. But love her he did. She would awaken eventually, and he had to banish any trace of post-coital angst. Nothing must cast a shadow over this time with her. Maybe one of the last times they would spend time like this. He wanted to enjoy it, revel in it and forget his duty to the DEA, if only for a day.

He felt her shift into a lighter stage of sleep. She began to move closer to him, if possible. Her eyelids fluttered. A barely audible sigh escaped her lovely lips. He gently stroked her eyelids with the pad of his thumb and traced the angle of her sculpted cheekbones. Her eyelids fluttered open.

"What—mm." She looked about in momentary confusion. "I forgot you were here."

"Yeah, still here...for now," he murmured and began to nibble her delicate ear lobe. He only knew one way to banish his pain. Rilla was more than an antidote, she was fast becoming embedded in his heart and soul, and losing himself in her was the sheerest heaven he knew.

Rilla caressed Mac's cheek with her fingertip. His face was so fine, so strong. "When are you leaving?"

"Tomorrow."

It was already after midnight. "So...this is..."

"...our last time together."

She sat up and choked out the words. "I need some sleep. You need to go."

"Come with me."

"Go with you?" If only she could. The thought of never seeing him again wrenched through her. She bit the inside of her lip. No point in letting him see her pain.

He shifted and leaned toward her. Moonlight shone through the window, casting a luminous glow over his muscular body.

"The DEA could use you. You're too good for this town. Your talents are wasted."

"No." She shook her head. Didn't he know anything about her? Didn't he know he'd asked the impossible? "I belong here. I have to finish out my father's term. We're short-handed now, what with R.J.'s death and Bellows in custody."

"So you're all about the job? No time for more than a quick roll in the hay?"

His terse tone knifed through her. "It's not like that. And you damn well know it. I'm realistic. I have responsibilities and I'm tied to this county. You're a government agent. You'll go on to your next assignment, and I'll decide whether or not I'll run for office in November."

"You haven't decided yet?"

"No." If he wasn't going to leave her bed, she would. His heat was too seductive. All she wanted was to surrender to his arms again.

"You won't come with me?"

"I can't. What word didn't you understand?" Dammit, yes. The idea was intoxicating. But how could she? Her father had betrayed the very people he'd sworn to protect. She had to show everyone—and herself—she was made of sterner stuff.

"And there's my mother..." She groaned. "I want her to move in with me, and I don't know how long she has."

"Even though she abandoned you as a child? You want to take her in?" He put his arms around her waist, nuzzled her neck and let out a sigh. "You're the best human I've ever known, Rilla Devane. Bar none."

Her throat closed with the love and agony flooding every cell of her body. "I'm just doing what's right."

"I love you, woman."

He loved her. Disbelief rocked her through her mind and body. He'd actually said the words. Words she'd never thought to hear from him. She gazed into his eyes. He was so dear. "I'm in love with *you*. But it's not enough. We're too different. Our lives are going in different directions."

"But they don't have to."

God, had she said the words? Yes, she loved him. As independent as she was, she felt safe, complete with him at her side. Why couldn't he...?

No. She couldn't ask him to give up his career any more than he would insist she leave her home. And Cherokee Springs *was* her home, and the people were part of her extended family. It was the one constant in her life.

"No." She gazed into his eyes and shook her head as the grief welled and gathered in her heart. "You know I'm right." She grazed his unshaven cheek with a fingertip and loved every inch of his sandpapery skin.

His gaze softened. "Rilla..." He cradled her face gently between his strong hands, placing a tender kiss on her forehead. "You're not giving me much of a choice here."

The regret in his voice sent a sickening lurch all the way to her stomach. Was she making a mistake? Letting him go?

Probably. She loved him too much to keep him in a backwater Tennessee town. It would be so much simpler if he'd truly been a writer. "You're making this so hard. Please leave."

He caressed her cheek, then wiped away her tears. "I don't want to hurt you, just love you..."

She tried to smile, but tears stung her eyes and a lump lodged in her throat and wouldn't go away. She swallowed. "If you don't leave now..." She sat up and swung her legs over the side of the bed.

"I'm staying the night." Barely above a whisper, his tone infected her with his urgency. "Let me love you one last time."

A moan ripped from deep inside her. She lay down beside him. Her arms went round his neck and she buried her face in his shoulder. His heart pounded against her chest as he encircled her in the warmth of his arms.

Mac held her as gently as a child. How could he bear to leave this woman?

"No rush this time, Rilla."

"But—"

He stopped her protest with his lips. He claimed her mouth as if surrender were her only option.

And it was.

Wondering if he would ever have the strength to leave her, he freed her hair from the braid and let it spill across the pillows like watered silk. For the last time. "God. You're lovely."

She trembled in his arms. "Mac..."

"Shh. I'm in charge."

He left a slow trail of kisses from the hollow of her neck, to her breasts, her belly and finally down to the crisp, dark curls at the apex of her thighs.

He parted her legs and inhaled the scent of her musk, separated the delicate folds and flicked at the sensitive nub with his tongue.

Her thighs trembled and her hips gyrated from side to side.

She breathed his name, a soft, sweet sigh.

"Not yet, babe." He settled his body over hers, his erection hard against her belly. Replacing his tongue with two fingers, he plunged them deep into her wet warmth. She arched and met his slow deep strokes while his thumb kept pulsating contact with her clit. He grasped a puckered dark nipple lightly between his teeth and raked it lightly.

Again she cried his name and begged him to take her.

"No." He cupped her other breast and nibbled the sweet chocolate tip, circled it with his tongue. He sucked, mimicking the rhythm of his fingers.

Her nails raked his shoulders. Legs wide apart, she rubbed against his cock until he was ready to explode.

He backed away. "Slow down, baby. Not yet."

Another trail of kisses back down to the delicate lips. He sampled her moisture. Her honey tasted so good, The scent of her...he never wanted to forget.

God. How could he leave her?

Her head whipped from side to side. He plunged his tongue in and out, deep inside the silken walls which were already twitching from their lovemaking.

Her hips arched against him. Her breath came in gasps, the sweetest music to his ears. He licked and circled and sucked her folds like a man starved.

She moaned and thrust to meet him.

He cupped her ass in his hands and buried his face in her wet pussy and licked her to completion as she spasmed and cried his name.

He moved up along her body, clasped her wrists over her head and nudged her slit with the head of his penis.

"I can't..." Her breath came in ragged gasps against his neck. "Yes..."

He thrust into her wet warmth and nearly lost control.

Slowly...

He kept a slow, tantalizing pace. Her body surrounded him. Her female scent seduced him. She was his... He didn't want to leave her.

The fire grew in his groin. He couldn't last much longer, quickened his pace. Thrust after thrust, his breath ragged, he groaned, "Come, baby. Come for me."

She met him stroke for stroke, her skin fever-hot to his touch. Deep, burning need overcame conscious thought as his body drove him on and on, growing frantic for completion.

"Deeper, harder," she begged, twisting and moaning beneath him with each driving thrust, sweeter and hotter than the one before until she gasped and cried as she came.

Tears coursed down her cheeks, but she gave no quarter, grasping and releasing until she propelled him to the heights with her. His body trembled over hers, their sweat mingling, as he plunged deeper and deeper into her body and soul.

He shuddered, and with a last frenzied thrust, pushed her over the crest again.

After their lovemaking, Rilla once again slept peacefully in Mac's arms. He pressed a kiss on her brow. How could he leave her? She had her life and he certainly had his. Heaven only knew where he'd be sent on his next assignment. Heaven only knew when he'd see her again.

Slowly he pulled away and eased from her bed.

Coward? Maybe, but he couldn't face any more of Rilla's tears. Each one seared his soul and made it more difficult to leave.

Chapter Twenty-two

The next morning Rilla called and arranged to meet Liz for coffee at the diner. She let her gaze travel up and down her mother's gaunt frame. In spite of her bony elbows and shoulders poking through her uniform, Liz's brown eyes sparkled.

She brought Rilla a fresh cup of coffee and one for herself, then sat across from Rilla. "You don't look like you got much rest last night?"

Rilla grinned, remembering... "Not much." She took a sip of hot, steaming coffee and swallowed.

Liz sighed. "You're young. Live life while you have time. That's all the advice I'm going to give you."

Rilla hesitated for a moment, then plunged ahead. "Miss Tweedy says you're sick. That you're seeing an oncologist in Nashville."

Liz shrugged and tugged her shirt sleeves down over the bruises. "What's the matter? You disappointed I'm not a junky after all?"

A sick guilt settled in her gut—why had she suspected the worst from her mother? Why couldn't she have seen how obviously her mother was ill? "How bad is it?"

Her mother turned away. "Don't act like you care. You already made it clear how you feel 'bout me. I don't need your pity."

"How bad?"

Liz whipped around, her lips drawn back in a grimace. "Bad enough. They took half of my left lung. And gave me enough chemo and x-ray treatments to kill a horse and light him up like Two-Mile Island."

"I'm sorry. I jumped to conclusions. I've been a real bitch."

"No kiddin'." Refusing to meet Rilla's gaze, her mother leaned against the back of the booth and stared out the window at what passed for rush hour in the Springs.

Rilla leaned forward. "Is there anything I can do? If you want to move in with me, I have plenty of room." She added a teaspoon of sugar into her coffee and stirred it with a spoon.

Her mother shook her head. "I'm fine at Miss Tweedy's."

Rilla swallowed. "Did the doctor say how long?"

"'Bout a year...give or take a couple of months."

"Look, you don't have to work those two jobs. You should—"

"Do what?" Her eyes snapping with fire, Liz faced Rilla. "I won't take charity. No matter what you think, I've always worked. I'll pay my way as long as I can."

"I can help you. My God, Mama, you saved my *life*."

"I don't need your gratitude...or your charity." Liz fiddled with a folded paper napkin. "I already told you."

"But I want to. I was wrong." Rilla reached for her mother's hand, but she pulled it out of reach.

"Not completely." Liz's expression was contrite. "I wasn't cut out for being a mom. I stood it as long as I could. Left the first chance I got."

"But Daddy would want me..."

Liz let out with a harsh laugh. "Your poor daddy probably would turn somersaults in his grave." She glanced away and gave a brief wave at a passing customer.

"You're wrong. Daddy never married again. He never stopped loving you, and I know he'd want me to help you." She had to make it right with her mother. Somehow.

"Honest?" A small, pleased smile tugged at her mother's lips. "I knew he didn't remarry, but I figured I ruined him for other women." Her mother let out another bark of laughter.

The diner was filling up with the morning regulars. Heaven only knew what they all thought. "That's what he let people think. But he'd get this look in his eye when he talked about you. He didn't very often, but I used to ask him about you—how you met, was I anything like you—that kind of thing."

Liz shook her head. "No. He blamed me. He must've."

"No." Rilla shook her head. "He told me you loved me, but—like you said—you weren't cut out to be a mother." She smiled at the memory. "He said bright-lights, big-city was your middle name."

"He got that right." Liz let out a loud sigh. "He deserved better. You did, too."

"I can't complain. I had a good life. For a long time I was too young to understand." She took another gulp of coffee. The smell of bacon frying back in the kitchen filled the air made her stomach churn.

"But since I've recently had to accept my father was human and capable of making some pretty bad mistakes, I need to accept you that way, too."

Her mother flashed Rilla a shy smile. "That sounds mighty grown-up of you."

"Anyway, Ralphie will love your company. He won't have to spend so much time with me at the office."

Her mother's gaze softened and her eyes grew shiny. Then she glanced away for a second. Was she afraid to let her daughter see the hope in her eyes? "I don't mind keepin' your dog company. But you'll be pretty busy. I don't expect you to babysit me."

"Please." Rilla reached for her mother's hand and this time wouldn't allow Liz to pull away. "Let's start from now. There's nothing we can do about the past, but we don't have to let it keep us from getting to know each other."

Pink spots appeared on her mother's cheeks. "All right then. We'll start fresh."

"It's settled. I'll come by Miss Tweedy's when I get off this evening, and I'll help you pack."

"All right," Her mother nodded. "I'll be through here at two."

Rilla drained the last of her coffee, then stood. "I'll let you get back to work." She walked from the diner, and for the first time in a long time, inner peace was more than a psychobabble catch phrase.

Washington, D.C.

"Mission accomplished. Good job." Havers extended his hand to Mac.

"Thank you, sir." All right, he'd shown Havers and Roxy Quinlan. He'd proved he had the right stuff. Why didn't it feel better? Why did an emptiness still gnaw at his gut?

"I'm ready for the next gig." He grinned to show how ready he was. "No rehab this time."

Havers leaned back in his chair, a frown creasing his ruddy, weathered face. "Sit down, Mac." He opened the folder lying on his desk.

Mac's stomach plummeted, but he mustered a casual, "Problem?"

"Take some time off."

"Time? I'm in top condition."

"You need to be certain undercover is what you want."

"Give it to me straight, Havers. What's in the folder?"

His boss sighed. "I hate this. Your psych eval indicates you're not as suited for deep undercover as first thought."

"So you're cutting me loose on the basis of some lousy shrink's report?"

"Cutting you loose? Hell, no. You're too valuable. There are plenty of positions in the Agency you're more suited for."

"Yeah? A desk job will drive me nuts in less than two weeks."

"You'd be a great instructor, Mac."

"Yeah, right." He swallowed the bitterness. "You know the old saying: Those who can, do. Those who can't, teach. No thanks."

He spun on his heel and strode from his former boss's office. He'd succeeded in his mission, cleared the case, and the Agency in their highly vaunted wisdom had deemed him unfit for undercover work? If the agency didn't need him, then the reverse was true, too. Screw 'em.

He walked from the Arlington, Virginia building and dashed across the street. His step was light. Dammit. His heart was lighter, too. Lighter than it'd been in months. For the first time in his adult life, he had no ties. No responsibilities.

And there was this woman he loved in Tennessee.

Rilla wiped the sweat from her forehead with the back of her forearm. "When is the A/C guy gonna get here? Anybody know?" she yelled at no one in particular.

Crap.

She checked the duty roster one more time. Losing R.J. and that bitch Bellows had left positions which couldn't be easily filled.

Three more months to serve of her father's term. Would she run? The local weekly had already been hounding her for an answer. Who would step forward if she didn't? No matter how much she wanted to leave all the politicking and handholding behind, she couldn't desert the office or the county. She owed them that much.

Duty and service were in her blood. She had her father to thank for that...and a few other things best not thought about if she didn't want to spiral further into the depths of depression.

She glanced at the calendar. Had it only been seven days since Mac left like a coward, sneaking out of bed and town after making love to her until she was senseless?

Don't be hankering after something you can't have. Forget him. That was her mother's advice.

Easier said than done.

"It's too damn quiet around here." She glanced down at Ralphie, who lay curled and snoring under her desk.

Even the dog agreed with her.

Deputy Paulson stuck his head in. "Hey boss," he said with a wide smirk. "Buster Villines wants to talk to you. Says he needs to show ya somethin'."

"No way! Last time he was in here, he tried—never mind. Just tell him I'm in a meeting. Tell him anything—"

"Rilla, do you mean me, too?"

Her head jerked up, startled by the sound of an oh-so-familiar voice. Her heart tripped into overdrive. "Mac—I thought—"

God. Just the sight of his lean-muscled form leaning against the door, wearing a dark brown leather jacket and a pair of jeans had her babbling like an idiot.

He eased into her office, obviously feeling quite pleased with himself, if his wide, shit-eating grin was any indication. He sat across from her and leaned his elbows on the desk. Next came his killer smile followed by a broad wink.

She cleared her throat. "That'll be all, Paulson."

Once her getting-smarter-all-the-time deputy had shut the door, she nailed Mac with a glare. “Slumming, DEA Agent Callahan, or whatever your name is?”

“Still Callahan, but I’m not with the DEA anymore.”

She folded her arms across her chest, mainly to keep him from seeing her heart pounding like fury. “Is that so? Why not?”

“Long story. I’ll tell you over dinner.”

“I’m pretty busy.” She gathered the papers on her desk and arranged them in a stack—anything to keep him from seeing how his sudden re-appearance had shaken her.

“Seven-thirty? My place?”

“Your place? What are you talking about?”

“You know—the one on North Main. I bought it. It’s mine now—for real.”

He bought the Victorian?

She stood and placed her hands on her hips. “Sonofabitch. You left my bed and ducked out of town without another word. What makes you think I have time for dinner with you or anything else? I haven’t heard a damn word from you in a week.”

He grinned, his gaze warm and seductive, but when wasn’t it?

“Now, hon, I’ve been busy. Buying a house and finding a new job takes a little time.”

“A new job? Hmph.” What was the man trying to pull now? “So, you’re going to be a real writer now? Going to write about all your adventures as an undercover agent? Or how about the one where you seduced the sheriff?

“Baby, that’s old news.” His expression took on a hangdog look. “Seven-thirty and I’ll tell you all about it.”

“I might have something planned.” She shrugged, then sat. “I’ll check my schedule.” She took her time pulling it up on the computer. There was nothing scheduled. No surprise there.

"Well, it appears I'm free," she said as casually as she could manage. "But I can't promise I'll make it. You know how it is. A wreck on the freeway, a drug bust or a hangnail—anything could happen."

"It's a date then," he said, still grinning like a perp who'd buffaloed the sheriff out of charging him. He stood and snapped her a cheeky salute. "I'll cook."

"Don't go to any trouble. I didn't promise I'd be there."

"You'll make it."

The nerve of the man. "You—"

He walked around the desk. All the strength leached from her muscles when he reached for her and pulled her to her feet. "I've never seen you at a loss for words."

His blue eyes shone with warmth. He wrapped his arms around her and kissed her—a long, warm passionate kiss which left her breathless and weak-kneed and ready to fall in love with him all over again.

"God, I've missed you." He eased her back into her chair. "I'll see you at seven-thirty."

She nodded and watched him stride down the hall. He'd sucked the air from her lungs. Her heart was dancing to some kind of crazy, hip-hop, syncopated Buck Dance.

And she didn't know if she was up or down or somewhere in between.

Nervous as a long-tailed cat in a roomful of rocking chairs, Rilla rang the bell, then waited for Mac to open the door.

And open it he did, wearing only a wide smile and a pair of jeans. She smiled. His six-pack certainly hadn't lost its definition. The light fur mat across his upper chest brought back the memories of their lovemaking.

Be strong, Rilla

She tried to hand him the bottle of wine she'd brought. "Here—my contribution to dinner."

"Great," he said, ignoring the bottle. It'll go well with what I've planned for dinner." He grabbed her hand and pulled her inside and led her into the living room.

"Not so fast, bud." She sniffed the air. "Odd. I don't smell anything cooking."

"That's because I'm having *you* for dinner," he said with a lecherous grin which sent a burst of heat to her core and did serious damage to her equilibrium.

She tried to back away. "Of all the arrogant—" She jerked her hand from his.

"No, you don't." He pulled her into his arms. "Okay, here's the deal. I quit the Agency. I'm working for your old pal Jason."

Disbelief, then a great mental sigh of relief flooded through Rilla. "You joined the TBI?"

"Yes. I can't quite believe it myself. And they're quite happy to have me."

No, this was too good to be true. There must be a catch. "But isn't it quite a comedown—from Fed to State?"

"Not if I want a life with you, Rilla—working with you, living with you. I can't imagine a better way to spend the rest of my life."

"You want to spend the rest of your life with me?" The wine bottle slid from her hand and thumped on the oriental carpet. "Have you lost your mind...or have I?"

Please, God, don't let this be some kind of cruel joke.

His gaze grew more sincere than she'd ever seen it. "Even if I have, will you still marry me? My God woman, I want to make babies with you."

She gazed at him, still not quite believing he was serious. "But—"

He stopped her questions with his lips. His mouth claimed her for all time. Without a doubt in her mind, she belonged to this man who'd given up his job and come back to love her. Kissing Mac was the closest thing to heaven on earth. But making love with him...beyond description.

He pulled back from their kiss. "I love you, Rilla, and coming home to Clinton County is the best move I ever made."

God, how she'd missed him. Her body melded to his and lost all sense of separation. She was aware only of one living, loving body.

They sank to the floor, their clothes torn away as they clung to each other in a frenzy of lips and hands and legs.

"Now..." she gasped.

Her legs wrapped around his waist as he thrust deep into her willing body and even deeper into her heart.

Home.

They met and balanced, lingering on the precipice ever so long, then spiraled ever skyward in a fiery burst of heat that threatened to consume them both.

About the Author

Romantic suspense author, Marie-Nicole Ryan, was definitely born in Kentucky, but defies anyone to discover and/or reveal the year. After graduating from Henderson County High School, she mistakenly decided nursing school was her ticket to riches and happiness. Another career detour found her going to interior design school, which was frankly a lot more fun than nursing school and even more work.

Through all these career stops and starts, she devoured books by the thousands: romance, science fiction, mysteries. After receiving a lot of encouragement from an on-line writing community, she decided it was time to plant her butt in the chair and bring her stories to life.

Her first book was released in May 2002. Since then she's had three more books published

Ms. Ryan has one son, lives in a suburb of Nashville, Tennessee, and has thrown caution to the winds by abandoning her R.N. job and is now a full-time author.

To learn more about Marie-Nicole Ryan, please visit http://marienicoleryan.com. Send an email to Marie-Nicole Ryan at marienicoleryan@comcast.net or join her Yahoo! news group to join in the fun with other readers as well as Marie-Nicole Ryan! Just send an e-mail to: Marie-NicoleRyanNews-subscribe@yahoogroups.com.

Trapped in a war zone, wanted for murder and standing on a landmine: sometimes life doesn't quite go as planned.

Running Scared

© 2007 Caitlyn Nicholas

Poised and sophisticated, Julie Marchant lives for her job. Buying gems, she travels the world mixing with the rich, the famous and the sinister.

Throwing caution to the wind, Julie is swept away in a night of passion. When she wakes to find herself alone, she thinks she'll never see archeologist Mitchell Cartwright again. However, fate has other ideas. She travels to Laos and they meet, just as the country teeters on the brink of civil war. Trapped, they flee together, but their past history and a murderous secret mean the road to safety, and love, is complicated and treacherous.

Printed in the United States
128620LV00001B/526-573/A

"Read 'em their rights and take 'em away," Rilla said. "I'm sick of the sight of them."

"You stupid, bitch." Kit yelled from the Jeep. "I fooled you for two months."

"Keep your trap shut," Kurt yelled over his shoulder. "I'm warning you."

"It's a little late, dip-wad," Rilla snapped. "Kit says she wants a deal, and I'm sure the D.A. will come up with something if she sells you out."

Disgusted by the two, Rilla turned her back. Where was the satisfaction she was supposed to feel after finding the man responsible for her father's death and the deaths of two teenagers?

Mac bundled Kurt into the back of Roxy's vehicle and locked the door.

The town could breathe easier now—why couldn't she? Maybe Mac was right and the shooter was still in the area. And maybe he was sunning his worthless hide somewhere on the French Riviera.

She glanced over at Mac where he stood talking to Roxy Quinlan and Jase. "I'm heading back to the office…"

"Paperwork?" Mac asked with a smirk.

"Let's see. My lockup, three agencies involved… Yeah, I guess there's some. And I need to pull in Rob Wyler. I'm sure he'll only be too happy to cooperate since we have his boss."

"We're right behind you," Mac said.

In a motel room at the edge of town, Liam looked in the bathroom mirror and checked his disguise. Gone was the salt-and-pepper hair. He'd shaved ten years off his age with the color. Contact lenses turned his eyes brown. The false mustache added to the younger, "with it" appearance.